SAVAGE AX

THE HIDDEN REALM
BOOK 1

D. N. HOXA

Copyright © 2022 by D.N. Hoxa

This book is protected under the copyright laws of the United States of America. Any reproduction or other unauthorized use of the material or artwork herein is prohibited. This is a work of fiction. Names, characters, places, and incidents either are the product of the author's imagination or are used fictitiously, and any resemblance to actual persons, living or dead, business establishments, events, or locales, is entirely coincidental.

ALSO BY D.N. HOXA

THE PIXIE PINK (COMPLETED)
Werewolves Like Pink Too
Pixies Might Like Claws
Silly Sealed Fates

THE DARK SHADE (COMPLETED)
Shadow Born
Broken Magic
Dark Shade

THE NEW ORLEANS SHADE (COMPLETED)
Pain Seeker
Death Spell
Twisted Fate
Battle of Light

THE NEW YORK SHADE (COMPLETED)
Magic Thief
Stolen Magic
Immortal Magic
Alpha Magic

THE MARKED SERIES (COMPLETED)
Blood and Fire
Deadly Secrets
Death Marked

WINTER WAYNE SERIES (COMPLETED)
Bone Witch
Bone Coven
Bone Magic
Bone Spell
Bone Prison
Bone Fairy

SCARLET JONES SERIES (COMPLETED)
Storm Witch
Storm Power
Storm Legacy
Storm Secrets
Storm Vengeance
Storm Dragon

VICTORIA BRIGHAM SERIES (COMPLETED)
Wolf Witch
Wolf Uncovered
Wolf Unleashed
Wolf's Rise

STARLIGHT SERIES (COMPLETED)
Assassin
Villain
Sinner
Savior

MORTA FOX SERIES (COMPLETED)
Heartbeat
Reclaimed
Unchanged

1

Nikki Arella

"You're so freaking bitter, I love it," Anya said as she fell on the bench next to me, the scent of lilacs that always hung about her invading my nostrils.

"I didn't even say anything," I muttered, taking another sip of my vodka.

She laced her arm around mine and pulled me to the side. "You don't have to, sweetie. It's just the look on your face." She grinned like the mischievous brat that she was.

Here I thought I was doing a good job keeping a neutral expression. "What about the look on my face?"

"Nothing. It just says that you want to murder everyone here."

"I don't." I did—and it wasn't even their fault.

"Oh, c'mon. I am *not* judging. See Simon Range over there?" She nodded ahead at the other side of the bar, at the skinny guy who was telling his bad jokes to a group of four to get them to laugh until they forgot to check their pockets. Vampires were very aware of their surroundings. Our instincts were sharp as hell, but enough alcohol in our system would make even the strongest of us as clueless as a mortal. "He's been stealing things all night, and everybody's too drunk to even notice. I, for one, would have no trouble seeing his head cut off."

I rolled my eyes. "You wouldn't hurt a fly." She just had a big mouth.

"Not me, silly," Anya said, batting her lashes with a sweet smile. "I mean *you*."

I laughed, then threw back the last of my vodka. I loved the way it burned me on the way down, and the way it made every thought in my head too blurry to make out properly.

Now I needed a refill.

"You want me to go kill Simon Range because he's stealing, even though he hasn't stolen anything from me?"

"I'm just saying it might help with whatever's got you looking so bitter."

I pointed my finger at her face. "I am *not* bitter." I just had an overcrowded mind.

"Sure, sweetie." She patted my back. "And the Hidden Realm is full of flowers and rainbows and unicorns. Just look outside."

She waved left toward the door and the only windows of the bar at its sides. All we saw was darkness and some lampposts in the distance. *Nameless* was not located in a good—or even decent—part of the Realm. It's where vampires came to get properly shitfaced. That's why it was my favorite. Definitely no flowers or rainbows around here.

Waving her off, I made to stand, but I must have underestimated how much I drank since sundown because the entire room swam before my eyes and I almost fell on the bench again.

"Whoa," I breathed, holding onto the table.

"And that's your cue to get the hell out of here," Anya said. "C'mon, let's get going. You need to sober up in time for practice. A glass of warm blood will do the trick."

"Fuck that. I'm getting another drink." I still had another hour to kill. Did she have any idea how long an hour could truly be?

But Anya grabbed me by the arm before I could take another step. I was really much more drunk than I thought because a little tug and my ass hit the hard wood of the bench again. It just made me laugh. How many of those glasses had I drunk? I tried to count the empty ones on the table, but fuck, they kept on moving.

"There's only so many passes Master can give you," Anya said as she pushed my hair behind my ear. I kept cutting it close to my chin, but it was time I let it grow out so I could pull it back and not have to deal with it anymore. "Look at me, Nikki." She didn't sound as cheerful anymore, and when she pulled me by the arm, my stomach turned. If I threw up right now, I was going to be so pissed. That shit cost money. "Jokes aside, this is too much. *You know* it's too much."

"Then leave." I jerked my arm away from her reach. But Anya was Anya, and she knew how to be a pain in my ass better than most. Though, to be honest, it's not like people had to try very hard for that. It was enough that they existed.

"Don't make me get Ivan."

I flinched. "Is that supposed to scare me?"

Because it did. Not that I was afraid for my life—I wasn't. But Ivan was the commander of the Redwood army—and Anya's brother—and since I was just one of the pointless soldiers of our beloved coven, he was in charge of me. He could order me not to leave the castle, and I couldn't afford that. I really, really couldn't.

"I know it does," Anya said, crossing her arms in front of her. Her chestnut brown hair shone in a way mine never did, and even though she was petite, her eyes were big, her features sharp, and she could give you a real scare when she got mad.

Still, I was drunk, so the sight of her with her lips pressed together like that made me laugh. And wasn't that beautiful? Just to laugh at the face of whatever was in front of you, not take *anything* seriously, and just enjoy this miserable existence people called *life?*

"You're a mess, Nikki," Anya said before she gave me the other look—the one that said she was *sorry* for me. Now *that* look I couldn't stand at all. It made the blood in my veins boil instantly. "You're better than this and you know it."

"Why are you here, Anya?" I spit, all the good feelings I'd had a second ago now vanished. "Nobody invited you. You don't drink. You don't dance. You don't fuck. Why in the world do you keep following me around? It's fucking annoying."

And *that* was too much, too.

Regret made its way down my throat, burning me worse than the vodka. The instinct to tell her that I didn't mean it, that I was just drunk and in a shitty mood, had my mouth open halfway before I caught myself. This was the point. Anya was too good, too pure to be in this place. In this part of the Realm. *With me.* She had no business here, even though nobody would dare even look at her twice because of Ivan. She needed to stay away from this place. And from me.

"Because I remember," she finally whispered. "I remember you, Nikki."

My gut turned again. I didn't want to fucking hear it.

But before I had the chance to storm out of the bar and find another one where I could drink in peace, the double doors opened.

The silence that followed a second after was absolute.

There were plenty of people who were feared around here just as much as Ivan, and one of them was Michael Ferrera—the Master of the Redwood coven army. He was Ivan's second in command and in charge of training soldiers for battle for no fucking reason at all. There were no wars in the Hidden Realm. There were seven covens that hated each other's guts, and there were plenty of fights between us on the daily, but nothing that couldn't be handled with a slap to the wrist. So, what was the point of having soldiers?

"Shit," Anya whispered when Master Ferrera stepped inside, and…his eyes stopped on me.

Double shit.

I swallowed hard, half sober already, and the whispers in my head were getting louder. There was just something about the green of his eyes and the line of his lips permanently etched downward. Rumor had it he was over three hundred years old, and a three-hundred-year-old vampire could do a lot of damage to anything and anyone without making an effort. Just the thought that I'd almost killed him once—by accident, of course—had chills rushing down my back.

Nobody moved a single inch as he slowly came into the bar, eyes still locked on me. I knew what he was thinking already, and it went perfectly with the slow, haunting music playing in the background that nobody had dared to pause yet. *Disappointment. Pathetic. Weak.* Exactly as I felt.

His footsteps dug holes in my brain, and the closer he came, the clearer I saw his face. His black hair was grey around the ears and his beard was grey at the tips, too. His thick eyebrows seemed to always be narrowed whenever he looked at me lately. He was a big guy—over six foot two, not overly bulky. He moved faster than any vampire I'd ever seen in my life, and if I tried to make a run for it now, chances were he would catch me before I made it to the door.

He stopped on the other side of the table, and he actually flinched at the sight of all the empty glasses in front of me.

"So sorry to interrupt your fun, Nicole," he said, barely moving his lips, but I still heard the whisper.

"It's okay," I mumbled, trying to straighten my shoulders. Unfortunately, I was still way too drunk to properly coordinate my movements, so all I managed to do was look more hunched than before.

"Is it?" the Master said, bringing a hand to his chest. "Well, then that's a relief."

I gritted my teeth. If he was here to make fun of me, I could be a bitch. He knew exactly how much of a bitch I could be, despite his creative punishment ideas.

"Training doesn't start for another hour." Hence why I drank vodka like water, just to make it in time for training.

"Get up, Nicole," he said, like he was already exhausted. "Go clean yourself up. Mr. Jones wants a word with you."

Well, damn. My knees shook as I stood up, holding onto the edge of the table.

"About what?" Sweat beads lined my forehead. I was having a little difficulty breathing, too, and the voices in my head were already relentless.

"Go," the Master said. "And brush your fucking teeth. You stink."

All the hatred in the world reflected in his eyes as he looked down at me, then spun around, his long black cape swooshing behind him. My eyes were stuck on the back of his head until he walked out of the bar and the people went at it again.

They were all watching me now. They all had something to say, something to *think* about me. Good thing I couldn't care less about anybody's opinion anymore.

Was this *it*? Was this as far as I went? Had they already had enough of my shit?

It looked like it. Because Abraham Jones, one of the three rulers of the Redwood coven, didn't speak to soldiers like me. I hadn't even seen him personally in over a decade, and now he wanted a word with me?

I'd have been tempted to believe it was a lie, but Master Ferrera himself had delivered the invitation. And Master Ferrera wasn't a fucking delivery boy.

"C'mon, let's get going," Anya said, and despite what I said to her earlier, she still looked terrified for me. It helped in making me feel even shittier than before, but I took her outstretched hand anyway. She slowly guided me around the table and out of the bar.

★★★

I hissed when the ice-cold water touched my face. I splashed some more anyway. It burned me, but it sobered me up somewhat, too. Now I wished I hadn't drunk all that vodka, but it was already too late.

When I looked in the mirror over the sink, I wished I'd combed my hair, too. It was a mess of ash blonde waves, too thick to be tamed down by anything. Running my wet fingers over it would only work until they were dry again, but it was the best I could do for now.

A second later, the door to the toilets opened. I heard the footsteps, and now that I wasn't that drunk, I smelled the scent, too.

That's why I kept my eyes on the mirror and pretended not to notice.

"Why do you keep doing this to yourself?"

I saw it in the mirror when I turned a shade paler. My mouth opened to tell Master Ferrera exactly why I kept doing it to myself. I turned to him, too, determined to not back down, everything else be damned. If he was inside my head, inside my body, constantly trying to block out my demons, he'd have been the same as me. Probably even worse.

But one look at his face, and he didn't look pissed anymore. He looked…tired. Even a little sorry.

"I was just having a drink," I ended up saying.

"One of these days, I'm going to have enough of your excuses," he said, then offered me a glass I'd been too distracted to notice in his hand. It was half filled with cow's blood. A bit warm, too.

As much as I wanted to knock it out of his hand, I resisted. It was the only thing that was going to sober me up enough to get this whole thing over with.

"Until that day comes…" I whispered, patting my hands dry on my skirt before I took the glass and walked out the door with my head up.

I didn't owe anybody any explanations, but fuck if they didn't know how to make me feel like shit every single day. Maybe it was my doing. Maybe I was just a fuck up. And if that were the case, why not just leave me be? Kick me out of the army. Kick me out of the Realm. Kill me altogether.

Why the hell hadn't they done it yet?

But the more stairs I climbed to get to the tenth floor of the castle, the more I realized…they were. Abraham Jones had called me up to his office—they were finally doing it.

And I couldn't even say I regretted it. If anything, it made me hurry up the stone stairs until I was in the hall of the tenth floor with half a dozen guards staring at me through their dead eyes.

Straightening my shoulders, I drank the cow blood. It tasted awful, but blood was blood.

"Mr. Jones asked to see me," I said, putting the empty glass down on the floor. Somebody would probably take it to the kitchen.

One of the guards to my right stepped in front of the double doors designed with golden vines and pushed one open. The others only watched. They didn't search me. Then again, it would be an insult to take my weapons off me. It would mean that I had the chance of hurting Abraham Jones with them, which was ridiculous. He was one of the most powerful vampires of our time. It was going to take a lot more than the knives strapped to my thighs to hurt him.

I walked through the door, expecting the fear to take over me—after all, there was a good chance that I was about to meet my end tonight. Jones had finally come around and he could see things for what they truly were. What they always had been.

That should have made me at least a little bit afraid.

But I got nothing.

The wide hallway on the other side of the main doors was full of guards, too. Lush carpets and fancy chandeliers, the smell of blood hanging in the air like a fragrance. These fuckers definitely knew how to set the mood. Nobody stopped me as I went down the hallway, looking at the closed doors on either side and the lamps spilling orange light, casting shadows every few feet that looked like monsters waiting to devour me whole.

When I reached the very end, the hallway opened into a round room with a desk on one side and fancy leather armchairs on the other. Paintings—all of them mostly red—hung on the walls, and the windows behind the desk were floor to ceiling, looking out at the center of the Hidden Realm, half of it hidden in the dark of the night.

"Ms. Arella, welcome," the woman behind the desk said before she stood up. Her smile was ice-cold, her grey suit without a single wrinkle, and her gold rimmed glasses were just for show. Vampires didn't get weak eyesight. Just one of the perks of walking around with an undead virus in your body.

"Mr. Jo—"

She didn't even let me speak. "This way, please," she said, and stepped away from her desk to show me to the doors on the other side of the room. I followed, looking down at her high heels in wonder. Toothpicks were thicker than that. How the hell did she not fall on her face walking on those things?

The sound of the doors swinging to the sides when she opened them echoed in my head. The woman moved away, and I saw into the room.

Three sets of eyes were on me.

"Please," she said, waving her hand for me to enter.

No going back now. Locking my jaws, I focused on breathing and keeping my heartbeat calm, and I entered the room.

The doors behind me closed. The silence in here wasn't all that different from the one outside, but there was just something about having three of the most powerful vampires in the world pick you apart with their eyes, trying to see under your skin, straight into your mind. It made the voices in my head get louder for a second before I pushed them down with all my strength again.

Abraham Jones was standing next to the large cherrywood desk in the middle of the room. He hadn't changed a bit since the first or last time I saw him. He was on the skinny side, which didn't really mean much, and his eyes were pitch-black, just two bottomless pits you could easily get lost in if he willed it.

Fortunately for me, right now, he was not impressed by the looks of me—and neither were the others. Curt Vanner sat on my left, a glass of whiskey in his hand as he watched me, brows raised to the middle of his forehead, his eyes more orange than brown under the light of the crystal chandelier. Next to him was William Reinhart, the shortest and chubbiest of the bunch, with hair cut so short it looked like a shadow over his skull. His brown eyes were *warm* compared to those of his friends. Together, they ruled the Redwood coven, one of the biggest vampire covens in the Hidden Realm—and the strongest, though I'm not really sure how they measured that anymore.

I stood before them with my head up, looking from one to the other, wishing they'd just start talking already.

But they took their sweet time—and the more of me they saw, the less pleased they seemed. I understood why. I wore a short, *short* skirt, had knife holsters strapped to my thighs, boots that went up to my shin, a crop top with a skeleton drawn on it that had holes in a few places, topped with a black leather jacket that had seen better days. And my face, too. I loved my black eyeshadow. My eyes were more grey than blue and pretty big, and the eyeshadow made them look especially scary, like the eyes of a mad woman. The mess of waves in my hair probably didn't help, either.

Good thing I didn't give a shit about pleasing anyone.

"You stink of alcohol, Nicole," Jones said, wrinkling his long nose. His voice sent shivers down my back despite my facade. It was powerful—powerful enough to be wielded as a weapon on its own, and I hated all the memories it brought back to me.

"I was out drinking with friends."

He raised a brow as if he knew I was full of shit. I didn't have any friends. Anya was different—she was almost a decade younger, and I couldn't tell her half the shit that went through my head. I couldn't tell *anybody* that, but still. I wouldn't curse her by calling her *a friend*.

"Since when?" Curt Vanner said. "Last week?"

Ha-ha, the fucking prick. "Just an hour ago." Though it had probably been two.

He then turned to Jones. "Are you serious, Abraham?"

"Bad idea," William Reinhart muttered, shaking his head to himself.

"Master said you called for me, so…" I shrugged.

"She can barely stand," Curt Vanner spit again.

"Actually, that is true. Can I just…" I made for the only empty chair on this side of the desk, but Jones wouldn't have it.

"Stay," he commanded, and my body locked down instantly. *Fucker.* He'd always been able to do that to me. When I was a little girl, just the sight of him made me want to run and hide.

"Look—I don't know what I did to be here. I swear I didn't hurt anyone." I flinched. "On purpose."

The men looked at one another and their concern only grew.

Jones sighed, lowering his head for a moment.

"If you could just tell me what it was, I can promise I won't do it again." Would I? Well, I would *promise,* though it was difficult without knowing what it was first. Had I picked a fight with someone lately? Hard to remember. But if I had, Master or even Ivan would deal with it, same as always. Jones wouldn't have had me here in his office and not even let me sit down.

So…

"You've gotten worse than I was told," Jones finally whispered, sizing me up again. Something in me twisted—hatred, raw hatred, and also guilt so deep it would have suffocated me if I let it. As it was, I raised up my chin.

"Like I said—I was just out drinking. I didn't know I was going to have the pleasure of seeing you today. It's been ten years," I said through gritted teeth.

Jones shook his head, half disgusted, half disappointed. "We have a job, Nicole," he started, and by the sound of it, he regretted every word even before he said it. "We have something that belongs to us out in the human realm, and we need to get it back."

"I see." I *didn't* see at all why I was here, though.

"It will take three days, give or take, to get to it, and another three to come back," Jones continued.

"Mhmm." Nope—still didn't see it.

"It's very important that it gets here safely." Jones looked at me from under his lashes. Gone was the disgust and the disappointment. The coldness with which he watched me now left no room for doubt about the kind of monster that he was.

"And you're telling me that because…?"

"You're going to be the one to get it."

Definitely not what I was expecting.

I smiled. "You want to send *me*…" I pointed at my chest and let that sink in for a second, "…into the human realm?" Was that what he said? Because if he did, then he was a *way* bigger idiot than I could have imagined.

"Yes—because he's lost his damned mind," Curt Vanner told me.

Unfortunately, I had to agree.

"We're teaming up with Sangria on this one, Nicole," Jones continued like his friend hadn't even said anything.

I smiled bigger. "*Ha-ha*. Right."

Out of the seven covens in the Hidden Realm, Sangria was our biggest rival, our worst enemy—and the only coven with more numbers in their army than us. They hated our guts. We hated theirs. We didn't *team up* with them, nor they with us, for any reason.

But it was nice of Jones to make that joke, anyway. Maybe he wasn't as uptight as I thought, either.

Except…the way he was looking at me, not a single emotion on his face…

"Every coven in the Realm will be going after it," he continued, "which is why a deal with Sangria appealed to us."

"But…but…" They were *Sangria*. They were assholes. They were bullies—murderous bullies who got away with almost everything around the Realm.

"No buts," Jones said, leaning against the desk's edge. "We've already decided that this is the best way. You will team up with them and you will get this done, Nicole."

It sounded an awful lot like a warning.

I was suddenly feeling really hot. I didn't work well with people—Jones knew that. He was there while I grew up, and I was still that same girl. He could ask anyone, and they'd tell him. If I *really* had to go out there in the human realm to find something, I was better off on my own. Way better. And less annoyed. And free to do this however I wanted. Just the thought that I would have to be in someone's company for six whole days made me shiver.

I swallowed hard. "Who are they sending?"

At that, Jones and the other two looked at each other intently again before they turned to me.

"Axel Creed," he finally said.

Now I knew for a fact that they were fucking with me.

"C'mon. Who are they sending, really?"

Jones raised a brow. "Axel Creed."

The smile was frozen on my face still. "Axel Creed," I said with a nod. "Savage Ax—*that* Axel Creed?"

"Correct," Jones said. "Which is why it's important that *you* handle this operation."

For a moment, I just stood there and expected them to start laughing. *We got you, Nicole! You should have seen the look on your face, ha-ha-ha. We got you good!*

Except that didn't happen.

"It's suicide," I spit. They knew this. Everybody knew this. Savage Ax was a monster—a bigger monster than any vampire in the Realm. Maybe an even bigger monster than *me*. He was the reason why Sangria had gained so much power over the past few years—that asshole went around like a fucking shadow, kidnapped people and had his way with them whenever Sangria needed it. He played dirty and there was never any evidence against him. Most people had never even seen his face. He hid behind their fortress, and he never came out unless it was to kill someone who refused to obey Sangria.

But Jones looked me dead in the eye and said, "Not for you."

That's when I knew the real reason why I was here in the first place.

I stepped back, shaking my head. I wouldn't do it. He couldn't just put me out there in the world with a murderer and hope I didn't lose my shit at any given second. Had he forgotten how he found me almost thirty years ago?

Had he forgotten what had been around me?

"Out of everyone in the coven, you are the only one who can handle this," Jones said.

"No," I whispered.

"Yes, Nicole. You will because you have to."

"He's a monster," I whispered, and though I was talking about Savage Ax, I was talking about me, too. The last few years, the whispers had gotten more violent than ever. It took a lot out of me to even control them here in the Realm. But out there in the human world? "He doesn't play by the rules. He's—"

"Merely a vampire with a reputation," Jones cut me off.

"Then why not send someone else? I am not fit to go out in the human realm. You know this. They know this." I pointed at Vanner and Reinhart. "I'm drunk as many hours as I'm awake. I can't remember the last time—"

"I know you're afraid, Nicole," he cut me off again. Damn right I was afraid—just not for the same reason he thought. If he were inside my body, inside my mind, he'd be terrified, too. "But this is too important. I will not compromise."

My heart thundered in my chest. Turning my back to them, I squeezed my eyes shut for a moment and just breathed, trying to calm down. We'd been down this road before. He knew very well how it ended, but that didn't stop Jones. It never had. He wanted me to become what I'd been avoiding my whole life, even knowing what it would cost me, but he didn't give a shit. Why would he? I was never more than a soldier—a weapon at his hand, even if I'd believed differently in the past. This is what I was here for. Why he hadn't killed me when he should have.

It was stupid.

More than that—it was *dangerous*. And that's exactly what Jones was counting on.

I wanted to laugh. He was a smart guy, I'd give him that. And his word was law. If he said I was going, then I was. I couldn't walk away from this no matter what.

But I'd made myself a promise a long time ago, and I'd only broken it when I lost control. That's *before* I'd discovered alcohol. So, if Jones thought he could take advantage of *that* part of me while I was out there, he was dead wrong. I would do whatever it took to keep myself in check, and if Savage Ax killed me because of it, well…it was a win-win for me.

When I faced the men again, I was calm. I was sober. My mind was sharp and my eyes on Jones's.

"What is it? What am I to find?"

"It's…complicated," he said and leaned away from his desk again. "We need to find a vampire."

I narrowed my brows. "What do you mean?"

"Exactly that. We need to find a vampire and bring her here."

Even Vanner and Reinhart were looking away from me.

"Did she escape?"

"No, she's never been here before."

What the… "Then how is she out there?"

It didn't make any sense. Vampires lived in the Hidden Realm, not out there in the world. It had been that way since the treaty with the sorcerers about twenty years ago.

We still went out there, specific groups from every coven, to get supplies. We had everything the humans had, as long as we could afford it. I couldn't since I spent most of my money on alcohol, but we had the latest cell phone models, TVs, and 5G, too. Booze, food, anything you could think of. The Hidden Realm was like a big city, not very different from the ones in the rest of the world.

But the rest of the world was full of sorcerers, too. They had a lot of magic to wield, and they could sense vampires from half a mile away, give or take. They didn't attack vampires who went out on behalf of their covens—it was allowed in the treaty as long as they kept away from humans, but the rest were fair game. Especially those who thought it was a smart idea to escape from the Realm. They never made it far. Either the coven they belonged to sent someone after them or the sorcerers out there killed them dead.

Come to think of it, I'd heard plenty of stories about Savage Ax being sent out to hunt vampires who'd escaped in the past decade, no matter the coven. Were those stories even true? If they were, he was already far ahead of me as I hadn't set foot outside the Realm in the past twenty years.

"That's not important," Jones said, pulling me out of my trance. The way he looked away from me for a second said he was a fucking liar. "You leave tomorrow at sundown. I will have the maps and details sent to you once we hear from Sangria."

"Who turned her? Do we know?" I asked, my mind still buzzing.

"Not at present, no," Jones said, and he didn't sound happy about it.

"But there must be—"

"All we have is an address. She's in Atlanta, Georgia," he cut me off.

Shit. "That's far." The Hidden Realm was in North Dakota.

"You'll have to travel the road on foot. It's safer that way. Cars aren't worth the risk."

"Walk all the way to Atlanta?" Was he serious?

"Run the highways. Walk the rest. You'll be aware of your surroundings at all times like that." He did have a point. We were faster than cars at full speed, but still...

"It's a *long* way," I insisted.

"And everybody else will be taking it. They could ambush you easily when you're in a car, and you won't even see it coming. You'll need your focus about you at all times."

I sighed. Fine—no cars. Whatever.

"Clean up. Rest. And no alcohol," Jones said, and by the sound of his voice, he was done with the conversation.

I held his eyes for a moment and *begged* him to reconsider. He really didn't want to send *me* out there with so many humans. I could hurt them, and I wouldn't even be able to stop myself. He had to know how wrong this was.

But Jones didn't give a shit.

"Go, Nicole. Bring her to us no matter the cost," he whispered.

My gods, he was *really* doing this. He'd given the order—I couldn't walk away from it now. I was actually going out into the human realm tomorrow. Out of all the impossible things that would have *never* even occurred to me, this definitely topped the list.

And Jones was done. Knowing that no matter what I said, it wasn't going to change his mind, I turned around to leave, my mind in a chaotic state.

"Nicole?" Jones called when I opened the door. "One wrong move and you have permission to kill him. No questions will be asked."

My flesh rose in goose bumps. I slipped out the door and closed it behind me, ignoring the woman in the hallway completely. A free pass to kill Savage Ax. What a fucking mess. *No questions asked*. And if Jones said that to me, there was no doubt in my mind that Robert Sangria said the same to thing to Axel Creed.

Yeah, this was definitely going to go badly and end even worse—probably with one of us dead. But I'd lie if I said I wasn't looking forward to seeing who the bigger monster was.

2

Ax Creed

Too many people. Made me wonder why I hadn't moved the chambers under my own house yet.

"Just bear with me," Lucien said. "It's going to be the best restaurant in the Realm."

"The private rooms, man," his twin brother Raphael insisted. "We have it all figured out. Nothing beats private rooms—they're literally like rooms with beds and everything. Completely *private*."

I looked at him. "What—like a person's *home* would be?"

"No, no—not like that," Lucien shot from the other side as we reached the main stairway leading down. "Homes are *boring*. But a restaurant where they can have their private fun away from people's ears and eyes? C'mon—you gotta see it, man! It smells like money!"

"All we need is a little loan," said Raphael. "And we'll pay you back in five years. We've got the numbers down—five years."

Grinning, I rushed down the stairs, but the twins had set their minds on it, and they weren't going to back off that easily.

"C'mon, Ax," Lucien said. "It's just this once."

"Just this once?" I laughed. "What about the convenience store? And the liquor store? Not to mention your brilliant cow-milking invention just last year?"

"But those were *nothing*," Raphael said. "Lucien's ideas—*this* is different. It's a restaurant. It's gonna work!"

I stopped walking when we reached the end of the stairway. "How about this: get the designs, numbers, and everything you have on paper, and I'll look over it."

Since I'd known them, they'd been pitching business ideas to me thinking I was a bottomless pit of wealth. Which I was, but that was beside the point. I'd invested in three of their genius ideas so far, knowing they would tank, but I was starting to think they were *never* going to actually learn from their mistakes. Still, it was time they did their homework and stopped wasting my fucking money.

"Fine," Raphael said. "We can do that. We can put everything on paper."

"We got a location. We know exactly how it's gonna look." Lucien grinned proudly.

"Good. Now will you two get the fuck off my back?" I had shit to do, people to torture.

"Oh, look at that," Raphael said instead, slamming his hand on my chest, making me wonder why I hadn't broken it yet. He knew I didn't like being touched, but he didn't give a shit. If I hadn't been the one to save them myself, I'd have gotten rid of them both a long time ago.

I looked ahead—at the woman swinging her hips to the sides, a seductive smile on her perfect face as she came toward us, eyes locked on mine.

"Oh, man. I'd give up my left nut for that," Lucien whispered, completely in awe.

"She can hear you, dumbass," Raphael said—and Ariel smiled, even though she was at least twenty feet away from us still.

"*That's* the kind of woman you mate," Lucien continued. He couldn't care less if Ariel heard him.

"Yeah, Ax. Fuck, yeah. It's time you gave that some real thinking." Raphael pressed his finger to his temple.

"No, thanks. Mating's not for me." And now I had to keep them here until Ariel walked away. Otherwise she'd be on me, too.

Fuck.

"Mating is for *everyone*," Lucien said. "Women are all over you—just pick one and be done. Seriously, before you get old and weak."

I laughed again, putting my hand on his shoulder. I squeezed—harder than I needed to, just to make sure he got the point. "I don't mate, little one. Women know that. They come to me when they need a good fuck. I do the fucking, and that's that." I said it loud enough for everyone around us to hear it. Especially Ariel, who was almost to us now.

"All right, all right, all right, I get it," Lucien said, moving away from my hand, rubbing his shoulder.

"Hey there, handsome," Ariel said as she stopped in front of me, way too close, then put her hands on my chest and leaned in to kiss my cheek. The scent of her, something sweet and nauseating, overpowered my senses completely for a moment.

The twins by my side were already drooling. So fucking boring, I could claw my eyes out.

"Hey, Ariel," I said, looking down at her hands, long nails painted black that looked like claws, still on my chest. "Keep your hands to yourself, darling. You don't want to wake up and find them missing, do you?"

She laughed an icy sound but got her hands off me.

"Always so funny," she said, pushing her long black hair behind her shoulder dramatically.

I laughed. "I'm really not."

She ignored it. "What are you up to? Wanna go somewhere? Let me make you feel good," she said, her dark eyes scrolling down my chest and lower. The twins almost collapsed when she let out her tongue and licked her lips slowly.

"You'll make me feel real good when I see that ass walking away," I said, and she laughed again. Whether she pretended not to know I meant it or she chose not to was a mystery to me.

"One of these days, Axel," she said, shaking her finger at me in a way she probably thought was seductive. I stepped to the side and let her make her way up the stairs, smiling.

"Now *that's* a good ass," Raphael whispered as we watched her walk up slowly, swinging her hips in those tight leather pants that were going to explode off her any second. Come to think of it, I did want to tear those off and see her ass bouncing while I fucked her. Maybe it wasn't a bad idea to give her a call later.

"Juicy and plump," Lucien said, nodding.

"I would give up an arm to mate with her," Raphael said.

I stepped back. "Maybe you should try it. Cut off your arm and take it to her. Who knows? She might like it," I said and finally got the hell out of there.

"Hey, wait!" The twins followed, making me groan. I rushed down the second hallway of the ground floor and didn't stop. "Hold on, man. Why are you so pissed all the time?" said Lucien.

"We're your buddies. We want what's best for you, that's all," said his brother.

"You want my money." If they thought I didn't know that, they were worse than I gave them credit for.

"Spending money is good for the soul," Lucien said. "That's why we want it."

"How about we continue this conversation downstairs?" I pointed at the door at the end of the hallway and the two guards in front of it.

The twins flinched right away and stopped walking. I grinned. "Oh, c'mon. You're not scared, are you?"

"No, no—we just know you're busy," Raphael said, moving backward now. "We get it—you're a busy guy. So we're just gonna let you go be busy."

"You sure? Because I got refreshments down there," I said, but they were already all the way to the middle of the hall.

"Just go do your thing! We'll be here when you're done," Lucien called, and they took off running to the other side as if they thought I was going to drag them down to the chambers by force. Twenty-six years old and they still acted like teenagers.

Laughing, I made way through the door the guards had opened for me. Those boys annoyed the shit out of me, but I did get a good laugh out of them more often than not.

I walked down the narrow stairway and into the chambers beneath the Sangria castle. It was a neat little place I'd made for myself, with rooms carved inside the stone and bars as thick as my arms that would make a lot of noise and be a bitch to bend if my prisoners ever hoped to escape. Currently, though, I only had one, and I kept him at the very end of the room, in a cell with a door instead of bars. A special cell I'd been inspired to design especially for him.

Guards were stationed every few feet, though I didn't get why. All the other five cells were empty, but oh, well. Coven money, not mine.

"Evening, fellas. How are we today?" I said as I passed them by.

"Good, sir," they all said at the same time, without moving an inch from their place.

"Keep up the good work," I said, already excited for what I'd find on the other side of that door.

I opened it, a big smile on my face, and...Finley was still alive.

Damn. The fucker was tougher than he looked.

"Evening, Finley," I said, locking the door behind me. The old fuck raised his head, his overgrown hair and beard all over the place. "Sorry I'm late. I got held up in a meeting. You know I hate those, but Robert insists." And if Robert wasn't the ruler of the coven—*and* the man who'd saved my life—I'd have sent him to hell a long time ago, too.

"Please," Finley said with a tired voice as I washed my hands in the small sink by the door and went to him.

All that was left of him was bones and skin. I hadn't fed him blood in over two weeks. The triangular structure he sat on that I'd carved with my own hands out of white stone still held. I had his arms chained to the walls with him sitting on the tip of the stone with his legs spread to the sides. Gravity was doing a hell of a job pulling him down. I could smell the wounds on his ass and balls and legs. That thing was going to cut him all the way if I just gave it enough time.

Sadly, though, I was bored out of my mind with the old fuck. I was going to finish him today, and that stone would remain there for the next asshole who deserved it. Maybe then I'd have more patience and see it through.

"You'll never believe what happened, Finley," I said, putting my hand on his shoulder. He flinched. "Some poor schmuck tried to steal an SUV right in front of the gates of the castle," I told him. "When they brought him in front of me—guess what?" The man blinked his dull brown eyes. "He pissed his pants, Finley." I laughed, and the man tried to do the same, because he thought it would please me. His bony shoulders shook. "He pissed his fucking pants in front of the entire board." I laughed some more.

Finley did, too. The sound of it was like needles in my brain, and as much as I'd have loved to drag this on a little longer, I couldn't.

I slammed my hand on his chest and sank my fingers under his skin all the way to his ribcage.

His laughter turned to a deafening scream instantly. Such beautiful music to my ears. His fangs came out all at once, his eyes darkening instantly.

"Were you laughing like that when you locked those girls in your basement, Finley?" I asked, and he began to hiss, trying to bite my face off—the vampire instinct in full swing. He tried to pull the chains from the walls, too, and the walls groaned. Weak or not, a vampire's strength was a lot, especially a vampire who knew he was going to die very soon.

I dug my fingers deeper in his chest.

"I didn't…I didn't…they consented…" he stuttered, just like he'd been doing for the past two weeks.

"Oh, yeah? Is that why you drugged them? Because they consented?" I could feel the vibration of his racing heart on my fingertips. Yum. His face was twisted, his dark eyes those of a monster, which was what we all really were.

"I didn't…I didn't…" he kept on going, and it made me laugh harder. He looked so weak and innocent right now, but he wasn't, not really. It took a lot to actually drug a vampire. It took a lot to even get a vampire drunk, but Finley here had been a pharmacist in his human life, and he knew how to mix his shit, get the job done.

Lucky for me, I'd found out about it before his coven, so it was only fair that *I* got to serve him his punishment, not them.

"Please," he said, even as he tried to bite my face off still. He could beg all he wanted—I was here to play, and I wasn't done until I got all of my fun out of it. "Please…oh, God…"

"Haven't you heard, Finley? God's not here. He took some time off from this place, left me in charge. This whole mess is way too much for Him, but me?" I grinned, pushing a bit deeper, breaking some of his ribs in the process. He howled like a wolf at the moon, but no matter how hard he tried, he couldn't move away from my grip and the chains. "I have no problem with it whatsoever." His heart touched the tip of my middle finger. All the blood that was left in him called out to me, but I resisted. Vampires were more than capable on living on animal blood, which was how it was in the Hidden Realm for decades now. But human blood was different. It filled us on a different level—as did vampire blood.

But I'd be damned if I took the rotten blood of this fucking creature.

"Get ready, Finley," I said, taking my hand out of his chest, watching his blood dripping down my fingers. "This is gonna be a while."

I got to work as he screamed his guts out.

3

"Another fucking meeting? Are you kidding me?" I said as I closed the door behind me.

Robert raised a brow, standing from his chair. "You didn't give me the chance to talk to you after the first. You just left." He seemed pissed about it, too.

"I was in a hurry."

He sighed. "Still dealing with the rapist?"

"Not anymore," I said with a grin, then sat down across from him.

"You could have spared yourself the trouble and just killed him on the spot," he said.

"But I needed to make an example out of him."

"No—that is *not* your job, Axel," Robert said.

"I made it my job." If it wasn't for that, what the hell else was I supposed to do in this place? "It's more fun than what you have me do here, anyway." Which was boring fucking meetings that were designed to fuck my mind up.

"You want to be the hero, I get it, but—"

"A hero?" I laughed. "You don't get shit. Why do you think they called me *Savage* in the cage?" I leaned closer and put my elbows on his desk as he flinched. He never wanted to talk about—

or even remember—the time before the Hidden Realm was created. "It's because I'm the fucking villain. I like hurting people, Rob. I like hurting bad people in very bad ways."

He fell back on the seat, running his hands over his shiny hair. Looking at Robert Sangria, you'd think he was in his thirties, just a young lad trying to make his place in the world. You'd also be dead wrong. He was almost two hundred years old, and he'd built an entire empire for himself over the last decade when he discovered Peridot gemstones deep in his lands in the Realm. All that money bought him men. Fancy things. Power. And he ruled over them all by himself.

"Talking to you is the most exhausting part of my day," he muttered.

"Believe me, I'm more than happy to get the fuck out of here." I'd been in this very office just hours ago, and I'd thought I was done for at least a week, but as soon as I'd come out of the chambers, he'd called for me again.

"I need you out there, Axel," Robert finally said, straightening in his fancy chair.

"Out there, where?"

"The human realm."

I squinted my eyes at him. "Are you serious?"

"I am, unfortunately," he said with a sigh. He intertwined his fingers and squeezed so hard his knuckles turned white. That's when I realized how stressed out he was, how his heart had picked up the beating and how his palms were a little bit sweaty, too, which was unlike him.

"What's going on, Rob?" I asked. "We talked about it last time I killed those sorcerers. We weren't gonna send me out there again." It had been inevitable—I'd been out searching for a rogue who escaped the Realm over two years ago, and the fucker had somehow gotten two sorcerers to cover for him. They'd attacked, had tried to keep him from me, so I'd killed them. I'd caused a mess that wasn't worth my—or Robert's—time.

And honestly, the outside world was a bitch to be in. Too many humans. Too much blood. Too many temptations. Not to mention the Vein spirits I couldn't kill with my fangs. I'd wanted to retire from that part of my life for a while.

"A vampire," Robert said. "Out there in the human world."

"Another escapee?" But he shook his head. Now *that* was interesting. I leaned back on my seat. "How?"

"Fuck if I know. Nobody's escaped here that we know of for the past year," said Robert. "But we have proof that she's there, and we need to get her back. As soon as possible."

"Proof from whom?"

"Not important." He looked down at his desk. "I need you to go out there and get her for me."

"You mean *kill* her." Because she was probably turned by a rogue.

But...no, it didn't make any sense. If there were rogue vampires out there and *we* didn't get to them first, the sorcerers would. They always did.

So how was she even turned?

"No—not kill her. Bring her here, unharmed."

"Fuck, Robert," I said with a sigh.

The human realm. It had been two years since I'd set foot out there. It was the same world we lived in, but ours was separated by magic. A limbo on Earth's surface made by the sorcerers themselves. We couldn't coexist. We'd tried since the beginning of time—and we always ended up killing each other. There was no stopping it.

The fact was, sorcerers had a lot of magic. There were a lot more of them in number, too, and they slaughtered vampires every single day before the treaty. They and the Vein spirits, too. Not that you could blame them considering humans ended up sucked completely dry on the regular, but still. It had taken the rulers of the covens a lot to make that treaty, but we were all alive because of it. We'd avoided an all-out war because of it. We'd made a home out of the Hidden Realm, far away from humans, and we lived well. We had livestock, more than enough to supply everyone with blood. We had food. We had technology—everything those bastards had out there.

It was peaceful here, but the more days passed, the more it looked like *peaceful* was not really the way for me. I'd lie if I said I wasn't a little bit excited to be there again. Not because that world had any appeal. Having to hide your true nature from everyone all the fucking time was exhausting, but it would be something to do. Something out of the ordinary. Something to get my blood rushing, at least.

"There's another thing," Robert said. "We're working with Redwood for this."

That was definitely more surprising than anything else he said. "Did you say *Redwood?*" He nodded, making me laugh. "Why?"

"Because it's too important. We don't really know what's out there or who that vampire is with. You're gonna need a hand."

I wasn't laughing anymore. "I don't need a fucking babysitter."

"Not a babysitter. Every coven will be sending out their people. It's already decided. Two are better than one—at least until you find her." He leaned closer over the desk. "It's very important that you find her, Axel. The most important thing you'll ever do."

Well, shit, now I got the chills. "I'll accept," I said. "On one condition. Is the secret I'm gonna find out at the end of this gonna be worth it?"

Robert closed his eyes with a sigh, and his heart skipped a beat. More than a good enough answer for me.

I stood up, suddenly feeling more alive than I had in a long time. "Who're they sending?"

"Nicole Arella, I think," he said.

"Never heard of her."

"Me, neither."

That bothered me. "They're sending a nobody for something this important?"

Robert looked up at me. "Abraham Jones is no fool. There's a reason why he's sending her. Keep your eyes open, Axel. And if it comes to it, kill her."

"With the utmost pleasure, Robert," I said with a grin.

"You leave at sundown. Here's the map, and I'll be loading up your old bank account for anything you'll need. You still got the card?" I nodded, though I wasn't sure it hadn't expired yet. "I'll let Redwood know you'll be waiting for their representative outside the Gates at sundown." He gave me a small leather bag with a folded piece of blue paper inside. I took the map, put it in my back pocket, and left the fancy bag on his desk.

"Axel," he called when I was already out the door. "Do not screw this up."

I winked and slammed the door shut.

★★★

The way the sky turned a deep orange just an hour before sundown had always been my favorite part of the day. Not because it was pretty to look at, but because back in my old life, that was *my* time. I wasn't required to be doing anything just before nightfall, only relax. Prepare. Become the man they called *Savage*.

Those had been good times for the most part, and it had gotten even better after, but lately, it felt like I'd gone a bit tame. That didn't sit well with me.

I drank the water, eyes stuck to the sky outside the large open windows of the guest room. It wasn't my bedroom, but the view was almost the same from here. The sun was about to retreat, and most of the Hidden Realm was right below me, even though I couldn't see all of it beyond the surrounding walls of Sangria's monstrous castle. To the naked eye, it looked just like an ordinary city. There were no skyscrapers here, but there were tall buildings. Homes. Businesses. Vampires everywhere you looked. Except during the day. It was quiet when the sun shone. Vampires slept until nightfall, so the streets were empty, the true face of the Realm right there for me to see.

But this was no ordinary place. The trees I could barely make out in the distance didn't grow there by accident. They marked the edge of the Realm. They hid the large, thick wall that encircled this entire city, heavily loaded with magic. The sorcerers had made it especially for us, to lock us up in here and keep the world safe.

A fucking cage.

It seemed like I was never going to really get out of those.

But at least I wouldn't be caged while I was out there. It was the perfect distraction, one I didn't even know I needed. This life here tied me down. It made my limbs heavy. I tried my best to survive, but it was getting difficult. There was only so much trouble vampires could cause. There was only so much pain *I* could cause here.

A trip to the outside world was exactly what I needed to get me out of this slump. And I suddenly couldn't wait to get the fuck out of here.

I put the bottle of water on the table and grabbed my jacket from the floor. The bed of the guest room in my house was as big as the one in my bedroom, except this one was already taken. Ariel slept on her stomach, the black sheets draped over half her legs, her naked back and ass in full display. I'd caved last night and given her a call because I was bored, and I didn't have the patience to go out. She hadn't complained, though. She'd submitted to my every order gladly, and we did have a hell of a night.

But it was done now. I'd let her sleep here because why not? It wasn't my bedroom—I never brought women back in there. I liked my sheets scentless when I did lie down.

And I did, every once in a while. I still hoped that I'd fall asleep someday. It's what vampires did—they fell unconscious into a coma-like state during the day, and they awoke with the night. Not me, though. I'd only slept seven nights in total in the twenty-five years since Robert turned me. Why, I'd probably never know.

When I got to my bedroom across the hall, I opened the windows there, too. The sunlight and the heat made me uncomfortable. It was just something to feel. A long shower awaited me, but before I slipped into the bathroom, I took a look at the sky again…and the Redwood castle in the distance. I'd never met any one of their rulers. I'd never met whoever they were going to send on this mission with me.

It was okay, though. I wasn't worried. Whoever she was, I would kill her before we left the woods outside the Gates.

Then, I'd go back to the real world after two long years.

4

Nikki Arella

Half an hour until sundown. I could have slept for at least another twenty minutes, but the whispers in my head were relentless since last night. Wandering the hallways of the soldier dorms until it was time to leave wasn't very appealing. About a hundred other vampires slept in the small rooms, and none was a friend.

It had been a while since I woke up this early, and if I weren't about to walk out into the human realm in just minutes, I might have even forced myself to wonder *why* I'd returned to the castle in the first place. Why I spent all my money on booze. Why I didn't just rent a place away from this hellhole.

Instead, I made my way to the top of the second tower, knowing very well that the sun would be out in the sky still. Lately I couldn't seem to make a single smart decision, it seemed.

Though the sun didn't really hurt us much—we didn't turn to ash right away when sunlight contacted with our skin. Far from it. I'd read plenty of vampire stories, and we weren't what the world imagined us to be. Our bodies were still alive. We still functioned just like every other living creature out there, but all our senses were enhanced. We had much more speed and strength, too, if there was enough blood running in our veins. It is true that vampires can't be born, though, just turned. You'd have to bite a human, then feed them your blood for the process to be completed and for the vampire virus to take hold of the body. And we weren't truly immortal—we still aged, though very, *very* slowly, and it would take over half a century of time to kill a vampire. Nobody survived that long without getting killed. At least they hadn't so far.

But the truth was, it was difficult for us to see properly in sunlight. Our eyes were much better equipped to see in the dark. The heat was a problem, too. We hated it. It made our limbs heavy. We much preferred the cold. Daylight just dragged us down. We were much more lively in the dark. That's why we slept all day and stayed up all night.

That's why I should have stayed in my bed until Anya came to get me—I had no doubt that she was already up, too, counting the minutes.

Letting go of a deep breath, I put my hands on the cold stone ledge and looked at my surroundings, hoping to clear my mind of the whispers. And the thoughts.

The castle was huge, with three towers, the tallest in the middle standing a hundred feet high. It was made of grey stone blocks, surrounded by a large wall that went all around the property. It looked like it was placed there by accident compared to the rest of the buildings in the Realm.

The balcony at the top of the second tower was narrow, but it completely encircled the tower. Behind the castle, I could barely see the three separate training areas. That's where I spent most my time—*training*, though I didn't even know what for. There was no point in having soldiers when there were no wars to fight. But I guess I shouldn't have complained. I had a roof over my head and money in my pocket. Who cared about purpose, right?

The heat of the sun had my skin covered in a layer of sweat in minutes. I walked to the other side of the tower to find some shade, and I looked at the city, almost completely silent like I'd never seen it before. Vampires didn't wake up until nightfall. And just now, under the light of the setting sun, the buildings didn't look so dull. The air didn't seem so heavy. The streets didn't seem so empty, even though they were.

It was almost beautiful.

In the distance, I could see the Sangria castle standing proud in the middle of ordinary buildings, the stones of it yellow, polished, its seven towers placed in a circle probably just for show. Who needs seven towers, anyway? But Robert Sangria had a lot of money. He needed to spend it somewhere. There was only so much one could do in the Hidden Realm.

The way I figured, if Jones was willing to cooperate with him, chances were that this mission was much bigger than I even realized last night. *Way* bigger. It also meant that both men were scared shitless that other covens might get their hands on that vampire first, and they were truly willing to do *anything* not to let that happen.

Why? Why would they go to such great lengths for a vampire? There were plenty of us in the Hidden Realm—over ten thousand. We weren't all that special. And if there truly was a vampire out there in the human world, what were the odds that she hadn't gotten killed by sorcerers yet?

When I heard the footsteps through the half open door of the balcony, my entire body froze. I expected it would be Anya come to drag me downstairs to make sure I wasn't late, but one sniff at the air and I realized it wasn't her at all.

Two seconds later, Abraham Jones pushed the door open all the way and stepped onto the balcony, his dark eyes on me.

I raised a brow. "Couldn't sleep?" I'd seen him just last night, and I thought it would be another decade until we met again. There was just something about the air around him that spoke of power, that tried to get you to submit to his every order. It had always made me uncomfortable. It still did.

"It's a beautiful day. I wanted to see it before it slipped away," he said, coming to stand beside me, hands folded behind him. He wore his black suit proudly, and his chin was raised as he looked ahead to where I was looking—the Sangria castle. I studied his sharp jaw and pointy noise for a second. So little about him had changed since I first saw him almost thirty years ago. He was basically the same man still.

"Here I was, hoping you'd changed your mind about me," I said, only half-jokingly.

"I haven't," he said without missing a beat. Damn. "It's almost time, Nicole."

Just the way he said my name brought back memories I was perfectly fine without. And now I regretted leaving that bottle of vodka in my room.

"I haven't been out there in twenty years," I reminded him.

"It's the same as everything here," Jones said, his eyes searching the grey sky that was getting darker by the second.

"Except there's sorcerers there," I said. "And spirits from the Veins."

That's what the sorcerers called the Ley lines spread all over the world, like a network of invisible rivers underneath the ground. They were endless sources of magic, and all kinds of spirits lived in them, creatures that sometimes escaped and killed, and sometimes they even latched on to a living being, too. To a vampire, they were even more dangerous than sorcerers because only magic could get rid of Vein spirits.

Jones stayed silent for a long moment.

"You will be safe, Nicole. You *know* you will," he finally said.

I smiled, despite the pain my memories brought. Or maybe it was *because* of it.

"Do you remember the night you found me?" My voice was barely a whisper. I blocked the images from my brain even as I spoke because I could handle the pain just fine. But I didn't need to feel every other emotion attached to that story, too.

"Oh, yes," he said, and his lips stretched. "I certainly remember." It was nothing to smile about, though.

"Why did you take me in?" I'd asked him this question once before. He'd refused to answer. His smile vanished, but he still didn't look at me. He still didn't speak. It made me laugh bitterly. "You saw me. You saw what I did. You kept me, anyway." And if he thought I was *accusing* him, well…he was right.

"You were a kid," he said, pushing all my buttons at once just like that.

"I was *not* a kid!" I suddenly snapped, way louder than I intended. But the whispers in my head were already getting louder.

"Yes, you were." Jones turned to me, but I refused to meet his eyes now. "You were six years old, Nicole."

"It doesn't matter. I am not who you think I am."

Jones thought one of those Vein spirits had *touched* me, that I had merely been in the wrong place at the wrong time. It wasn't *my* fault that it had happened—it was just fate. But he kept overlooking one simple truth my whole life—vampires and magic did not mix, not for any reason. I was a vampire, and if a spirit had truly gotten into me, it would have killed me, as simple as that. Jones refused to acknowledge it still, apparently, and I was going to paint the picture for him. Again. "I'm a monster. I will be out there with humans and sorcerers, with actual Vein spirits—"

"And you will come back to me," he cut me off. I saw his hand moving before he touched my chin with his fingertips and turned my head to him. His eyes had become even darker, or maybe I just saw them better now that the sky was all but black. "Our nature is not our responsibility, Nicole." But all the lives lost at the hands of *my nature* would be.

"I haven't seen you in a decade. Why now? What's so special about this vampire that you would risk sending *me* out there?" I asked, even though I knew Jones well enough to know he wouldn't answer.

"I've given you as much time and space as I could, Nicole," he said instead. "I know what happened with Ezra—"

"*Don't.*"

At the mentioning of that name, I move my head away and stepped to the side to give myself some room to breathe. The voices in my head reacted immediately, so I squeezed my eyes shut and just focused on pushing them down for a second.

"This has nothing to do with that," I lied. "This has everything to do with *you*. You should have killed me, Jones. I can't be trusted." I hated that he made me say it when he knew it very well.

"If there is one person in the world I would trust with my life, it would be you."

Even my heart stood still for the second that it took me to raise my head and meet his eyes again.

My gods, he was serious.

"Whatever you've become now, this isn't who you are, Nicole. I've seen you fight your own self since you were a child, every single day. You never had a reason to do it—you chose to. I never made you or taught you—you *chose* to, simply because you knew it was the right thing to do."

I swallowed hard to push back the tears next. Why did everyone always have to be so goddamn sentimental?

"You've given up. I don't blame you. Sometimes it's just easier to let go. But it's time to wake up now. It's time to take your life under your control again."

He strode to me slowly because he wanted me to see his every movement. And when he put his hand on my shoulder, it took all I had not to jerk away.

"You will be safe from Vein spirits. You can fight the other covens. You can handle Savage Ax and everything else the world throws at you. But Nicole," he dug his fingers into my shoulder, and I moved my eyes to his immediately, "don't expect it to be easy. It will be hard," he whispered. "And it will be worth it."

Goddamn him and the sun and everything else on the face of the earth.

I stepped back. It was time for me to go.

"I'll bring her back, Jones," I told him. "But after that, I'm done."

I would no longer be a soldier. I'd tend bars or work in retail or whatever. There were jobs in the Realm. Somewhere where my patience wouldn't be tested every day. I'd been stuck in my comfort zone for so long, I was terrified to even think about leaving it behind. But I'd make another comfort zone away from this castle. Jones was right—it was time to take control. Just as soon as I came back.

But the way he suddenly smiled gave me the chills. "Bring her back. Then, we'll talk about it," he said. "Things are changing, Nicole. And we will both be here to witness it." For some reason, his words sounded like a *promise*.

Before I could think to ask a single question, he moved so fast he practically disappeared from my sight and into the tower again. I couldn't even hear his footsteps as he went down the stone stairs.

With a sigh, I turned to the dark sky as if searching for an answer. When I received none, I walked back inside, too.

5

"You're all set," Anya said as she pulled my jacket over my shoulders. "All set. You got everything you need, right?" she asked for the fifth time.

"Yes, Anya. I'm all set. I got the map, the blood, and the money." *And the liquor*—but I didn't say that last one out loud.

"What about your phone? And your charger?"

"Yep. I got all of it," I said, patting the pocket of my jacket.

"Great," she said, breathing heavily. I heard her heart hammering in her chest, too. I loved that girl, I really did, but I wished she wouldn't have worried. "Anya, just go. Get back to bed. You—"

But before I could finish speaking, we heard the footsteps falling on dry leaves. We were outside, surrounded by the large trees at the edge of the Hidden Realm. Anya had driven me here because she actually owned a car, but the road was a few minutes away from the large gates half shielded by the trees—and a shitload of magic.

A second later, we saw Ivan and two Redwood guards striding to us with their heads high and their shoulders rigid, moving the same leg forward at the same time. So fucking dramatic, I could die of cringe.

"Please tell me you're going with her," Anya said to her brother even before he stopped in front of us.

"Anya, c'mon," I said, but Ivan was already at it.

"No, I'm not. She's going alone," he told his sister. "And if she drinks that bottle in her bag, she's gonna die in the first hour out of the Realm."

I rolled my eyes as Anya turned to me, shocked. "What? What bottle? You didn't say you were taking a bottle?" She made to grab my bag, but I moved it to my other arm. It wasn't her fault that she hadn't smelled the bottle—I'd put it under the stacks of money they'd given me. Money had a very strong scent because of how many times it changed hands on the regular. Plus, Anya wasn't very attentive.

That—or she just trusted my word that much, which wasn't very smart.

"He's just joking," I said, then looked at Ivan—the spitting image of his sister. Same chestnut hair, same brown eyes—except his had much more depth. They were sharper. Nothing ever escaped those eyes.

"Do you have everything you need?" he asked me, looking me up and down. His heartbeat picked up a bit right away. I knew he had a thing for me—he always had. And honestly, I never knew why when he was hot as hell and women fell all over him all the time.

But he wasn't my type because he wasn't made out of glass and he didn't contain liquids that could wipe my mind clean of thoughts for hours at a time.

"Yep. All set. If you could just get these babies for me." I nodded at the massive gates that were easily fifty feet high. Who had even brought them here? I had no idea, but Ivan nodded and stepped forward, toward the keyhole that was bigger than my head.

He had the key for it, too—just as big as my arm that one of the guards was carrying in a leather bag.

Anya was already shaking. I took her ice-cold hands in mine. "Just breathe," I begged her.

"You got the blood, right?"

"Yes, I got the blood right here." I touched my bag and the thermos full of cow blood she'd prepared for me. "And they make all kinds of foods in the human realm. I'll be fine."

"Okay, okay," she said, and when Ivan put the large key in the keyhole and began to turn it, she wrapped her arms around me tightly.

Fuck. Not that I'd ever admit it out loud, but I was going to miss her so much. I hugged her to me for just one second, just so that she had that small thing from me in case I never made it back.

"Go," she whispered, eyes filled with tears. "And come back, okay? I'll be waiting."

"I will, Anya. I'll be back." I tried to put as much resolve as I could in my voice. I don't know if it worked.

"You need help with that?" I asked Ivan when I went to the gate. It looked to me like he was having trouble turning the key—and I couldn't blame him.

"No, I—" he said, but I'd already dropped the bag and grabbed the other end of the steel key to help him. A tiny pull was all it took, and the monstrous gate roared as the lock clicked open.

Ivan left it there and stepped in front of me, brows narrowed, brown eyes wide and honest. I hated this part so much, but I smiled anyway.

"Don't drink, Nicole," he whispered. "Without alcohol, there's nothing out there you won't see coming. You're the best soldier we have when you're sober." He put a hand on my arm, and it was all I could do not to flinch. "You're smart. *Be* smart. It's different out there."

"Thanks, Ivan. I appreciate it. I'll see you when I get back, okay?" Too much pressure getting all sentimental like that. I swear, everybody wanted to do it at some point—even Jones—and I was sick of it. Feelings belonged on the *inside*, where we could lock them up and pretend they didn't exist, and when pretending didn't cut it, well…that's where alcohol came in.

"I'll see you when you get back," he said with a disappointed nod. I was used to those, so it didn't even hurt anymore. Putting his large hands on the gate, he pushed it open with all his strength, and it barely moved a tiny bit.

"That'll do," I said, even though I'd have to squeeze through the opening to get to the other side. I just wanted to get out of there. "Thanks, Ivan. Anya. And you two." I waved at the guards I didn't know. They didn't wave back.

"See ya, gang." I slipped through the small opening between the large gates. They were as thick as me, maybe even a little more.

I almost couldn't get my bag through, but Anya helped from the other side, and then I could see her eyes staring at me. I waved again, the brightest smile in my arsenal stretching my lips as I walked backward.

A second later, Ivan pulled the gate closed.

I stopped walking and smiling and let out a long breath.

Outside. I was outside of the Hidden Realm. Outside in the real world full of humans. And sorcerers. I hadn't been out here in twenty years, not since I was fifteen years old.

Shit.

I turned around and looked up at the full moon, at the large trees over me, heard the sound of the mockingbirds chirping in the distance, smelled the million things that lived all around me. I felt eyes on me, too, but I couldn't see the small animals watching, only smell their fur. And it was nasty.

"Here goes nothing," I muttered to myself and started walking.

I wasn't afraid exactly, but I wasn't completely calm, either. It was a mixture I didn't recognize very well, and it was already uncomfortable. Feelings sucked balls.

Only after I'd taken the tenth step did I feel the change in the air. It was like, one second it was heavy, weighing on my shoulders in a way I hadn't even recognized, and the next, it was…*free*.

The air was light, the smells so much more intense, my sight near perfect. I turned to look at the trees that shielded the walls of the Hidden Realm that you couldn't see at all from out here, apparently, and I breathed deeply. Just trees, trees, and some more trees all around me.

The magic.

The magic the sorcerers who'd made this place for us as part of the treaty was gone. It ended here—and now I could breathe free air again. What a difference. Had I even noticed when we all first came to the Realm? My gods, it was really a different world out here.

Despite everything, I smiled. Maybe this wasn't such a terrible thing. Maybe Jones knew what he was doing when he put me up to this. Maybe…just maybe, I'd actually enjoy the ride. Just a little bit. The night was still too hot even though it was September, but I didn't even mind it. I was suddenly eager to see more. The Realm was hidden by miles and miles of woods on all sides, and it was going to take a while to get to civilization, but…

My nose caught a new scent—something that wasn't an animal. Something…vampire. All my good mood went down the drain instantly.

Savage Ax.

Fear gripped my insides as I turned around and searched for him. I was supposed to meet him right outside the Gates, but he wasn't here. I couldn't hear him or see him—only smell the scent he'd left behind. Leather and mint and unmistakably vampire.

I waited for another minute stuck there in the middle of the grass that reached my knees. I waited, ears open, eyes sharp, but he didn't come. I knew he knew I was here—he could probably smell me, too.

But he wasn't coming.

With a sigh, I put my bag over my shoulder again and I started trailing his scent. The fucker was probably playing games with me. Did he even know who I was? I doubted it. At first, when I was turned, I was the most curious thing any vampire had ever seen—a six-year-old with fangs. It's why Jones always kept me hidden, had me staying with other vampires he trusted for months at a time before he came, picked me up, and dropped me off with someone else. It was a miserable childhood, but I was always safe. Always protected. Always had blood and food, a roof over my head. And plenty of loneliness.

But by the time the treaty was signed and the Hidden Realm was created, I already looked pretty much as I do now. I grew up much faster than the normal human. The virus had me looking like a teenager at nine years old and like an adult at thirteen. I pretty much stopped aging since then, and I would remain the same for another couple centuries. *If* I even made it that far.

Very few people knew my story, so I doubted Savage Ax had heard my name. As much as it made me cringe now, I'd been a *good* girl most of my life. I'd done as I was told. I'd stayed out of trouble. Had hated alcohol with a passion.

I'd had Ezra.

The familiar stab in the gut hit me all at once, taking my breath away. Squeezing my eyes shut, I focused all my being into drowning the emotions that wanted to spill over me. Bad shit happened when I lost control and let them out. It was best they stayed in.

I kept on walking, getting distracted by the trees, the birds, the little animals watching me curiously and running away whenever I got close. It helped in keeping the whispers at bay.

But half an hour later, there was still no Savage Ax.

The smell of water and the sound of it falling caught my attention, and for a second, I stopped following his scent. I wanted to see where all that noise was coming from and that smell that was more pure than anything else in these woods.

Two minutes later, I reached it. There were no trees around and the moonlight gave me a clear view of even the smallest details. The ground rose a few feet and ended with a pile of rocks shaped like a hook. Underneath that hook, water came out of the stones—so much of it—and it fell down at least thirty feet into a large green pool right past the edge of the grass. All of it shone with a beautiful silver hue.

Dropping my bag, I went as close to the edge as I could without falling. A freaking waterfall, though not as big as some pictures I'd seen, but definitely just as beautiful. What's more—the sound of the water falling drowned every thought in my head until all I could focus on was *it*. The most beautiful thing I'd ever seen in my life.

And…Savage Ax was watching me.

I could feel his eyes on me like a physical touch. I turned slowly and looked all around me, but I couldn't see him. Way too many places to hide—the grass was tall, the trees large, the leaves huge. I smiled at myself as I took my jacket off and let it fall to the ground. He wanted to play fucking games with me? Fine. I'd play, too.

I took off my crop top next, extra slowly. Still no movement. I unzipped my skirt, too, and let it pool around my feet. Next went my panties, my bra, and I left the boots for last.

A minute later, I was standing naked in the middle of the woods, with only two holsters strapped to my thighs.

No Savage Ax.

Oh, well.

I turned around and jumped off the cliff, straight into the pool of water thirty feet down.

The feeling was incredible. The wind blowing on my face was different from when I ran at full speed. It was *free*, and it lasted a long time before I finally touched the surface of the water and slammed into the pool.

Cold. Ice-cold. The water was heaven all around me. The pool was deep, too. I stayed under the surface for as long as I could hold my breath. I *never* wanted to come out. The small fish that swam around me, the uneven rocks of the bed I sometimes touched with my feet, the cold and the darkness down there was like a sanctuary.

But eventually I ran out of air. Raising my arms, I started swimming up to the surface. The moon was so bright that I saw everything in perfect clarity. I saw the rocks from which the water fell…and the black silhouette of the man on top of it, looking down.

I broke the surface with a huge smile on my face, eyes on the silhouette. I could barely make out his face from the distance, but it was him. It had to be.

Such a *guy*. All it took was stripping off my clothes and he came running.

At least now I knew where we stood.

Leaving the water behind wasn't something I wanted to do, but night had long since fallen and I had to keep moving. I started climbing the sharp rocks up to the woods again. My muscles were strained, but with every new movement, my strength came back to me. The cold of the water still hanging on my skin helped, and every new breeze against it fueled me.

I made it to the top, breathing heavily, but smiling so big my cheeks hurt.

When I stood up, he was right there, barely ten feet away from me now, and I finally laid eyes on Savage Ax.

I'd heard the stories about him—everyone had. They were whispered among vampires in bars, in the streets, inside homes. He was a psychopath who loved violence, and he was pretty much unstoppable with Robert Sangria at his back.

But none of the rumors had ever talked about the looks of him. At least not that I remembered.

He was just over six feet tall, with big shoulders and narrow hips, his chest and stomach defined to perfection with all that muscle that I could see because he wore nothing but a black leather jacket and a pair of loose faded jeans. There were scars everywhere on his torso, and they kinda looked like tattoos, but nothing came even close to the blue of his eyes. It was icy, and when I blinked, it almost looked green before it transformed to blue again. It pierced right through me.

There was a scar on his face, too. It started on his left temple and went all the way over his ear. His hair was dark, cut close to his head, and his stubble was much the same length. His full lips didn't smile as he watched me, but his hands did pull up in fists when those eyes scrolled down my face to my tits, then lower to my stomach.

"See something you like?" I teased, then bent down to grab my clothes—extra slowly.

He leaned his head to the side but didn't say anything, just watched me intently as I put my panties on, then my skirt. The way he looked at me, you'd think he was calculating all the ways to eat me raw. I wished he'd make a move so I could see what he was made of. That's why I held his eyes as I smiled, then put on my bra, and my crop top. He didn't move an inch, but that heart of his…oh, I heard it. I fucking heard how it turned up a notch. Just a tiny bit.

"I like you already," I told him with a wink.

Finally, when I put my jacket on, I opened my bag. The moon was up so it was fair game. I took out my bottle of vodka, opened it, and took a long sip.

Ah, yes. It burned so beautifully, I could drown in it and be a happy woman.

At that, Savage Ax smiled a little bit.

Putting the bottle back in the bag, I brought my finger to my lips.

"*Sshhh*," I whispered, then took off walking through the woods again.

He'd follow me—I knew he would. He'd played his hand and I'd played mine. Now that we'd seen each other's faces, we could move on. We didn't even have to go the same way, so long as we reached the same destination at the same time.

But it wasn't meant to be.

I heard it the second he moved—and the fucker was fast. I barely managed to drop my bag and turn before his fist was in front of my face.

The thing was, I was fast, too. I moved away and his knuckles barely grazed my chin. I grabbed his arm and pulled him to me, and my knee was up and waiting. It buried in his gut and emptied his lungs, but it wasn't nearly enough damage. That's why he recovered and slammed his fist on the side of my waist hard. I'd been expecting it, so my muscles were clenched, but damn. He could throw a fucking punch, at least. Even though tiny stars still danced in my vision, we were close enough that I didn't need to see all that well to grab him by the back of the jacket and slam my knee in his gut one more time. And when he tried to punch me again in the chest, I ducked down and kicked him in the shin with the tip of my boot hard. Bone cracked but not a sound left him.

When I came up again, he had one arm around my shoulder and a large hand around my arm to try to get me to hold still. His other hand came for my neck. Before he could reach me, I slammed both butts of my fists onto his ears hard, and had he been a little weaker, his skull would have cracked. As it was, he only squeezed his eyes shut for a second. His grip around my arm loosened, and it gave me enough time to slam my fist in the middle of his chest once. I went for it again, but the fucker recovered way too fast. Much faster than the other soldiers I sparred with at home. His large hand wrapped around my fist and he squeezed. My knuckles cracked, but I gritted my teeth to keep from screaming. The pain was quickly washed away by the adrenaline, and I grabbed the side of his neck, but it was too damn thick to try to strangle, so I did the next best thing—I stabbed him with the long fingernail of my thumb. Skin broke and blood came out, and it must have hurt because he hissed before he squeezed my fist a bit tighter, then had no choice but to move back a bit, away from my fingernail.

My fist was a mess, but fuck if I wasn't having a good time.

And if the wide smile on his face was any indication, he was, too. He was a handsome bastard, but when he grinned like that, showing me all of his teeth, the canines slightly crooked, he looked crazy. Mad. Completely insane with those sparks dancing in his eyes. He moved away from me for a good minute, while I ducked away from him, too.

But then I got sloppy.

I saw his fist coming, and I knew I'd dodge it in time, but I should have paid attention to where his other hand was, too—right on my other side, ready to grip me by the back of the neck and pull me to him so hard, I had no chance of stopping it. I slammed onto his chest, and when he wrapped his other hand around my neck, I didn't stop him. My hands were busy, anyway, and he saw why when the tip of my knife pressed against his Adam's apple.

We both stopped moving, chest to chest, breathing heavily, our noses barely an inch apart. His hands were around my neck, and my knife was pressed to his.

Which one of us would be faster?

Oh, I couldn't wait to find out.

"Is this about the booze?" I whispered. "Because you're gonna have to get your own. I don't share."

Those yummy looking lips stretched and stretched into a wide smile again, and the way his chest was pressed to my boobs every time he breathed made my thighs clench a little bit. A man who could actually hold his own in a fight. Maybe the rumors about him were true, after all.

"Just checking to see if I can trust you to watch my back out there," he finally said. His voice was just as sexy as the rest of him, rough and a bit hoarse. Perfect for whispering dirty things in a woman's ear.

Damn, I needed to get laid.

But those lips, though. I watched them, and my imagination got away from me. I felt my tongue coming out to lick mine. His eyes fell on it, followed its every movement, and the whites of his eyes slowly began to turn to red.

Got'cha.

I slammed my forehead on his nose with all my strength.

He fell back a couple of steps before he began to laugh, a tiny drop of blood coming out his nostril. Shit, my forehead was pounding, but I didn't let it show. I kept a smile on my face and watched him as he laughed, wiping the blood off his nose with the back of his hand.

Damn, he was hot—and with a touch of crazy, which added a lot to his appeal. Not to mention that throaty laugh...

"Just checking," I said with a shrug and picked up my bag from the ground again. My hand still hurt—vampires healed fast, but it was going to take a few hours for my cracked bones to heal.

"Who the fuck are you?" he called after me.

"Maybe I'll let you know when I figure it out," I called back and kept on walking. My ears were sharp, my head no longer pounding.

But Savage Ax didn't attack me again.

6

I smelled two more of our kind by the time we reached the edge of the woods. A two hours' walk—how nice. It was worse that we couldn't run. Running was fun, not to mention *fast*, but you couldn't keep quiet while running, and you couldn't be sure about what was around you. Also, the strength it took us to use our full speed would leave us easy prey for a stronger vampire for at least a few minutes. Out here in the open, that was a no-go.

But whoever it had been I'd smelled, they probably smelled me, too, and they stayed away. Good for them.

And me.

Ax kept behind me at all times, though. I could never see him when I looked back, but I smelled him. Heard him. Imagined him laughing just fine, and I'll be the first to admit that I wasn't proud of all the minutes I allowed him to be in my mind. It went from imagining what his lips would taste like, to thinking about how he'd kiss me—probably violently, with a lot of teeth and blood. He'd probably grab my hair and slam me to him, too, then leave a trail of bruises down my neck because he seemed like the type to want to mark his territory, and…*shit*. There I went again.

I could smell the asphalt about fifty feet away, and I decided that that was the best place to stop for a breather. And a swig of vodka. Soon, I'd be out there in the middle of the human world, and though I was up to date with all the movies and all the viral videos, it was a bit scary. Exciting, too, but mostly scary. Who knew what having all that human blood right under my nose would do to me? It had been a long time.

Dropping my bag on the ground, I found a nice thick tree root to sit on and rest my back. Not that I was tired, but I was irritated because it had been two hours since night fell and I wasn't drunk yet. The whispers were in my head, and as much as the woods had provided distractions, it all looked the same to me now. It was definitely time to fix that.

"Tired?"

His voice came from higher up, and I didn't even need to search for longer than a second before I found him atop a tree, feet firmly planted on a thick branch like he couldn't care less if it broke. Of course, he didn't—he was a vampire. The fall wouldn't even sprain his ankle.

"No, just catching up with my buddy here." I showed him my bottle of vodka.

He jumped off the tree and onto the ground almost completely soundlessly. Even though barely any moonlight made it down here, I still saw him. Saw every shade of him, every shape, the glistening in his gorgeous eyes.

He stopped a few feet away from me, looking around, eyes searching every tree and every leaf hanging on them.

"You don't have a bag," I said in wonder. I had one. I didn't take much—just a change of clothes and my essentials.

"I don't need one," he said, raising a thick brow as he looked down at me. "Are you always so slow?"

I grinned. "Pretty much, yeah." He knew why I was taking my time walking through the woods very well.

"Maybe I should carry you on my back then. That way we have hopes of getting to our destination in a couple days."

"Actually, that is not a bad idea." I took a swig of the alcohol again. "You could totally pass for a horse."

The next second, he was squatting right in front of my feet. I didn't see it coming, and it did give my heart a little scare, but if he heard it, he didn't comment.

"And you could pass for a schoolgirl," he said, looking down at my flared black skirt and crop top.

Well, damn, he was making me blush.

"You don't like my skirt?" I put my hand on my knee and slowly dragged it up my thigh to the hem of my skirt, then pulled it up a bit until he could see my panties.

I swear, to see his eyes light up like that was fucking hilarious. Impossible not to laugh.

"It looked better when it was off you," he said, then sat down on the ground, eyes on my legs. Couldn't blame him. They were fine legs.

I raised a brow. "Now you're just being nice."

"Do you always take your clothes off when you can't find who you're looking for, Nicole?"

"It's Nikki. And absolutely. Chasing bores me. I'd much rather make them come to me."

His eyes didn't give away anything, and the small smile curling half his lips could have meant anything. I couldn't figure him out now that he wasn't lusting after me.

Which was a bit strange, to be honest. One minute his eyes were bloodshot, and the next, he was completely composed. Made me wonder if he'd faked it. If he was playing me the same way I was playing him.

Damn.

"You're not what I was expecting," he said, and he sounded surprised. Well, he wasn't what I'd been expecting, either.

"What did you think—that I'd be a little damsel in distress, waiting for a savior?"

"A little bit, yeah," he admitted with a shrug. At least he was being honest.

"Sorry to disappoint, but I am no damsel." He could see that for himself. "So, tell me, Axel," I said, drinking a little more of my vodka. I didn't want to overdo it—I still needed my senses sharp for out there, but a little buzzing in my head wasn't going to hurt me. "How many times have you fantasized about fucking schoolgirls?"

My question didn't surprise him in the least. "I don't fantasize," was what he said.

I rolled my eyes. "Can you get any more boring?"

A spark lit up his eyes again as he grinned. I liked that much better.

"How many times have *you* fantasized about getting fucked like a schoolgirl?" he said.

"Oh, I lost count a long time ago."

His smile only widened. "You like being a little slut, don't you." It wasn't even a question.

And had I given just one tiny little fuck, I'd have probably been offended.

"I like taking what life has so generously given to us. We have bodies for a reason. Sex feels the way it does for a reason. Why would I be stupid enough not to take advantage of that?"

Big talk. I wouldn't even remember what sex felt like because I hadn't had it in almost two years. There's just something about nameless men in your bed that makes you feel *worse* afterward, instead of *better*. Besides, I had alcohol. I didn't need a man—much less one who was going to stick his knife in my back when I wasn't looking—and then *die* because of it, too.

Unscrewing the cap of the bottle, I took another big sip. Fuck having my mind sharp—the memories needed to go asap.

"So, what do you say, Axel?" I teased, raising my leg a little bit. "Do *you* like being a slut, too? Shall we take advantage of the situation? Nobody's around for miles."

But he already knew that I was fucking with him, just like I knew he was fucking with me. We were testing each other, searching for limits still. "No, thanks, Damsel. I've got enough women begging for seconds as it is," he told me. "Besides— whatever you're used to that's left you so unsatisfied all your life, I'm not that kind. Schoolgirls can't handle my cock, but maybe, in a few years…"

His voice trailed off as he shrugged.

I burst out laughing. That was *good*. It was really good.

But now I was thinking about his cock, too. That's why I looked at it like a damn fool.

And when I saw the bulge in his jeans…oh, man. "I think your cock wants to make up his own mind about me, Axel." I laughed some more.

He wasn't shy in the least. Which was a shame because I really wanted to see him blushing. "He'll get over it in no time."

"Are you sure?" Because he was hard, and damn if I wasn't a little bit wet, too. I was still just teasing him, but the mind wandered and the body responded—for the both of us, apparently.

"Yep. I've already seen all there is to see. There will be no need for imagining."

Well, damn. Now I almost wished I hadn't taken my clothes off at the waterfall. *Almost*.

"On the contrary. All the ways your cock could teach me a thing or two about what I've been missing…imagine what *that* would be like."

He tried to hide it this time. He really tried—and though he didn't blush, I was perfectly satisfied with the way his eyes widened for a second and the way his heart skipped a beat.

It was plenty of proof that he was just a man, despite his reputation, just like Jones said.

And as much fun as this was, it was time to drop the games.

"We've got a small town coming right outside these woods," I said, nodding my head to the side.

His brows shot up as if he was having trouble focusing. It would have been so easy to tease him again, but I was tired of it. All that talk was making *me* horny, too, which defeated the purpose. I wanted *his* mind wandering, not mine. I wanted to see how easily *I* could distract him, not the other way around.

Taking the map Jones had given me from my bag, I unfolded it as I held his eyes. Ten seconds in, he was perfectly composed and not even hard anymore. Color me impressed.

I sat up on my legs and spread the map of the United States of America in between us. It didn't escape my attention how his eyes stopped on my cleavage when I bent over to straighten the wrinkles on the paper, but I bit my tongue to keep the smile off my face.

I don't fantasize, my ass. Savage or not, Axel Creed was definitely just a man.

And now we could actually do what we were here to do.

"All the other covens are going to take the obvious route," I said, showing him the black line I'd drawn the night before that would lead from the edge of North Dakota, all the way to Atlanta, Georgia. The fastest way would be through Iowa and Illinois, which was how I knew that every other asshole who was on this with us would go that way. "But if we take this route and go through Nebraska, there's a good chance that we'll make it to Atlanta first, especially if we run the highways at night and don't run into any trouble."

"That's stretching it," he said, eyes on the map now, too. "There are sorcerers and spirits out there. Trouble will be inevitable, but as long as the other fuckers keep away, we'll get there in three days, even using the main route."

Unfortunately, he was right. "We're going to have to handle the sorcerers and keep away from spirits, but I'd rather not have to worry about the other covens, too." We could actually run fast without fearing we'd get ambushed any second.

He looked at me from under his lashes, which were longer than mine. "Except you don't know for sure that we won't be followed. You don't know for sure where the others are going to go." Shit. Right again. "A fight with them can't be helped—we'll still need to take them all out before we can get that woman."

"Fighting them doesn't concern me. Them getting to her first and hiding her does."

"Our options are limited. Let's get to the first town and see what we're dealing with first."

"You've been here before, haven't you?"

He nodded. "Plenty of times. But things change fast in the human world."

"So, how're we gonna do this?" I folded the map again and put it in my bag. As much as I itched for some more vodka, I resisted. "Are you planning to drive?"

"Driving out here would be stupid. Five other vampires around us, not to mention the sorcerers," he said. He and Jones would probably get along just fine.

"How will we know if the other's in trouble?"

He grinned again. "We'll be together, won't we?"

I raised a brow. "We'll kill each other before we get to the next state."

"I don't kill schoolgirls."

"Well, I do kill savages."

He laughed—and the sound sent vibrations throughout me. Completely involuntarily, I might add.

"There's a reason why our rulers sent us here, Damsel. I think we'll survive."

I squinted my eyes at him. "Is that nickname supposed to make me feel small and weak, and give you the impression that I'm in need of saving?" It was the second time he'd called me *Damsel*, and as much as I didn't give a shit, I was actually curious.

Or was it because of what I said to him earlier, about me not being a damsel in distress?

"You're not small or weak. And I don't think you need saving," he said, leaning his head closer to me as he whispered. "It's just to remind the both of us that no matter how big your mouth, you're still the prey, Damsel. You can still get devoured."

That sonovabitch. *Devoured*. And the way he said it—so fucking dirty. Yeah, his voice was definitely made to talk dirty like that.

"Maybe I have no problem with being devoured," I whispered back, fighting to hold my smile.

"Believe me, you would." It sounded so *final*.

He stood up then and spun around slowly, still searching our surroundings while I searched every inch of his body. Fine specimen. I could fuck his brains out without feeling bad afterward.

Too bad he was a monster—and worse: a *Sangria*. I wouldn't touch him with a ten-foot pole.

But I did know him a little better, which had been the point of this sit-down. I was confident enough that he wasn't going to stab me in the back the moment it was convenient. At least until we got to that woman.

Once we did, it was game on. We were both going to try to kill each other, and right now, I wasn't as certain in my ability to survive—or keep my control—as usual. He could throw a punch and he was fast, but he also got distracted easily. And until that day came, I'd learn more about him. As much as I didn't want him to stick around most of the time, it was smarter to have him there.

With that thought in mind, I made my way toward the highway behind the trees.

"Coming?" I called, but Ax didn't answer.

For the rest of the way, I could barely tell he was following.

7

Not a soul in sight.

I looked ahead at the wide, empty street, scratching my cheek. It was already midnight, but I'd expected Lowin to be a bit livelier. It wasn't. Lampposts were on every few feet, some of them broken. The houses were all one story high, lights turned off, while the people in them slept. I faintly heard a few heartbeats, and they were coming from all around me, all at once.

The thirst reared its ugly head up instantly. Drinking cow blood from a glass was one thing. But sinking my fangs in a human neck, while warm fresh blood slipped into my mouth…my eyes squeezed shut as another set of even uglier memories came before my eyes.

Stop.

Pulling my bag off my shoulder, I searched for the thermos with cow blood Anya had prepared for me and took a sip. It was necessary, at least until I got a bit used to my surroundings. The blood was a bit warm on my tongue. It didn't taste like anything in particular—I'd trade it for a juicy steak any day, if I could survive off juicy steaks without losing my damn mind. But the thirst took it, and I put the thermos back in the bag before I started walking down the street.

A look behind and I saw Ax standing barely ten feet away, looking around. Now that there were no trees around us, he wasn't going to be able to hide from me. Not that I cared—if he attacked, I'd hear it. There was a light buzzing in my head from the vodka, but now that I'd drunk the blood, it was going to chase the tipsiness away in no time. One of the reasons why I hated vampirism—you could only stay drunk for a couple hours at best no matter how much you drank, and if you drank blood right after, it gave strength to your body and sobered you up in minutes. All that wasted vodka, but it was still better than letting the thirst put ideas into my head.

Eventually, when I reached the middle of the empty street, curiosity got the best of me. I began to go closer to the houses, inspect their yards, and when that didn't tell me anything, I looked through the windows, too.

So ordinary. Living rooms, kitchens, hallways. I'd had a place like that once, when I lived with Ezra. Now, I couldn't afford a place of my own because of the booze, so I lived in the soldier dorms with about a hundred other noisy vampires. All I had was a room and a tiny bathroom, but the apartment Ezra and I had rented was pretty much the same as what I was seeing here. Nothing different—except for the bikes and the colorful hopscotch drawn in the driveways for kids. There were no kids in the Hidden Realm.

I turned two corners, going deeper into the town of Lowin, before I actually heard a voice. I stopped in my tracks, heart beating steady, until three boys turned the corner ahead of me, talking among themselves, laughing. Much drunker than me, too. I was jealous.

But they definitely didn't look threatening—just some teenagers out past their bedtime. I kept on walking, searching behind me for Ax, but he wasn't there. Probably doing his own exploring.

A sharp whistle reached my ears.

"Hey there, beautiful!"

All three boys had set their eyes on me. They stopped on the sidewalk, right in front of a barber shop, and grinned brightly at me across the street. All their hearts were beating fast, their delicious blood rushing in their veins…

"Hey there, handsome," I said with a wink, slowing my step.

"You're not from around here," one of them said.

"Fuck, you got gorgeous legs," said his friend.

I laughed. "Thanks, sweetie."

"Hey, wait a minute. Where you going?" the first one said again. "Where you from? Are you staying? 'Cuz we can show you a good time."

"Thanks, boys, but I'm in a hurry. Maybe some other time?" I said and kept on walking. Being closer to them and smelling all the goodness in their veins wasn't going to do any of us any favors.

They turned around, too, as if they planned to follow me. Only mildly annoying. I could disappear from their sight in the time it took them to blink.

"Hey, wait up! C'mon, we can—"

They were all talking at the same time as they dragged their feet after me, and then they were cut off abruptly.

I turned to see that Ax had simply *appeared* right in front of them and was looking down at them like he was seconds away from cutting off their heads.

And the boys were scared shitless. Their hearts beat a mile a minute and their blood rushed even faster.

"W-w-who are you?" one of them asked in a low whisper.

I rolled my eyes and continued walking.

"I'm the reason you're *never* going to be out of your house after ten p.m. again."

I almost burst out laughing but held myself. He didn't need to do that. They were just kids, for fuck's sake. So what that they were drunk and wandering the empty streets?

"You've got five seconds to get the fuck outta here," he told them, and the boys were barely breathing.

"Just leave them alone," I said. The boys wouldn't hear my voice, but Ax would.

"Five…" he said, and they all started running at the same time, one of them even screaming as he went.

Shaking my head, I laughed to myself and kept going, until I turned another corner and…heard another heart beating steadily not too far away from me.

A little girl was standing all alone in the middle of the street, barely twenty feet away from me, wearing a white pajama gown, her black corkscrew curls tied behind her head in a pink ribbon.

She held a doll tightly to her chest and her big black eyes were right on me.

I stopped walking for a second and looked around at the houses and the closed stores. Nobody was there.

What the hell?

I continued walking, eyes on the girl so I'd see it if she spooked and ran. She was so tiny—couldn't have been older than six or seven.

"Hey there, little girl." I stopped about five feet away from her. "What are you doing out here all by yourself?"

Maybe she was sleepwalking? Vampires didn't—we didn't technically sleep during the day. It was more like a coma state, but I'd read about sleepwalking. I was pretty sure I used to do it as a kid, too, back when I was human. And had a family.

The girl blinked but didn't say anything, just held onto her doll.

"Do you need help finding your house?" I asked the little girl.

And she…smiled.

"*Sorcerer.*"

I heard Ax's whisper as if he were right behind me.

And then a blinding blue light came from the right and hit me on the shoulder without warning.

The pain of the magic was so intense, I hardly felt it when I slammed against the wall of a store to my right, then hit the sidewalk on my face. My instincts took over immediately, and I stood, completely disoriented, jaw uncomfortable by how fast my fangs were coming out. Six grown people were slowly approaching the little girl still standing in the middle of the street with that doll, smiling sneakily at me.

The little brat.

The magic was retreating from my body, and it left a sour taste in my mouth. More than that…it left my chest feeling like it might explode when the hunger took over me, and…something else. Something far more monstrous than a vampire could possibly be. The whispers took over my head, too, and though I could never understand them, I knew what they wanted. Those people—dead on the spot, their lifeless eyes staring at the sky.

Stop.

It took all I had to force my eyes to close. It took everything to push down the hunger and every fucked up part of me that came alive the second I was taken by surprise. Why the hell would they attack me sneakily like that? Had they no idea what it was like in my head?

Grunts and growls left my throat as I pushed and pushed so hard, I thought I might pass out.

By some miracle, I didn't. When I opened my eyes again, the sorcerers and the little girl were still there, half of them watching me, the other half watching Ax who was coming up the street slowly, a small smile playing on his face.

It's over. I breathed and it didn't hurt. My fangs were still out, but that was okay. I was in control. I wouldn't use them. These people weren't human—they were sorcerers, and sorcerer blood could be deadly to a vampire if we took too much. It was their ultimate protection against us.

My hands were still a bit numb from the magic I was attacked with. The Veins must have been strong around here. More than enough magic supply for the sorcerers, who called themselves *guardians* of the humans. It was a fucking pain in the ass to deal with, though, but if I were lucky, there would be no more blasts of magic thrown my way tonight.

Shaking my hands to get the numbing sensation out, I slowly made my way to the street again. The dent I left in the wall I hit wasn't my problem—it was theirs.

And Ax…he was full-on grinning now, and he sat down on the sidewalk, made himself comfortable as he watched me, as if he were preparing for a show. I rolled my eyes and turned to the sorcerer again.

"You have no place here, bloodsucker," one of the men keeping his hand on the little girl's shoulder told me.

Bloodsucker? "How original." I stopped a good distance away from them. I didn't want to provoke them. "Look, we're just passing through. We don't want any trouble." I searched their eyes, hoping to see who it had been that had attacked me, but they all looked the same. Same wide eyes, same hatred reflecting in them. Same scent of magic hanging onto their skin. "And that was pretty damn low, by the way. I wasn't prepared for an attack."

The man who'd spoken first flinched like my voice disgusted him.

"This is a human town," he reminded me, as if I didn't know. "You were attacking my daughter."

"Yes, I know where the fuck I am—and I wasn't *attacking* her," I spit, then swallowed hard again.

A second later, Ax was right behind me.

"That's *it?*" he whispered. "That's what you're gonna do—*talk* to them?"

Fisting my hands until my fingernails dug into my skin, I let out a long breath. I was *not* going to let this asshole get to me. So, I turned to the sorcerers again.

"Like I said—we're just passing through. We have permission from our covens to be here, and we don't want any trouble. We'll be out of your hair in a minute."

I leaned down to grab my bag, touching the bottle of vodka to make sure it wasn't broken. It wasn't—which was how I knew these sorcerers were damn lucky.

In all honesty, I expected them to attack me again. The stories we heard back home about them were pretty terrifying. But to my surprise, when I started walking, they all moved backward to the other side of the street, never looking away from me for a second. Good thing I'd thought to mention the covens.

"Are you serious?" Ax tried again, coming after me, but I didn't dare look at him. The last thing I needed right now was to be more pissed off. There was only so much I could do to hold myself back without alcohol in my system.

Luckily, he didn't say anything else, and my head was turned back as I walked away from the staring sorcerers, still there on the sidewalk. They weren't going to come after me. They weren't going to attack me again.

What a fucking relief. If every other encounter we'd have with sorcerers until Atlanta would go like this, I wasn't half as afraid as I was just minutes ago.

And then…

"*It has already started.*"

I stopped and turned around again. None of them were speaking, but I'd heard that whisper. Whichever of the three women said those words, I heard them. And judging by the way Ax was watching them, I'd say he heard it, too.

"Let's go," I said and turned around to leave again.

It was the first time in my life that I had actually met a sorcerer, and maybe, if I got *really* lucky, it would also be my last.

★★★

The city of Bismarck was something else. Still not as lively as I'd hoped, but considering it was after two in the morning, I'd say it was okay. Lights and cars and noisy people…and I still couldn't force my mind to shut up.

All that blood around me…all those hearts beating fast, all the people who were drunk and wouldn't even be able to tell if I bit them…temptation was a real bitch.

Ax was nowhere to be seen, which was for the best. I just needed a second—and all that vodka in my system. I'd be good as new in no time. So, I kept on walking and drinking, forcing myself to be curious about all the cars and the restaurants and the grocery stores I passed by. So many lights. So much noise.

For minutes at a time, I couldn't hear my own thoughts through it. Yet every time my mind wandered back to the town of Lowin and the way those sorcerers had attacked me, my instincts screamed. They wanted revenge. They wanted blood.

And I wanted nothing more than to pass out already. So fucking tiring.

The sun was just a couple hours away from shining when I decided that I wanted to spend the day here. It was just the first night. Tomorrow, I'd be more careful. I'd keep myself in check. I just needed to forget for now. Maybe even find someone to keep me distracted until I dropped unconscious. It was a big city, after all. Plenty of *fresh meat,* so to speak. And the best part was that I'd never have to see them again. The perfect scenario to end my dry spell.

Finding a dark alley wasn't hard, not at this time. It was completely empty, and the smell had my stomach twisting, but I just needed a second to gather myself and drink some of the cow blood in my thermos before I could allow myself to entertain the idea of being in a closed space with so many humans around me.

The blood was going to erase the effect of the vodka, but there was more to drink. I was so used to this game of drunk and sober, it was ridiculous. I could find a bar. I could find anything in this place now. It was almost like I was *free,* and if I let myself get distracted for a minute, I'd even believe it.

Except…

A body slammed onto mine out of nowhere and pushed my back onto the wall of the alley before I had the chance to walk out into the street. Ax's scent filled my nostrils, chasing away that of piss and vomit sticking to the broken asphalt.

"For fuck's sake," I growled, trying to push him off me, but he didn't budge.

"Now *that* was very interesting what you did there, Damsel," he whispered, pressing onto me for a second. His heart beat a little faster than usual, too. "What are you hiding from me?"

My own damn fault. Had I not been so distracted by my own thoughts, I'd have heard him coming. As it was, I forced myself to roll my eyes, and when I pushed him off again, I put my back to it. He finally moved.

"Wouldn't you like to know." Avoiding his eyes, I made for the street. But his hand wrapped around my wrist too fast for me to move away, and he pulled me back.

We were face-to-face again, and I was about five foot six, so he towered over me.

It didn't scare me, not even a little bit.

"What?" I spit, and if he knew what was good for him, he'd have let it go right then and there. I was not in the mood. I was pissed—I'm pretty sure he could see it. He just didn't care.

"Why don't you drop the tough girl act for a second and just be honest with me," he said, those blue eyes of his piercing through mine. "Why are you here in the first place? Why would Abraham Jones send a drunk out into the world for this?"

Motherfucker. I pulled up my knee, but he saw it coming and moved away at the last second. Good—I needed more space to breathe.

"Fuck you, Axel Creed. You don't know shit about me." The whispers were already back. Great.

"I really don't. But I'm stuck with you in this thing, and I'd like to know how badly you're gonna fuck me over so I can be prepared for it," he said with that awful, sinfully sexy grin of his. It just pissed me off more.

I stabbed him in the chest with my finger. "You think you're tough, don't you? You think you're scary and strong, but guess what? You're just a little boy starved for attention. You can't fucking stand that I couldn't care less about who the fuck you are," I spit. "Stay out of my way and I'll stay out of yours. When we find that vampire, we'll make our way back."

His eyes widened for a second and his smile faltered. I really thought that was the end of it. He'd leave me alone and I'd be on my way.

But just as I moved, he slammed me against the wall again and lowered his head until all I saw was his eyes. All I felt was an infinity of rock-hard muscle pressed to my chest. I was definitely not expecting that, so my breath caught in my throat and my traitorous body was suddenly warm. My thighs clenched, too. He overwhelmed all my senses within seconds.

If he could only feel how much I hated his guts right now…

"You're not half as intimidating as you think you are, you know that?" I whispered, looking down at those lips, imagining what they'd feel like on my pussy. Which was *sick*, to say the least. This man was a fucking monster, no matter what he looked like, but my body had a mind of its own.

"Well, fuck, Damsel," he said as he grinned. "That would have hurt my feelings if you weren't lying through your teeth."

"You don't scare me, Ax," I said. At least not in the way he thought. "You just annoy the shit out of me."

Which was definitely the truth, so…why in the world wasn't I pushing him off me already?

"Aren't you forgetting something, though?" He came closer and closer, making me swallow hard. Fuck, our lips were barely an inch apart. I felt his warm breath blowing through my parted lips, and for the life of me, I couldn't think well enough to put my hands on his chest and just push him back.

"What's that?" Even my voice was dry, and my fucking ears were full of the sound of his heart thundering in his chest.

"I can smell your wet pussy," he said slowly and pressed his hips onto me.

Holding back the moan that wanted to rip from my throat was like knocking down a mountain all by myself. The fucking prick.

The shame of allowing myself to end up in this position brought me back my strength. Heat crawled to my cheeks, but I doubted he saw it when I kneed him in the balls and he bent over a bit, giving me back my personal space. Not a single sound left him.

He was fucking impossible, and I needed to be away from him asap. So, I turned to leave, this time prepared in case he grabbed me again.

He didn't, but…

"The next time you get wet for me, I'm gonna do something about it, Damsel. That's the only warning you get."

Shivers danced on my back. I didn't stop walking until I was out in the street.

The faces were blurry, the lights were blurry, and the need in me grew with every new step I took. The vodka wasn't cutting it, either, and I was so sick of it. So sick of trying to control my body. So sick of not letting go when I wanted to. When I yearned to.

So, I walked and walked until my feet started to hurt, never giving myself the chance to stop and think, until I saw a sign that read *Motel* on a building at the corner of a street. Finally. There was still time to get drunk and then crash until tomorrow night. The perfect way to leave this fucked up night behind and start fresh tomorrow.

The best part was the bar on the corner across from the three-story motel. There were three cars in the parking lot, which meant there would be rooms available. That's why I went straight for the bar first. There would be enough alcohol in there to keep my mind off the blood of humans. And even if Savage Ax came after me, I'd be too distracted to even look his way.

8

Ax Creed

It had been a long time since my limits were tested. Now, it was happening all at once. I was sitting in a shithole bar in the middle of a human city, with twenty-eight humans cramped up in there with me. All those hearts beating in my ears. All that blood luring me in with its scent.

I threw back the fifth shot of tequila, then downed half my beer. Maybe the little Damsel had a point with that bottle of vodka she carried around.

And *she* was testing my limits more than anything ever had.

My hand fisted over the table, and I had to remind myself that I didn't want unnecessary attention—which I would undeniably get if I broke the fucking table. But the lower she went on that guy, pressing her ass against him as she danced, the more it seemed perfectly reasonable to draw as much attention to myself as I could.

The smile on her face said she was enjoying every second. Her eyes were half closed—she was too drunk to even think right now.

Yet those eyes would stop on me every few seconds anyway. She'd wrap her arms around one of the three men she was dancing with—and look at me. She'd lean back against the chest of one of them, run her hands on the back of his head, down his neck—and look at me. She'd move those hips in a circle, bringing her ass right on one of their hard-ons—and she'd look at me.

Every time she did, her heart skipped a beat.

So fucking sick of it, I was about to lose my damn mind. I was right here. If she wanted me so badly, I wasn't going to fucking turn down a lap dance.

But she never even whispered anything my way. All she did was drink and dance with those men. *Human* men. Was she planning to bite them? Because I wasn't going to let her. Her control was admirable, but if she got them alone…

Fuck, no. She wasn't going anywhere alone with them. I had enough trouble on my plate with her as it was—she was a fucking drunk and a greedy little slut deserving of a good spanking on her perfect ass. I would put her over my knee and deliver it myself.

My cock twitched in my pants and my fists tightened. How in the world had she managed to get under my skin so fast? It had been *hours*. Was it when she'd taken her clothes off at that waterfall? I swear, I'd never been more caught by surprise in my life. She was most definitely *nothing* like I expected.

Or was it that she could fight much better than all the soldiers Robert trained at his castle, even with that vodka in her system?

Maybe…the way she defied me? In the Hidden Realm, everyone knew who I was. They acted like it, too. I was used to that.

And maybe it was the scent of her wetness every time she looked at my lips that drove me fucking nuts. How did she keep such good control of herself when her body was begging for me?

She'd tested me in those woods, and I'll admit it myself, I didn't do the best I could. Like I said—she caught me completely off guard and there was something about her wildness that kept distracting me.

It still did. I just couldn't figure it out.

I watched as she pushed two of the guys away, then wrapped her arms around the third—the tallest of them, with a strong jaw, an army jacket on his wide shoulders, and a hard-on the entire fucking bar could see.

His hands moved from her waist down to her ass, and he squeezed. I heard his moan all the way across the bar as she giggled.

What the fuck was she doing?

And why did I even care?

"Mind if I join you?"

I looked up at the woman with the long black hair who'd been watching me from the bar since I got here.

Distractions. *Other* distractions. That's exactly what I needed.

"Not at all," I said, pushing the chair next to me out so she could sit. She was a bit tipsy but not drunk, and her big lips were painted a blood red—my favorite color. They would look amazing wrapped around my cock.

"I'm Taylor," she said, offering me her hand. I took it and brought her knuckles to my lips. I licked her skin before I kissed her, and she giggled just like Damsel from across the bar.

Fuck.

"I'm Ax. Lovely to meet you, beautiful," I told her, and she instantly blushed. I heard the blood rushing in her cheeks. I felt her heart pick up the beating. It was just making my entire existence more miserable.

"So charming," she told me, batting her fake lashes at me. "What would a guy like you be doing in this hellhole all by himself?" she said, then slowly put her hand over my knee.

"Just passing by," I said, and my mind wandered again to that small town and those sorcerers who'd attacked Damsel. That's what she'd said to them—*just passing by*. Even after they attacked her without cause. Even after I *felt* in her that she wanted to rip their throats out.

So, why hadn't she? Gods know I wouldn't have stopped her—they deserved to die for being sneaky fuckers and using a little girl as bait like that. But she'd lowered her head anyway.

Why?

"Are you even listening to me?" the woman said, then turned to the other side of the bar. "What's so interesting over there?"

Fucking Damsel and that man's hand on her ass—that's what. I was going to fucking murder him. I was going to cut off his fingers one by one, peel the skin off his face, and break his ribs slowly, and—

"Of course, I am. You were telling me about your sister coming to live with you last month," I said. I was a vampire—I could hear more than one thing at a time. And even though I couldn't care less about the story she was telling me, I knew what she was saying.

Pretending wasn't hard to do. It didn't distract me as much as I'd have liked, but I was good at pretending. I asked her questions. I smelled her blood. Smelled her pussy getting wetter every time her hand moved farther up my thigh. And when I touched her wrist, just a little bit, her heart skipped a beat, too.

But Damsel was still going at it with Army Jacket. I was gritting my teeth so hard, there was a chance I'd break my own fucking jaws soon.

"Why don't you just tell me something about yourself?" the woman asked after she was done telling me all about how her sister was making her miserable since she got here. "Where do you come from? What do you do?"

"But you're far more interesting than me," I told her with a smile that women usually loved.

She giggled, her cheeks flushing once more. "You're such a gentleman." I really wasn't.

But through the corner of my eye, I could see just fine how Damsel spun around and pressed her back to Army Jacket's chest. I saw his hands moving up her thighs, over her holsters and under her skirt.

I'd never wanted to hold a man's heart in my hands so badly. A different kind of monster had taken over my mind tonight, and it wanted his blood so bad my hands were shaking. It wanted his eyes off his skull and each one of his fingernails pulled off slowly, one by one, until he passed out from the pain.

"You know what?" My voice sounded like a stranger's. I threw the rest of the beer back and stood up. "How about we get the fuck out of here. Let me show you a good time, beautiful."

The woman giggled again—she liked it when I called her that. It didn't matter to her that I'd forgotten her name—that one she liked better. Suited me. And that mouth of hers was going to distract me just fine. There was a motel right next door, so that's exactly where I was taking her.

"I was hoping you'd say that," she said as she followed me, swinging from side to side. Maybe she was more drunk than I gave her credit for, but I'd make it worth her while, anyway.

A second before I walked out the doors, I felt Damsel's eyes on me like a physical touch on the back of my neck. I didn't turn.

I didn't think about her at all until we were inside the motel.

"I've never done this before," the woman whispered to me while I paid the clerk for a room. He asked for an ID, so I gave him an extra hundred-dollar bill. Not that I didn't have one, but the IDs we had in the Realm weren't going to seem familiar to him. "Are you going to take it easy on me?" she continued, snuggling under my arm, touching my chest. I didn't much like to be touched usually, but right now I didn't mind. I'd rather think about her hands.

"Not really," I told her. "I don't do easy."

Her eyes lit up instantly. "But not too hard, right?"

I only smiled. She'd like hard. I always made sure they did.

Five minutes later, I unlocked the door of the smelly motel room, and she had her arms around my neck, bringing her lips to mine. I slammed the door shut, and for a moment, kissed her on autopilot as my senses searched the room. Dirty. Spiders everywhere. The toilet was a mess. I could hear the TV in the room next door—porno—but there was nothing close to me even remotely threatening. The room was safe enough.

Then I got to work.

I undid the zipper of her dress as I stuck my tongue in her throat, then tore the panties off her, too. She cried out, more surprised than anything, but her eyes were on fire. She tasted of cheap liquor, and the red lipstick was smeared all over her face—and probably mine—but it would have to do.

"Get on your knees," I told her, and she didn't complain. She put her hands under my jacket and pushed it off my shoulders, running her fingernails down my skin. She kneeled before me and her hands shook as she undid my belt, then my zipper. She looked up at me, too, eyes full of wonder, the scent of her pussy so different from…

No.

I grabbed a fistful of her black hair when she took out my cock and wrapped her small hands around it, moaning. I put my other hand under her chin.

"Open wide," I ordered, and she did. I buried my cock in her mouth all the way until I touched her throat. She gagged, and the sound was exactly what I needed. Closing my eyes, I threw my head back with a sigh. Nothing better than sex to take your mind off things. Even though the sound of her heart was tempting, and the smell of her blood nagged at my brain, it was easy to ignore them. Easy to focus on the way she sucked my cock. She was good at it, too, and she was hungry, just like I liked them. The feeling took me higher—I didn't hold myself back, not tonight. I hadn't been so desperate to stop thinking for such a long time, and it was working.

Until…

"You better be naked by the time I open this door."

My eyes opened and I tightened my grip on the woman's hair to stop her from moving.

A lock turned. A door opened. And I heard that giggle.

Fuck.

I pulled the woman's mouth on my cock again and tried to keep all my focus on her tongue, her teeth, those lips wrapped around my base…but my ears were fucking impossible. My attention drifted away, down the hallway, right where I'd heard Damsel's voice…

Right where I heard it again.

Her moans filled my head instantly. The squeaking of the bed drove me fucking nuts. The grunts of that man had my body on fire within seconds.

"Stop."

I stepped back, closing my eyes and breathing deeply. This was fucking ridiculous. What the hell was wrong with me?

"Did I do something wrong?" the woman said, still on her knees, her breasts almost spilling out of her lacy black bra.

"No," I told her, feeling even more like shit with every new second and every new squeak of that fucking bed… "I'm sorry, beautiful. But I'm just not in the mood."

Her eyes moved down to my cock. It was rock hard still—just not for her.

"Maybe another time?" I pulled up my jeans, then gave her her dress. "Let me pay for the panties."

The woman was mortified. Tears pooled in her wide dark eyes, but she gritted her teeth and didn't let them spill.

Fuck, I must have really lost my mind.

I gave her two hundred bucks, and the way she looked at me, half-heartbroken, half-pissed, should have had me feeling like a fucking pussy, but it didn't. I just couldn't wait for the second she walked out of the room, her torn panties in her hand, and slammed the door shut with so much strength the walls shook.

And the sound of Damsel fucking another man returned full force.

I couldn't stay in there and listen to her fake cries of pleasure, hear the sound of that man slapping her, the way he grunted like he was about to fucking die any second…

I grabbed my jacket off the floor and walked out. The woman who'd been with me was already making her way back inside the bar, but I didn't want to go in there anymore. I just needed a second of silence.

So, I climbed up the yellow bricks of the motel building and I jumped on the empty rooftop.

The sound of her didn't reach me up there. The air was cold, the night almost ready to give way to day, and the silence was so fucking welcome.

I sat on the concrete rooftop, rubbing my face.

That was a first. It had *never* happened before in my life. I didn't make women leave without pleasing them first. I always made sure they left my room satisfied. If it hadn't been for the sound of Damsel drilling into my brain, this one would have been no different.

I just didn't get it. What the fuck was it about her? Was I so used to women falling to their knees in front of me without my having to even ask, that the first one who refused to do it did *this* to me? Was I so used to scaring everyone, that the sight of her eyes, not a hint of fear in them, intrigued me?

"Fuck, Damsel." I couldn't even think straight when I knew that another man's cock was buried inside her. I wanted it so bad to be mine, it was driving me nuts.

The mission, I reminded myself. The reason I was here in the first place. We still had that vampire to find, keep an eye out for sorcerers, and worse—Vein spirits. The most dangerous thing for a vampire in this world because we couldn't kill them. All we could do was get away, and that was a bitch to do because they moved pretty fast. They were the *real* reason why the covens had even agreed to sign the treaty and hide in the Hidden Realm. Sprits couldn't get to us there no matter what. The walls kept them out.

But out here, we were fair game. And despite everything, it was *a good* thing. Right now, it didn't seem like it because of the stupid fucking jealousy I'd been fine a lifetime without feeling, but it was. It was different. It was a change. I'd been yearning for a change, for something to kick the boredom out, and I got it. Not the way I'd hoped, but at least I wasn't fucking bored right now.

Walking to the edge of the rooftop, I looked down at the street, barely any humans around anymore. Maybe I needed to take some blood. Maybe that's what was going to put things into perspective again because right now, until we got to that vampire, there would be nothing to deal with except her.

And lucky for me, my eyes zeroed in on the guy I would *really* like to suck dry completely.

He came out of the motel, walking like he was drunk or high, that army jacket on his body, smelling of Damsel—vodka and something sweet, almost like cinnamon, that should have been sickening but wasn't. He stopped in the parking lot, texting furiously, and a minute later, his buddies from the bar came out, screaming and cheering. They went right up to him and high-fived him as if he'd won the fucking lottery.

Every hair in my body stood at attention.

"My man!" one of them said.

"How was it?" asked the other.

"Oh, man. Best pussy I've ever had," said the guy. My hands pulled up in fists. "I swear—she is properly *wild!* I can't fucking feel my balls, man!"

And they laughed.

I closed my eyes, hoping to be able to convince myself to just walk away, but I stayed right there instead.

"Damn, man. Fuck, you lucky bastard," said his friend, patting his back.

"I wanna fuck her, too," said the other. "You think she'll let me in if I go there? What was the room number?"

"Twelve," the man said. "And you definitely should. She'll let you in. I don't think she'll even realize it's not me." And he laughed harder.

I saw red, and I can't even say why.

The next second, I jumped off the rooftop and straight into the parking lot.

The men were all drunk but they heard me. And when they saw my face, they immediately started to back away.

"Hi, there," I told the guy Damsel had fucked. "May I have a word? It won't be long."

He narrowed his brows at me. "Who the fuck are you?"

I hated it when they asked me that question.

I stepped in front of him way too fast for him to even see my movement. It freaked him out so bad, he almost tripped on his own feet. I grinned when I grabbed him by the arm.

"I'm your worst fucking nightmare." Possibly the cheesiest thing I'd ever said, but fuck, it felt good because it was damn true.

I dragged him behind the motel while his friends screamed and ordered me to get my hands off him. They threatened to call the police. They threatened to *shoot* me, too.

But neither of them came after us.

9

Nikki Arella

I knew it the second I stepped in front of the bathroom door that something was wrong. I pulled the door open, not concerned with the fact that I was completely naked, having just come out of the shower.

But all thoughts of towels left me when I saw Ax standing in the middle of the tiny room, looking completely deranged. He was breathing heavily, too, his naked chest rising and falling…drops of blood on his skin and jacket.

He didn't look hurt, though. He looked *possessed* as his eyes scrolled down my naked body—so intently I almost covered myself with my hands. Despite the fact that I'd just had sex—*really* shitty sex, but still—and I'd finished myself off in the shower, the need rose in me again, just like that.

What the hell was it about him? He looked like a murderous psycho, covered in blood, and it *turned me on?* Something was very wrong with me.

And then he moved. There was something in his hand that I hadn't even noticed, and he threw it on the edge of the queen-sized bed.

A jacket. An army jacket half covered in blood. Fresh blood that I should have smelled first instead of getting caught on the scent of *him*.

"Touch another man and he dies."

He spoke slowly, his voice thick and hoarse, sending chills down my spine. It left no room for doubt that he wasn't completely serious.

My mouth opened but no sound left my lips. I couldn't form a sentence if I tried.

With one last lingering look at my legs, he turned around and stormed out of the door, slamming it shut behind him.

"Damn," I whispered to the empty room and went to inspect the jacket. Yep—definitely Jimmy's. It smelled like him. Poor fella. Was he dead already?

With a sigh, I took the jacket and put it in the shower to keep it out of my way. Then I finally dried my skin and hair, locked the door with the pathetic lock anybody could break, and lay down on the messy bed. The sun was minutes away, and I had absolutely no reason to stay awake. That I'd been able to pull that off made me almost proud—I'd had a human man in my bed, all alone, and I hadn't bitten him when his neck had been right there. It had taken *a lot* of alcohol and self-control to get there, but I'd done it.

For that alone, I deserved some sleep.

Granted—I wasn't safe out here in the open, but I was also a vampire. Unconscious or not, if I heard something, I would wake up.

And as much as it sucked, I heard *everything*.

Pulling the covers all the way up to my neck, I made myself comfortable, closed my eyes and forced my mind to shut down.

***

Had he really killed him?

I squinted my eyes as I watched his profile, and Ax pretended he couldn't tell. Had he really killed Jimmy? He'd been human. Harmless. His biggest fault had been that he came in thirty seconds, but that's it. He wasn't a bad guy.

And now he was probably dead, his jacket coated in his blood in the shower of that motel room for the cleaning ladies to find.

Fuck. This man was worse than I thought—and *he* left the bar with that woman first. I saw him. She was gorgeous, long dark hair, beautiful brown eyes, lips to die for, legs for days. I saw them leaving together—*not* that it mattered. That little spark of jealousy I thought I felt could have been anything and I was too drunk to tell because I couldn't care less about whom he fucked.

Why did *he* care about me?

"Did you kill him?"

My whisper hung in the air, as if the words themselves were afraid to get in his ear. The memory of him standing in the room, covered in blood, eyes filled with rage, had my breath hitching a little bit. Here I thought I was a normal person and smart enough to be disgusted by him, but no. I thought he was the sexiest guy I'd ever met instead.

Ax didn't flinch. He didn't even look my way, just continued to stare ahead at the grey sky, waiting for it to turn dark.

Shaking my head at myself, I grabbed the bottle of whiskey I'd bought as soon as I woke up and took a sip.

"You're a fucking hypocrite, you know that?" I said. Still no reaction, but he knew what I was talking about. He left the bar with her *first*. "I bet she felt great last night."

Take the bait, take the bait, take the bait…

He didn't. Not a single word.

I sighed.

"What do you think we're after here, anyway?" Too much silence, even though I could hear the city buzzing with life all around us. *His* silence weighed more than all of that, and I couldn't even say why. He looked pissed—not my problem. He'd probably killed a guy last night because I fucked him—still not my problem. He refused to even look my way since we left the motel—most definitely not my problem.

So, why was I making it my fucking problem?

"Vampire," he finally said, never moving a single inch. We were on the rooftop of a five-story building a couple blocks away from the motel, at the edge of the city. We figured we'd wait here for night to fall before we made a run for the next town. We had a lot of ground to cover today, but we were getting closer. By this time the next night, we'd be in Atlanta—or very close.

"Don't tell me you actually believed that," I said with a flinch.

That got him to turn his eyes to me for a second.

"Of course not. But he did promise me that whatever secret I found at the end of this was going to be worth it."

"It better be." I took another sip of my whiskey, then put the bottle away in my bag. The sky was dark. The night was already here. "Whatever it is, we need to be prepared for it because it's not going to be pretty." I knew that simply by the fact that Jones had sent me here. He was preparing for a disaster.

For a moment, I wondered if Robert Sangria had told Ax more. I wondered if he'd told him to kill me, too, just like Jones told me.

Asking him would be pointless, though. If he did, I'd find out.

Putting my feet on the railing of the rooftop, I jumped to the alley between it and the next building. My boots barely made a sound when they hit the asphalt. Without waiting to see if Ax was following, I put my bag over my shoulder and started walking.

I didn't see him again until Iowa.

10

Mason City wasn't half as noisy as Bismarck. The streets were wide, and not too many people around at almost two in the morning, either. Most importantly, nobody was looking at me.

Dropping my bag, I sat on the sidewalk to catch my breath. I'd been running for a long time, through field upon empty field surrounding the cities. I hadn't wanted to stop by a small town at all, hoping to avoid trouble that way. The darkness had helped in shielding me even if somebody had been out in those fields keeping watch. That's how I'd made it here in record time.

And now I was fucking exhausted.

My bag was full of protein bars and I grabbed one to snack on. I'd also gotten a delicious pizza before I left Bismarck. Vampires needed very little food to function. Blood did the trick for us, so we usually ate once a day, sometimes once every two days. But the protein bar was delicious. That's why I'd gotten a few to keep me company. And when that was done, I grabbed the bottle of whiskey, took a good long sip, then lay back on my elbows. An old man across the street watched me curiously as he passed, but he didn't say a word. His heart sped up at the sight of me, though, and I'd forgotten just how peaceful it had been in those fields without the sound of a human heart pumping blood in my ears. I still had half a thermos of cow blood with me, but I'd hoped to save that for the way back. If I needed it before then, I could always drop by a butcher's shop and ask for a refill. I had the money for it—and humans would sell you anything as long as you could pay, same as vampires.

The more minutes passed, the more my strength returned to me. It had been worth running the way I had, even if I felt like shit right now. A couple more minutes sitting here and I'd be good as new.

"Are you here yet?" I asked the empty street in front of me because I was too lazy to check with my eyes.

Three seconds in, I felt a whoosh of air somewhere to my right, and when I turned, I saw Ax standing in front of a large one-story building at the street corner. Yep. He was here. I hadn't felt him at all while running through the fields, which was for the best. I'd needed those hours to clear my head and get myself in control. Last night had been a mess because I'd been tired and caught off guard by him.

Now, I was much better prepared to handle him.

Or so I thought.

"What do you say we stop here for the day?" I asked as he approached slowly, his footsteps barely making any sound.

"It's still early. We can get to the other side of this city," he said when he stopped a couple feet away. I risked a glance at his face, and he didn't look as pissed off as before. He looked pretty calm, actually. And not at all tired. In fact, his heart beat steady, and there wasn't half as much sweat on his back as there was on mine.

I squinted my eyes at him. "Have you been running?"

"Yes. I was behind you." No smile. No tease. No nothing.

I didn't like it.

"So why aren't you tired?"

"I take ten minutes off for every forty of running. It keeps me from wasting my energy all at once," he said.

"Could have just told me that." I did take breaks but only for a couple minutes at a time.

Never mind, though. I was already feeling better. So, I took a couple sips of the cow blood and jumped to my feet.

"All right. Let's hope there are no sorcerers here."

"If there are, we'll know." He started walking down the street, leaving me to follow.

I did my best to look away, keep myself distracted by the buildings and the lights and the humans, but every few seconds, I found myself staring at his back. He certainly wasn't like the usual vampires in the Realm. It made me wonder what it was like in his head. I wanted to know what he thought about. *How* he thought. As much as it disgusted me, there was no denying it—he intrigued me. And I wasn't all that certain about what the rest of this journey would look like as I'd been in the beginning.

After about five minutes of walking, Ax stopped in the middle of the sidewalk abruptly. I stopped, too—I was still a good ten feet away from him. Close enough to hear it when his heart skipped a beat, just a second before he looked back at me. He wasn't smiling. He was dead serious instead, and that look suited him perfectly, too.

When he turned to the road and started running at full speed, I barely caught it. No warning, not even a single whisper, and he was on the other side of the street in a second. Cursing under my breath, I took off after him, thinking he'd heard something. Smelled something. Possibly sorcerers.

And the moment I stepped on the sidewalk on the other side, I smelled the magic, too.

I didn't need to wonder where Ax had disappeared to—the scent alone led me to him. He had stopped a couple of feet into a dark, narrow alley, looking up at the yellowish green shape hovering in the air at the end of it.

Every hair in my body stood at attention, and my heart skipped a beat, too.

It wasn't a sorcerer he'd smelled. It was a Vein spirit.

And its glowing eyes were on us.

The spicy scent of magic overpowered even that of piss and garbage. It was so much more intense than that of the sorcerers. I'd gone a lifetime without ever coming across a Vein spirit, and I'd considered myself lucky for it.

Now, it looked like I'd finally run all out of that luck.

I'd heard about them, read about them, but none of the stories had ever done them justice. The creature was floating on air, its face heart-shaped, its hair made of glowing strings floating around its head. We couldn't see its body from whatever was covering it, but we did see the hands—fingers twice as long as mine tipped with sharp claws. Claws that were made of raw magic and could rip me in half in a second.

Swallowing hard, I slowly dropped my bag to the ground. The Vein spirit's glowing eyes became bigger as they focused on me, and it slowly came closer, hovering a foot over the air. The way it moved was mesmerizing. It could hypnotize me if I kept my eyes on it for long enough.

And the closer it got to us, the heavier the air became.

"Start running east," Ax whispered so low, I barely caught it, and he took a step back.

"We can't outrun it," I forced myself to say. Master Ferrera hadn't taught us much about Vein spirits because they couldn't access the Realm, but we did know that the ones made out of only raw magic could get through anything at an incredible speed—wood, concrete, bricks. Those that were corporeal were much easier to handle—they had substance, a head to cut off, a heart to stab through, things that could give you time to get away. Unfortunately, those were much rarer.

"We have to try," Ax whispered, taking another step back until he was right by my side. And the spirit was still slowly floating toward us, eyes locked on me as it came. My gods, that face was going to star in every nightmare I'd have from now on. It freaked out even the voices in my head, which had turned to screams now.

And Jones thought *this* thing had gotten inside my body and had latched onto my soul?

"Damsel," Ax said when he moved back a step and I didn't follow. Instead, I reached for my knives.

You will be safe from Vein spirits. You know you will.

The words Jones said to me in that tower came back to me in a rush. He thought I was safe from spirits because they didn't attack each other, not unless they knew for a fact the other was weaker. So fucking hard to think with all those screams in my head demanding my submission, but I already knew we couldn't outrun this thing. We still had two hours before sunrise, but we'd eventually get tired if we ran at full speed. The spirit wouldn't.

Did I really trust Jones that much?

I couldn't make up my mind if I tried, not with those screams in my head.

"Damsel, move!" Ax outright shouted.

And I did.

I stepped forward.

The Vein spirit stopped moving. My hands shook when I raised my knives. Sweat dripped down my forehead. My heard thundered in my chest as I held its eyes.

A second lasted an eternity. I was perfectly aware of the colors that outlined the shape of it, glowing a sickening green. The magic of it pressed onto my skin, trying to get me to turn, to run, to scream my guts out.

But the pressure was nothing compared to the voices in my head. My mind was in chaos, and right now, a thousand bottles of vodka weren't going to clear it.

Any second now, the spirit would jump at us. Any second now, I'd *really* have no choice but to turn and run, and finally prove Jones wrong. My knives couldn't hurt it—it was magic. But it could hurt me. It could hurt *everyone*, including humans, who couldn't even see the shape of it. It could still suck all the good out of them, feast on their life force until there was nothing left. It *would* do the same to me.

But to my surprise, the Vein spirit pushed itself back a bit. There had been no mouth on the shape of its face until now, but there it was. The glowing light opened into a small circle, and the spirit cried out. Its voice was as haunting as the image of it. It wasn't loud, but it made the voices in my head quiet down for an instant. My whole life flashed right in front of my eyes as I waited, more scared than I had been in a long time…

The spirit moved.

It turned around lightning fast and flew right into the brick wall at the end of the alley, disappearing from our sight.

My muscles were still clenched. My hands still shook as I held up my knives, searching the wall, waiting for it to come back and devour me completely, too fast for me to even feel it…

Seconds turned to a minute, then two. The voices in my head had turned to whispers again, and my instincts relaxed, recognizing that the danger had passed. But my mind had yet to catch up, not only because I was afraid that it would come back.

But because of what it meant that it had left like that.

It meant that there was a good chance Jones was right about me.

My stomach twisted. My muscles screamed, and I finally let go of my breath, lowering my head. I heard Ax stepping closer to me again, his breathing even, his heartbeat steady.

"My, my, Damsel." His whisper sounded like he was in awe. "How in the world did you do *that*?"

Biting my tongue for a moment, I squeezed my eyes shut and took in a deep breath.

It was done. It was over. It didn't matter whether Jones was right or not—I would refuse to believe it until the day I died. Just the thought that I had that thing inside me made me want to stick my knives inside my own chest and be done with it. But it wasn't true. It wasn't possible—*I was a* vampire. Magic and vampirism could not coexist, and that was that.

Besides, there were much more important things at hand right now. More alcohol to drink.

So, when I turned to Ax, I was almost completely composed again.

"Do what? Stand in front of a Vein spirit and scare it away with my knives?" I tried, knowing full well he wouldn't buy it.

His smile proved me right. "That was not your knives, Damsel."

I shrugged. "What else?" Walking around him, I went to pick up my bag on the ground. "We got lucky. This spirit was weak. Let's hope we don't run into another soon."

"I suppose it's pointless to ask that question again, isn't it?" he called from the alley when I stepped into the street. He meant, *what are you hiding from me*. That question.

I said nothing, just continued walking.

***

Fifteen minutes later, we were pretty close to the edge of the city, and I was looking forward to finding a bed to rest in for the day. I'd had enough of magic for at least another century, and I couldn't wait to drop unconscious and forget all about the stupid Vein spirit, the way its eyes had looked at me, the way I'd spooked it away just by standing there.

It *didn't mean* that Jones was right. It just meant that whatever I was, that spirit wanted to have nothing to do with me.

Yeah, I'd keep those thoughts until the day I had solid proof of his theory. Which worked perfectly because that day would *never* come.

But it wasn't meant to be.

I heard the sound behind me clearly. It came fast and strong, and my instincts had me moving back a step even before I realized what it was.

The arrow buried in the white wall of the building to my side a split second later.

Ax, who'd been walking a couple steps ahead, turned around, eyes searching across the street, on the rooftops. My heart beat steady as I touched the arrow with my fingertips, and when no magic attacked me, I pulled it from the wall and brought it to my nose.

"Vampire," I whispered. The scent was unmistakably vampire. There was no magic sticking to it, and it didn't smell like a sorcerer.

"The other covens," Ax said, just as we heard the second whoosh coming for us—this one from the other side. I waited until the last second, standing perfectly still until I knew exactly where the arrow was coming from, and then I moved forward, just as Ax did. The arrow buried in the same wall, a couple inches higher than the first.

"Motherfucker," I spit, dropping the arrow and my bag on the sidewalk. My fangs were already coming out, and the thirst grew inside me. Fifteen minutes, and my mind was in chaos again. Couldn't I just catch a fucking break?

"Come out, coward!" Ax shouted into the night, at the empty street. "You don't have the balls to stand in front of me, so you're going to throw those pathetic arrows at me?"

"Ax," I said, despite my better judgment. I watched him step into the middle of the street, eyes searching the rooftops.

"C'mon, don't be scared," Ax called again, that mad smile on his face now, and his eyes sparkled like two precious jewels. He was actually enjoying this.

"Ax, we need to keep moving." Before whoever was attacking us showed their face. If they did, there would be a fight, that was inevitable. They were no Vein spirits. I couldn't send them away with a look.

And if there was a fight, there was also a very good chance that I'd lose my shit because this whole night had already been too much.

Ax shook his head. "Fuck that. This coward is gonna die first."

But the coward hid well. I sniffed the air every few seconds, hoping to catch their scent, but there was nothing there—just humans. And it was a relief, honestly.

I went to Ax and grabbed him by the arm. "Let's keep moving. We're close."

He turned to me, and the look in his eyes said he wasn't sure if I was serious or not.

"They're *attacking* us," he said incredulously.

"And we need to keep moving," I whispered, letting go of his arm. I grabbed my bag from the ground again and continued walking.

Ax burst out laughing the same second. I expected him to call *me* a coward, too. I expected him to go chasing after whoever was throwing those arrows at us.

But to my surprise, he followed me.

"You're tame, Damsel. You can send a spirit running, but you refuse to fight a vampire?" he whispered behind me. "Way too tame."

If he only knew… "Just keep moving."

The next arrow didn't come at us until we reached the end of the street.

Ax didn't wait around for me to say anything. He'd had enough of it already. With a growl, he jumped over the closest building to our right and started running over the rooftops east to where the arrow had come from.

"For fuck's sake," I muttered, shaking my head. But I didn't have any other choice except to follow.

I jumped on the rooftop, so pissed I was seeing red. Why couldn't he just keep moving? Half my mind was made up to let him go and just continue myself, but I couldn't because I had no idea how many people were throwing those arrows at us. What if all the other coven representatives had joined forces? Would he be able to kill them all himself? Five against one weren't good odds. Not even five against two—we were vampires. But I just couldn't turn my back and walk away right now, not when I didn't even know what was waiting for us in Atlanta.

Cursing under my breath, I ran just as fast as he did, jumping from rooftop to rooftop, barely managing to see which way he went before he disappeared from my sight again. At that rate, there was no way he wouldn't catch whoever had been throwing those arrows.

And when I saw him jump off the two-story building, I thought he had them. I picked up the speed and jumped myself, heart thundering in my chest.

But when I turned the corner, everything came to a halt.

Ax was standing in the middle of the street, arms loose by his sides, his back turned to me. On the other side of the street was a group of people—fifteen of them—and they were all watching us.

The smell in the air left no room for wondering. Magic, thick and heavy, and it was coming from them. Not as heavy as in that alley with the spirit, but heavy enough to make it difficult to breathe easily.

Sorcerers. *Here we go again.*

11

What in the fuck?

I'd smelled that arrow—it had been touched by a vampire. There had been no magic on it, just the scent of a vampire—a mixture of rot and rust, impossible to miss.

Forcing myself to breathe, I made my way to Ax slowly, eyes on the sorcerers in front of us.

"He led us here," he said when I stopped by his side.

"Did you see him?"

"Not clearly, but I saw his shadow," he whispered. "He led us here deliberately."

Unfortunately, it made perfect sense. "Hoping the sorcerers would finish us off."

"Or just stall us."

I sighed, dropping the bag to the ground yet again. "Just let me do the talking, okay?"

"Sure, Damsel. Sure. I'll wait," he said, and I heard the grin in his voice, but I didn't turn. Didn't dare look away from the sorcerers waiting at the end of the street.

But when I started walking, so did they. They met me almost halfway. Fifteen of them—all adults this time. Seven women, eight men, all of them brimming with magic, all of them wishing they could tear me apart with their eyes alone.

Damn, it was already exhausting. Wasn't that Vein spirit enough for one night, at least?

"Hi, there. I'm Nikki Arella. That's Ax Creed," I started, my voice calm, my arms at my sides, hands open so they could see I wasn't carrying any weapons. "We don't want any trouble, okay? We're just passing through."

All of them held their breath until I finished speaking. They were picking me apart with their eyes, analyzing every inch of me, same as I was doing with them. So much power. So much magic contained in those bodies. Here I was thinking I'd never have to meet another sorcerer again. Now I was looking at *fifteen* of them, just minutes after spooking a Vein spirit, too.

As much as I hated to admit it, I was nervous. I was scared. I couldn't wait to get out of this city already.

But before any of them could say anything, a guy to the right, just a little over five feet, with a long blond beard and small green eyes, stepped forward. He came closer and closer until barely two feet were between us. The sound of his heartbeat filled my head.

Shit—was he going to make me attack him?

"Rot in hell, bloodsucking whore," he hissed, then spit right on my left boot. I was too surprised to move back, even though I saw it all playing in front of me in slow motion.

Ew.

My blood was all but boiling, and my fangs were itchy. Every instinct inside my body demanded I grab his face and break his neck, then pull his head off his shoulders completely.

"Caleb, get back here right now," one of the women said, but Caleb grinned at the disgusted look on my face.

Could he not see how hard I was trying here? *Please see. Please stop.*

He didn't.

"You—"

That's as far as he went.

Suddenly, Ax was right behind him, his large hands on the man's head, and he twisted it to the side so fast, none of us had a chance of doing anything about it.

The next second, Caleb hit the ground on his side.

Somebody screamed.

Ax grinned at me.

"What the fuck is wrong with you?!" I hissed. Had he lost his fucking mind? There were *fourteen* sorcerers right behind him!

"If anybody's gonna insult you, it's gonna be me, Damsel," he said, perfectly calmly.

"You started a goddamn war!" I said, pulling up the sleeves of my jacket, knowing that any second now, magic was going to come at us from all sides. Any second now, those sorcerers were going to attack all at once.

Any second now…

Wait.

I looked at the sorcerers, half of them with their hands in front of their mouths as they stared at the body of Caleb, the other half looking at us still.

None of them moving.

Ax smiled as if he could read my mind. "Why don't you let *me* do the talking this time." It wasn't a question and he didn't wait for an answer. He just turned around to face the sorcerers with that smile still on.

He was mad. He was completely fucking mad—who even turned their back on fourteen sorcerers right after killing one of their own?!

"Right, so," Ax said, moving closer and closer to the group, who already had their arms raised. The air crackled with their magic. I moved closer, too, slowly, praying with all my heart that this didn't get out of hand. I couldn't afford to lose it right now. We were so close—tomorrow, we'd be in Atlanta. So fucking close.

"Anybody else wants to spit on her?" Ax said, pointing his thumb back at me. None of the sorcerers made a single sound. "No? Good then. Like she said, we don't want trouble. We're just passing through, that's all."

It made no sense. Those people, they were still not attacking. Their hands were raised but they...

"You killed him," one of the women said, her hand shaking as she pointed at us.

"Well, he spit on her. How the fuck would I know if that shit wasn't poisonous or if it contained a spell or some kind of magic? It was a direct violation of the treaty." He shrugged. He was not concerned in the least and everybody could see it. That's why they looked at him like he was a three-headed alien.

"You have no right to pass through here, Savage Ax," the man standing in the middle of the group finally said, his grey mustache hiding his mouth completely.

And just like that, I understood.

They knew him. They'd heard about Ax.

"Except we do," Ax said. "We're here with permission from our covens to look for a vampire. And then we go back." He nodded his head back toward me again. "She doesn't want to kill anyone, and I would have listened to her, but I don't take kindly to being provoked."

The man gritted his teeth so hard, I heard them cracking from seven feet away. His fingertips sparkled and purple smoke began to slip out of them.

Not only that, but every other sorcerer around him suddenly looked terrified. I heard their hearts as they picked up the beating, and I saw their hands shaking, too. I moved closer to Ax.

"There are no vampires here," Mustache Man said. His fingers shook as that purple smoke kept coming out of them in thin tendrils.

"Not *here* specifically," Ax said. "But we're going to be on our way now. If somebody tries to stop us, we *will* fight back." It was a threat, and they all understood it.

"Why are you scared?" I asked before I could help myself.

Mustache Man turned his brown eyes to me.

"Because they've heard about me," Ax said with a shrug.

"No, no, that's not it." They knew who he was from the beginning, but none of them was shaking like that until… "You know something."

Mustache Man raised his head and took a step closer. He lowered his hands, but that smoke was still coming out of his fingertips, and the closer he got, the heavier the air became.

"There are no vampires here," he repeated slowly, as if he were talking to a child. He was a tall guy, a couple inches taller than Ax, so it was easy for him to look down on us. But he really didn't intimidate me as much as he hoped. "Leave our city and don't come back."

I smiled. "Your pupils are dilated. Your blood is rushing. Your heart is racing, and your hands are sweaty," I told him. "So, why don't you just tell us what you know?"

But the man didn't budge. "You've already killed one of our own. You have two minutes to leave before we open fire."

He turned back to the others, took his place in the middle of them, and raised his hands again.

"You thinking what I'm thinking?" Ax said, rubbing his hands together.

I sighed. "No. It's not worth it. Let's keep moving." I went back to my bag, right next to Caleb's lifeless body. The way his small eyes stared at the sky was freaky, and his blood had already started to get cold, too.

"We can push them," Ax said. "We can make them tell us."

"They won't," I said because I'd seen it in that man's eyes. He wouldn't budge—and *he would* attack. We'd made it this far without too much trouble. We were almost in Atlanta. "Let's just go."

By some miracle, Ax listened to me. We kept our eyes on the sorcerers as we walked ahead, and they kept their eyes on us and their magic at the ready. The air had been so thick with all that magic that when we turned the corner and they disappeared from our sight, I breathed a hundred times easier.

Pressing my back against the wall of a building, I gave myself a moment to calm down. My fangs were already retreating. My instincts weren't on high alert. The danger had passed.

For now.

"You have to stop doing this," Ax said.

"This is what we agreed on—no trouble."

"He fucking spit on you and you were gonna let him get away with it."

"That's what *no trouble* means."

"It was your right to take his life," he insisted.

I rolled my eyes. "For fuck's sake, you didn't have to kill him. Do you have any idea what would have happened if they'd attacked us? And they'd have been well within their rights!"

But the lunatic grinned. "I was hoping they would."

"This isn't a fucking joke," I muttered, but I might as well have said it to the wall behind me.

"What are you hiding from me, Damsel? C'mon, just tell me. How did you do that with the spirit?"

I flinched before I could help it—and he saw it. That's why his smile grew wider.

"Stop killing people. Just stop, okay? Let's just get to Atlanta first."

"So, you're not curious at all about what they were hiding from us?" He came closer and closer, his wide eyes bright. "You don't want to know?"

"Of course, I do, but to make them tell us, we'd have to be prepared to kill them."

"Then let's go for it."

"You're fucking crazy." Fourteen sorcerers? That wasn't going to be as easy as he thought.

Suddenly, his hand was on the back of my neck. "Then be crazy with me," he whispered, his warm breath blowing on my lips. My breath caught instantly. "I know you want to. Just be crazy with me. Whatever you're holding onto, let it go."

Didn't that sound like a fucking dream.

Grabbing him by the wrist, I pushed his hand off me. "No more killing."

I took my bag and started walking again.

He didn't stop me, though I expected him to. And when I reached the end of the street, I turned around, but he wasn't there.

"Great," I muttered to myself. At least alone, I could make sure that nobody else ended up dead at my feet.

***

Half an hour later, Ax jumped right in front of me. Just popped up there in the middle of the street, put his hand on my arm and pulled me to the other side.

"Where were you?" He hadn't been following me—I'd checked. And if he'd gone back to mess with those sorcerers, I didn't even want to hear it.

"I went back." Yep. I didn't want to hear it.

I groaned. "For fuck's sake."

"No—I don't think they saw me. I just wanted to listen to what they were saying," he said.

Shit. Now I was curious. "And?"

"Nothing. They had that house so wrapped up in magic, not even a fly could fucking get through. Not from any angle." And he didn't seem happy about it.

"Whatever it is, it's not important," I said, a bit relieved. "We need to find a place to crash for the day, then we can keep going."

"We're not crashing here. It would be stupid," he said. "They might come looking for us. Not that it's a problem because I don't sleep, but you keep insisting not to kill them, so…"

I narrowed my brows. "What do you mean, you don't sleep?" What we did was not technically sleeping, but every vampire did it. It's how we recharged.

"I just don't," was all he said. "The next town should be safer."

He started walking and I shook my head at myself, smiling. "So, are all the rumors about you true?"

"Not sure. I don't keep tabs on rumors about me," he said.

"What do you do with your days, then?"

"I eat. I torture. I fuck. Not necessarily in that order."

I laughed. "You're fucking crazy."

Suddenly, he stopped right in front of me, his eyes on my lips. It was all I could do not to lick them.

"You keep saying that," he whispered, "but you like it."

It was incredible how I felt all the heat of his body on mine—and *liked* it. But to move away now would only give him more power, so I raised a brow instead. "If you think that, you're delusional."

He slowly leaned his head to the side. "You liked it when I watched you at the waterfall. You liked it when I watched you in the bar. I know you did—I smelled it all over you."

I wanted to deny it, but I also knew it would be useless. "That's before I knew you were *fucking crazy*."

His hand wrapped around the back of my neck, his touch gentle this time.

"You can match my crazy." He said it like he knew it for a fact.

His touch almost electrified me. Reason ran away from me for a second, and I actually considered leaning into his hand.

Thankfully, I caught myself in time.

"I don't think anybody can do that, Ax. Move out of my way," I said, and I tried to put as much resolve in the order as I could, but somehow, my voice came out a bit breathless.

Ax didn't move.

Instead, he sniffed hard, closing his eyes. "I fucking love the smell of you," he told me, pressing his nose to my cheek before he licked it.

I should have been disgusted to feel his warm tongue on my face like that. I should have pushed him off or said something to get him to move.

But my eyes closed, and my body was not working anymore, so I stayed right there like a fucking fool.

"You're wet for me again, Damsel," he whispered in my ear, and it was all I could do to keep from moaning. That voice of his was like a magic spell, rough and low and way too powerful to be fair.

"I'm not," I said, begging my own self to just move, do something, push him off.

"Yes, you are," he said, and his other hand came up to my face, too. He looked down at my lips like they were the object of all his fantasies. It was harder to breathe now than it had been in that alley with the spirit.

It was also *wrong* the way he looked at me. Wrong the way I looked at him. Somebody up there must have shown me mercy because my mind cleared for a moment. I put my hands on his chest and pushed him off me.

"I am *not* wet." Fuck this guy. This was ridiculous. He was messing with my head, and I wasn't going to let him.

But the second I moved, he was right behind me, arms wrapped tightly around my torso, his mouth right next to my ear. My body locked down again instantly.

"Let go of me," I hissed and tried to push him off, but he could have been made out of steel.

"You're a fucking liar, Damsel."

"I'm not—"

"Let's see, shall we? Let's prove it."

"What—"

His hand was on my thigh, moving up under my skirt lightning fast, and his fingers pressed over my panties, right on my clit.

"*Fuck!*" I cried, unable to hold myself. He growled and pressed himself harder against my ass, and I felt all of his erection on me perfectly. *Fuck, fuck, fuck.*

I held my breath as he slipped a single finger under the lacy fabric of my panties, and right between my soaking folds.

My eyes squeezed shut and my back arched despite my better judgment.

"Greedy little pussy," he whispered in my ear. My entire body was on fire, and as much as I wanted to stop it, I couldn't. It was impossible.

Especially when he swiped that finger up, nudging my clit on the way, and then took his hand from under my skirt. I watched, completely mesmerized, as he brought his middle finger coated with my juices right to his mouth and slipped it between his lips. He sucked hard, moaning like he'd never tasted anything better in his life.

I'd be damned if I'd ever seen anything sexier in my life.

"Fuck, Damsel," he growled, holding me tighter against his chest, and I still felt his hard cock pressed to my ass.

My gods, I wanted it so bad, my knees were shaking. This wasn't a game anymore. We weren't just teasing—I *wanted* him for real.

And it was wrong.

Slamming the heel of my boot onto his toes, I pushed myself off him, embarrassed, enraged, fucking incredulous that the past few minutes had even happened.

"Touch me again and I'll cut your dick off," I spit with all the hatred I could muster, then started running down the street like a fucking coward.

12

The inn we stopped at in the next town was so much better than the shithole motel in Bismarck. It had a clean carpet, crisp white sheets, and there was absolutely no rust in the bathroom.

The only problem was the connecting door on the left of the room, behind which was Ax.

I put the bag on the bed and took out my bottle of whiskey. It was just half an hour until sunrise, and I couldn't wait to pass out already. Until then, I'd just drink half this bottle as fast as I could. No need to think about the glowing spirit or the sorcerers or the mad vampire whose heartbeat had filled my head.

But even after the burning sensation took over my body, and my thoughts began to buzz lightly, it didn't take my mind away from the need clawing at me from the inside. No matter how hard I tried, I couldn't stop thinking about his face when he'd brought that finger to his lips and sucked all my juices off his skin like he was starved for me.

Great. I was getting turned on by a monster, and I didn't feel half as bad about it as I should have.

That's until the connecting door between the two rooms opened.

There he stood, a small smile on his gorgeous lips, wearing nothing but jeans that hung way too low on his hips, revealing the

V of his muscles to me perfectly. His eyes glistened with mischief, burning like two sapphires, making him almost too beautiful to be real. My thighs clenched at the sight of his curves and his skin covered in scars. The urge to know where each one of them came from was strong, but I bit my tongue. It wasn't my fucking business.

"What are you doing?" I asked with half a voice.

"Making sure we're both safe. Whoever attacked us with those arrows is still out there."

I narrowed my brows. "We are *not* sleeping with the door open." Had he lost his fucking mind?

"That's okay, Damsel. I don't sleep. I'll keep an eye out."

"You want to watch me sleeping like a fucking pervert all day?" I spit and stood up, so furious now I could explode. It had nothing to do with the situation, unfortunately, and everything to do with *him*. With *me* not being able to stop thinking about his fingers and his cock.

But I could pretend, couldn't I? I *would* fucking pretend until a miracle happened and somebody knocked some sense into me.

"I am not a pervert," he said, and his smile finally dropped. "There are people who want to hurt us out there. We won't know until it's too late if you're passed out."

"I can take care of myself, douchebag," I said, throwing the bottle of whiskey on the bed.

"The door stays open," he said.

My mouth opened to scream my guts at him. Who did he even think he was, touching me like that, then forcing me to sleep basically in the same room with him?

No. Just fucking no.

But I controlled myself. The more fuss I made about this, the more he'd know how much it affected me. I could handle myself, damn it. I'd been horny plenty of times before. Just last night, actually. Which was why I'd taken that human to my room.

I could handle Savage Ax just fine.

Not only that, but I would also make it *really* hard for him to handle me.

Locking myself in the bathroom, I stripped off my clothes and took a shower. I left the water nearly ice-cold because I needed to stop feeling so fucking warm and aroused tonight, just for a few minutes until I passed out.

Once that was done, I dried my body and hair with the towel, then walked out into the room again.

Completely naked.

He wanted to sleep with the door open? Fine. He wanted to look at me like a fucking perv while I slept—great. I'd give him something to look at. See if he liked it when he was hard and there was nothing he could fucking do about it.

"Damsel, I—" His voice cut off when he came to the connecting door and saw me drinking whiskey from the bottle naked.

I smiled, pushing my wet hair away from my eyes. "Sorry—I sleep naked. If that bothers you, feel free to close the door." And I winked.

He held his breath for a long second, and it wasn't helping that I could hear his heart tripping all over itself.

"You're the fucking devil," he finally said with a grin, then moved away where I couldn't see him.

Good. I'd rather just pretend he wasn't there at all.

I turned my phone on, knowing I'd have texts waiting from Anya. She'd want to know that I was okay. Four texts from her—and one from Ivan, too. *Still alive?* I replied to both of them quickly. *Yep. I'll be in Atlanta tomorrow.*

Now they knew I was okay…but was I, really? Sharing a room with a Sangria, unable to keep proper control of my own damn body. I'd always had trouble controlling the whispers in my mind, but these past couple days, the burden had only gotten heavier—and it was all because of *him*.

Grabbing the remote, I turned the old TV on, hoping to find something to keep me distracted for a few more minutes. Almost there. The sun was almost there.

But then I heard him dragging something, and he appeared right in front of the door with a chair identical to the one in my room near the tiny desk. He sat on it and made himself comfortable.

Right there, in front of the door, where he could see me and I could see him perfectly.

Fuck, he was impossible.

I pretended I couldn't tell he was even there. Turning the overhead lights off, I left the nightstand lamps on and sat on the bed. Not that he'd have difficulty seeing me in the dark—we were vampires.

Flicking through the channels, I felt his gaze on my body like a physical touch. Shivers danced on my back and my thighs clenched again, despite the ice-cold shower I'd taken. But I was determined to kill whatever time I had left with my eyes stuck to the TV screen and the shitty '80s movie they were playing. I would *not* look his way, not even for a second.

One minute turned to two, then three.

My eyes were glued to the screen, but I didn't see anything. All my attention was focused on him, sitting there in front of the door, watching me. It should have been creepy. It should have been scary.

Instead, I couldn't stop thinking about that dick pressed to my ass.

Reaching behind me for the whiskey, I risked a quick glance his way, then grinned.

"You got something in your pants," I said, and the heat of the whiskey going down my throat only intensified the heat between my thighs. He was hard. So deliciously hard, it must have been painful to keep those jeans on.

He must have thought so, too, because the next second, I heard the zipper.

Impossible not to look.

"I do, actually. Want to see?" Ax said, and just like that, he pulled out his cock for me to see.

Oh, fuck. He was big. He was *huge*, bigger than I'd ever seen before. My traitorous eyes were stuck on his smooth pink tip, the veins running the length of him, the way his hand gripped it tightly, then moved up and down slowly…

"What the fuck is wrong with you?" I hissed, blood rushing to my cheeks, heart beating a mile a minute. I was dripping between my thighs.

The asshole smiled, eyes half closed as he leaned his head back a bit and continue to jerk himself off as he looked at my tits. At my nipples that were rock hard.

Fuck.

"Everything's wrong with me, Damsel," he whispered, then moaned, throwing his head back. The sexiest sound I'd ever heard in my life.

"You're a fucking pervert," I spit and crossed my legs, turned my eyes on the TV—only for a second.

But he was impossible. This wasn't even funny—it was wrong. It should have *felt* wrong, damn it.

And I should have covered myself or walked out of the room or just slammed the door shut in his face.

Instead, all I could do was watch him with his cock in his hand, looking at every inch of me through half-hooded eyes, moaning and growling like a fucking animal.

I'd never felt more helpless in my life. My mouth was open, my eyes never blinking, afraid I'd miss a single second of the show he was putting on for me. My gods, I was going to explode myself. It wasn't fair that he looked like a fucking god like that. It wasn't fair that my pussy was pulsating between my clenched thighs. It wasn't fair that I wanted him in my mouth so bad, I was drooling.

"You're the most beautiful thing I've ever seen in my life, Damsel," he whispered, fisting his cock faster. A moan ripped from my lips when he threw his head back again. It was like I could *feel* his pleasure all over my body, and I wanted more.

I wanted to feel it, too.

The fucking pervert. If he could do this right in front of me without an ounce of shame, I could, too. My gods, if I didn't, I was gonna lose my shit. He was messing with my mind, playing me like a fucking fool.

And I was going to play him right back.

That's all the convincing it took for me to lean back on the bed and spread my shaking legs, put my heels on the edge of the mattress. He growled, eyes wide open now as he watched my hands squeezing my breasts. I pinched my nipple with one hand, imagining it was his teeth, and I moved the other to my stomach, then lower to my clit.

The second my fingertips pressed on it, I cried out and my back arched. In my mind, he was there, buried between my thighs. Fuck, it felt so good. So much better than it had in a long time. So good it was a bit painful to move my fingers up and down my soaked folds.

Ax stood up slowly from the chair, his hand on his cock still, his jeans gone. He stepped into my room, watching me like he was beholding all the wonders of the world, completely mesmerized by the sight of my fingers disappearing inside me.

My eyes were stuck on his hard cock, at the way his hand moved up and down, slowly now, and I was so close to the edge, I was going to burst any second just by looking at him.

"Let me take care of you, Damsel," he said when he stopped in front of the bed between my spread legs. I couldn't speak if I tried, and I couldn't stop moving.

Until he made me. He grabbed my hand and brought it up, then sniffed my fingers. I cried out, my hips still moving, my body desperate for release.

"Enough with the games," he growled and came closer until his thighs pressed against mine. Fuck, just that small touch and I was already drowning. "You and I both need to get each other out of our systems." His voice was low, rough, so fucking sexy I could come just listening to him talk, too. "Once. Just once." His grip on my hand tightened, like he was *begging* me.

"Once," I breathed, so desperate it was kind of pathetic.

"Say it. Tell me," he demanded, then slipped my fingers inside his mouth. My eyes squeezed shut as he licked my juices clean off my skin. The feel of his warm tongue seared me.

"Yes," I cried out, reaching my other hand between my legs because I couldn't wait. I'd never been more turned on in my life. And the way he hovered over me, that perfect face, those sparkling eyes…I was already doomed. "Fuck me, Axel. Just this once."

He let go of my hand and pushed the other away from my pussy with a growl. He grabbed me by the thighs and pushed me up on the bed before he lay over me. Fuck, his skin was warm like it was on fire. His tongue was in my mouth, devouring like a starved man. He pressed his hips down on me, and I cried out, desperate to feel that cock inside me. His hands came up to cup my tits and he didn't hold back. He squeezed my nipples like he meant to pull them off, then took my tongue and sucked it in his mouth violently. His hands moved down under my ass, and he dug his fingers in my skin like he wanted to tear me apart.

Fuck, I was so close to the edge I couldn't think. Running my fingernails up and down his back, I kissed and bit his lips until I tasted his blood. He moaned into my mouth and dug his fingers in my thighs before he pushed himself up a bit and guided the tip of his cock right between my folds. Charges of electricity took over my body. I locked my ankles around his hips tightly and pulled him as hard as I could.

"Easy, Damsel," he breathed, then sank his teeth in my jaw as he groaned, pressing his cock into me harder.

"Fuck easy," I said through gritted teeth and pulled him to me.

Half his cock slid inside me, making me cry out. I let go of his lips as my back arched, and the orgasm ripped through me mercilessly. Every muscle in my body clenched as I held onto him, digging my fingernails into his back. I saw nothing, heard nothing, smelled nothing else. My body was light as a feather, and I was soaring in the dark sky, completely free for a long moment.

Ax moved back a little bit, barely because of how tightly my legs were locked around him, and thrust back inside me with all his strength, burying all of his cock inside me at once.

All my being hung in the place where we connected. He froze for a second, holding onto me, face buried under my neck, cock pulsating inside me.

His warm tongue licked the side of my neck slowly, bringing me back to life, just like that. And my need returned, too, as if I hadn't orgasmed in years. Three seconds, and I was starved for him again.

Once, I reminded myself. Just this once. And then we'd be done.

"Clench that tight pussy around my cock," he breathed, and I did. He groaned, raising his head, running his tongue over my lips. I took it between my teeth and bit.

"Move," I whispered, and my hips rocked up, taking him even deeper. My gods, he filled me from head to toe. It was painful to adjust to the size of him but even more painful not to have him buried inside me all the way.

He moved his hips back just a bit before he slammed into me again, making me scream. Fuck, it hurt. It felt incredible. I'd never been more fulfilled in my life. Digging my fingernails into his hips, I pulled him to me every time he moved back. I bit his shoulder and he bit mine, one of his hands torturing my nipple, the other cupping my ass to keep me from moving every time he thrust inside me like he meant to cut me in half.

"Don't you dare come yet," I warned him. I needed to come with his cock inside me first. And he growled, picking up the pace, slamming into me like a real savage, until I could barely feel my legs.

"You're a greedy little slut, Damsel," he told me, biting my jaw as he raised up again to look at my face. "You want to come again?"

"Yes," I cried out, his words only intensifying the fire burning under my skin.

"You want to clench around my cock again?" He thrust inside me so hard I saw stars.

"Yes!"

"So fucking greedy," he said with a growl. I really was. "Eyes open, Damsel. I want to see how I break you from the inside."

Our eyes were locked as he kept slamming into me over and over again. His hand moved deeper under my ass, and I felt his middle finger as it pressed against my asshole, then the tip of it slipped inside without warning. The orgasm ripped throughout me the same second, wiping my mind completely clean again.

And once he felt my pussy clenching around him, he let go, too. The weight of him over me took my breath away, but the way his cock pulsated inside me made my orgasm last longer than ever before. We were locked in each other's arms, fingers digging, eyes closed, skin coated with sweat.

I didn't just feel light this time—it felt like I didn't have a body at all. Nothing was holding me down. I was free for real.

But soon, it was over.

Our heartbeats were already slowing down, and the sun was peeking through the window. I was so exhausted, I could barely speak.

It's over.

"Get the fuck out of my room," I told him, pushing his arms back.

He raised his head, a lazy smile playing on those beautiful lips that tasted even better than they looked.

"You're welcome, Damsel," he said and kissed me on the lips so fast, I barely felt it.

But he pulled himself out of me and stood up, looking down at my spread legs with so much longing, you'd think we'd been lovers for a lifetime.

"'Night, asshole," I mumbled.

The pillows were too far away so I grabbed the sheets, spun around and wrapped myself in them, eyes already closed.

13

Georgia.

It was an hour and a half until sunrise, and we were already in Georgia. *Halle—fucking—lujah*. Three more days and this nightmare would be over. I wouldn't have to be turned on by a fucking psychopath, and I wouldn't have to even *see* said psychopath ever again. He'd go off to his part of the Realm, *eating, torturing, and fucking* for the rest of his days, and I could go back to my booze, to having to worry *only* about the whispers in my head, not my traitorous body, too.

Really hard to have high self-esteem right now when I'd been fucked like that just last morning by a savage—and enjoyed every second of it. More than I ever had before. In my life. Ever.

Even with Ezra, which was saying something.

At least it helped that he kept away from me as we ran all night. I didn't stop—couldn't stop if I tried. I needed to keep moving if I was going to have any chance at forgetting about last morning and *never* getting wet for Savage Ax again.

Damn it, why couldn't he just be ordinary? Just another vampire like those in the Hidden Realm. I could get anybody to walk away from me within the hour, but not this guy. He pushed back just as hard.

And why did he have to sound like *sex,* and why did he have to make my pussy clench every time I felt his eyes on me?

That shit was reserved for when you actually *cared* for someone. And when you did, you spent time with that person, and eventually, if you were lucky, your mating instinct awakened and you got the urge to bite them, take their blood, become *mates*. That way, you have someone for life, and you are the most powerful version of yourself you can possibly be.

The perfect ending to a fucked-up vampire life.

But no—that was way too complicated for good ole me. Those first parts had worked out fine—I'd met Ezra, had loved talking to him, sleeping with him, fucking him. We were going solid for seven years, and I was so sure that the urge to mate would be upon us any day. I'd waited for it every single time we were together.

And then he'd just…sent it all to hell. All those years. All those promises. All that hope.

"Fucking feelings," I muttered to myself as I took a long sip of the whiskey. Two more of those and I'd be out. Good thing there were plenty of liquor stores in Atlanta.

"You got the address?"

Ax spoke to me from at least twenty feet away. I turned to see him leaning against a lamppost on the sidewalk, looking like a fucking painting rather than real.

"I do," I told him and looked ahead at the busy street. It was late, but there were plenty of people out and about in Downtown

Atlanta. Plenty of hearts and plenty of blood. The buildings were larger, the streets narrower, and way too many cars for my liking.

I turned to look at Ax again, and a flash of his face when he'd been right over me while his cock was buried inside me came before my eyes. I shivered.

"Race you?" I said and took off running before he could reply.

Yeah, I was a coward. Yeah, I was running from him, but it was for my own good. My own safety.

The address Jones had written down for me, according to Google, was in a neighborhood behind the Mercedes-Benz Stadium. We were so close now I could taste it. I could taste peace back in my room in the Realm, the alcohol going down my throat, knowing there was absolutely no reason to stay sober...

But the blood. I'd have rather been stuck in those thoughts, but the thermos with the cow's blood in my bag was empty, and I smelled it so much clearer in humans now. Had I been in this state two nights ago, I'd have never dared to take poor Jimmy to my room for fear I'd kill him.

I needed to feed. I needed to find a butcher and refill my thermos. Or I was going to fucking lose it, and I couldn't risk it. Not when I heard every heart beating within a half mile radius.

Focus, I told myself. We were almost there. Almost done. Just a few more minutes.

When I entered the neighborhood, I stopped at the beginning of the street to wait for Ax. Where the hell was he? I looked back, hoping to see him running, but he wasn't there.

Then...

"Hey, Damsel."

The voice came from ahead, at least ten feet away, and I finally saw him hiding in the shadows of a five-story building, arms crossed in front of him as he watched me. Show-off.

Rolling my eyes, I made my way up the street. "You're here. Good. Here's the plan—we go up there and knock on the door, see who answers."

Every building along the street looked the same, and the deeper we went, the stronger the smell of weed and alcohol. Groups of men hung out in the alleys, and they spoke in hushed voices as they watched us. Hopefully nobody would try to stop us, or Ax was going to kill again. I really wished he wouldn't.

And I really wished everybody with fresh blood in their veins would just stay away from me, too.

"What if she refuses to come with us?" Ax asked as he watched the groups of guys watching us. A smile was on his face and a glint in his eyes—he was challenging them. He was *hoping* they'd say something.

"Hey, knock it off," I said, slapping his chest. His *naked* chest. "If she refuses to come, we'll change her mind."

"And if *that* doesn't work?"

I gave him a pointed look. "We are *not* going to kill her."

"Unless we have to." He was serious.

"Are you kidding me? Redwood teamed up with Sangria for this. What the hell does that tell you?"

"That whoever we're here for is very important."

"Thank you!" At least his brain was working well. "No killing. We'll try to talk to her, and if it doesn't work, we'll tie her up and fucking carry her." Which was going to be a lot more problematic than even I realized.

"A car," Ax said. "We'll have to drive back to North Dakota."

"You said no cars. Jones said it, too."

"Well, I changed my mind—I'm not going to carry her all the way back. And Jones isn't here, is he?"

I grinned. "No, he's not." I wasn't going to carry a grown vampire over my shoulder for three nights, either. We'd rent a car and we'd drive it back. It would be slower, but we'd be careful. We'd take breaks and make sure we were not being followed. It would all work out.

"In there," Ax said, pointing at the building on the other side of the street. The number on it matched the one Jones had written. Finally.

The building was at least fifteen stories high, with dirty dark brown bricks on the exterior, a couple of the windows on the ground floor broken. The doors of the entrance were in pretty bad shape, too, and there were drawings on the walls everywhere I looked.

We sniffed the air as we went to the stairs, not bothering with the elevator. We could get up there faster by running.

"At least we're safe from Vein spirits," he whispered, and his smile said he was testing me. If I gave him the chance, he'd ask me questions again. I didn't want to fucking talk about it—or even *think* about it at all.

So, I didn't take the bait.

"Let's see what the fuss is about," I said and took off running up the stairs. I could hear the hearts of the people all around me in their apartments. I could smell their blood. I wondered if Ax felt it, too.

Come to think of it, he hadn't had any cow blood with him at all. Was he having trouble keeping his focus?

But every thought I had came to a halt when I stopped in the hallway of the tenth floor and smelled the spicy scent of magic lingering in the air. The apartment we were looking for was on the eleventh.

Ax was right beside me, his eyes closed. We didn't breathe, didn't move for a long moment, only listened.

"Sorcerers," I whispered, when it was clear that nobody was awake on that floor or the one above. I ran up the stairs to the eleventh floor, and I didn't even need to read the numbers on the doors to know where I was going. The spicy scent led me right to the one at the end of the hallway to the right.

The smell of magic was strong but not intense enough to make me think someone had used it in the past couple hours. Ax took his sweet time walking down the hallway, and by the time he made it to me, I'd already opened the door.

Unlocked.

And one look inside told me why.

"Fuck me," I whispered as I stepped inside the narrow hallway of the apartment. Things were on the floor—broken glass, broken wood, pieces of paper, sheets.

"Somebody's definitely been here," Ax said, pushing the door closed behind him. He was absolutely right—and whoever it had been, they'd made sure not to leave anything untouched before they left.

The kitchen and the living room were a mess of broken things thrown all over. Nothing was in its place. Broken plates, a broken TV, half of it still hanging on the wall, broken coffee table, chairs scattered everywhere.

By the time I took in everything in the rooms, Ax had inspected the bedroom and the bathroom, which were all empty. Nobody was here.

"Definitely sorcerers," Ax said, squatting down as he looked at the broken things covering the floor.

"They got to her." Of course, they did. Why wouldn't they? They'd made it their job to wipe us off the face of the earth, and when they couldn't do that, they just locked us up in the Hidden Realm. Since we weren't powerful enough to fight against them—and win—we had no choice but to go willingly. "Isn't it strange, though?" I said as I walked around the kitchen, then to the living room. "I don't smell vampire here." Only sorcerers.

Ax didn't say anything. At the far end of the living room, three picture frames were on the floor, broken. One was of a little boy on a bicycle, one was of a woman and a teenage boy, and the third was an elderly couple holding hands as they smiled at the camera.

I took the one with the woman and the boy. They had huge smiles on their faces, the same dark brown eyes, the same pitch-black hair. Definitely related.

Was this the woman we were looking for? She didn't look like a vampire, but maybe she took this picture before she was turned.

Which begged the question—*by whom?* Was it really possible that someone had somehow escaped from the Hidden Realm and hid out here on Earth without anybody knowing about it?

I sighed. "So, what now?"

"Don't ask me," Ax mumbled, hands in his pockets as he looked at me from across the room.

"What?" I narrowed my brows. "Why not?"

"Because all I can think about is fucking you, Damsel. I'm not good with ideas right now." He said it bluntly, like he was talking about something completely normal.

Chills rushed down my spine instantly. "You're fucking sick," I muttered—but I was no better.

"I am," he said, like I'd paid him a compliment. "We should go get a room."

I turned to him again. "Fuck that. You said *once.*"

He grinned and his face transformed completely. "I'm a fucking liar."

I rolled my eyes again, but the heat in between my legs kept on growing. "Well, I'm not."

"Yes, you are. Stop fucking lying to me, Damsel. I can smell your wetness."

I broke the picture frame, took out the picture, and put it in my pocket. I don't know why I wanted it with me, I just did.

"Then I'll just find someone to take care of it." I made for the hallway to inspect it, too, but he was suddenly right in front of me, looking down at me with no hint of amusement in his eyes.

"You want to be a little slut, Damsel? That's fine," he whispered, "but you're going to be *my* little slut while we're here, nobody else's."

Why in the world did I enjoy it when he talked to me like that? I should have been disgusted, but…his voice. It had to be that voice.

"I am *not* yours," I said through gritted teeth.

"Yet," he whispered.

Taking in a deep breath, I stepped back. This was pointless. Wasted time. "We need to find that vampire," I reminded him.

"It's almost daylight," he said, leaning his head to the side as he looked at my lips and practically set them on fire.

Pulling them inside my mouth, I slipped into the hallway. "We're not sleeping in the same room again, asshole."

And I'd be damned if I didn't keep my word.

14

He couldn't even be bothered to pick up the fucking phone.

"Damn it, Jones," I whispered to the night, then called his number again. Voice mail.

Taking in a deep breath, I forced myself to calm down for long enough to say five words. "She's gone. Sorcerers took her."

Now, if he could just deem it worthy to listen to that voice mail and give me a call back, that would be great.

I looked behind me at the hotel and shivers washed all over me. We were staying just a couple blocks from that woman's apartment because we wanted to go back there first thing tomorrow night. The sun was about an hour away from shining, and I'd never felt more helpless in my life. Even that pizza I'd eaten minutes ago hadn't really tasted like anything. Why hadn't I made Jones tell me more? A goddamn name would have been nice. And a Plan B, too.

Shit. If he didn't call me by tomorrow night, I was going to have no choice but to call Ivan.

I wondered if Ax had called his coven as I made my way through the revolving doors of the hotel. We were staying on the fourth floor, rooms across from one another, just like I liked it. I couldn't afford to be too far away from him right now when there were sorcerers out there—not to mention the vampires from the other covens. But across the hallway would do just fine.

I expected him to open the door when he heard me coming. He didn't, and I was thankful for it. What happened last night could never happen again. It was a mistake. He was my enemy, not to mention batshit crazy. Crazier than *me*, which was saying something.

The hotel room was an upgrade from everything else I'd ever lived in until now. Lush carpet, strawberry scented shampoos, a nice flat screen TV, and pillows stuffed full of feathers. The smell could be better, but I wasn't complaining. Especially not when the minibar was full of tiny bottles of alcohol.

After the shower, I grabbed a vodka and lay down on the bed to wait for the sun to come up so I could pass out. I'd have loved it if I could stop thinking for five minutes and just focus on the movie playing on the TV, but it was impossible.

Almost the entire bottle of vodka was in my system, and my mind wouldn't shut up.

Something was wrong here. How had Jones and the other covens even found out about a vampire living in Atlanta by herself? How had she managed to do that with all the sorcerers around who could feel her every time she was near them? Who was this boy smiling next to her in the picture I'd taken from the apartment, now lying next to me on the bed?

And most importantly, why hadn't that apartment smelled like a vampire at all? How long ago had she disappeared?

Maybe Ax would have more answers. Maybe he'd given his coven a call and they'd actually picked up, unlike Jones. Was I crazy enough to go knock on his door and ask?

Fuck no. That would be plain stupid. I knew he'd want to get in my bed again, and I was also perfectly aware of the fact that I couldn't fucking resist him if he pulled his pants down and showed me his cock again.

That fucking prick. Why wasn't I disgusted with this guy as I should have been?

Something was very wrong with *me*, too.

Jumping off the bed, I went and grabbed another small bottle of alcohol from the minibar, then paced around the room as I drank. Things weren't adding up right now, but they would soon. Once Jones got my message and called back with instructions, everything would make sense.

Hopefully I'd be home in a couple days and continue my life far away from the savage across the hall. And the stupid attraction I had toward him. Because despite the situation, and despite the fact that I knew who he was, my lady parts were on fire because a part of my brain was stuck replaying how he'd felt inside me last time. How warm his skin had been. How delicious the weight of him pressing against my thighs…

When I heard a door in the hall open, I held my breath and stopped moving. It was him. I knew it was him. I heard his heartbeat and smelled the strawberry scent coming off him. He'd showered, too.

Where the fuck was he going when it was half an hour to sunrise?

One step, then two…and another.

He stopped right in front of my door.

Gritting my teeth, I waited for him to knock. I wasn't going to open the door, obviously. And if he tried to break it, I was going to fucking murder him for real.

But…Ax didn't knock. I felt him right there in front of my door. I heard his heartbeat clearly and the way he breathed—slowly, steadily.

The asshole didn't knock.

What was he going to do—just stand there all day? It felt like he was breathing down my fucking neck!

He had issues, and I was worse. Closing my eyes, I lay down on the bed and breathed. My heartbeat had sped up, too, and I focused on that instead of what was outside the door—the very reason why I was so nervous in the first place. That asshole. I didn't even need to *see* him for him to play his fucking games with me. I could imagine him just fine.

That's why I opened my eyes and just stared at the ceiling, counting the seconds in my head. Why wouldn't he just go away? Why was the sound of his heartbeat echoing in my mind?

Don't open the door, my own thoughts warned me.

But it was already too late. The anger had grown the size of a monster inside me, and I no longer saw reason.

Cursing under my breath, I went to the door and pulled it open. Just like I expected, he was standing right there, hands on the frames of my door, wearing nothing but those jeans, and that mad smile that was a hundred percent *him*.

"*What?*" I spit, so pissed that he'd made me open the door I could burst. Worse—it made the whispers in my head turn up a notch, too. The second I started losing control of my emotions, they were the hardest to ignore.

"I thought you said you sleep naked." He made a point of eyeing my skirt and crop top.

"Get the fuck away from my door," I said and slammed it shut.

Or I was going to until his hand came up and pushed it right back open.

"I'm waiting for further instructions from the coven," he said. "The sun's barely thirty minutes away. How about you let me in? I can smell your wetness from across the hall, Damsel."

That fucking nose of his.

I smiled. "How about you go fuck yourself instead?"

"Tried that yesterday. Didn't work," he said, his eyes sparkling with mischief.

And now I was imagining him sitting down with his cock in his hands. Not helping.

"Then you should try again today," I said in a whisper like I was letting him in on a secret, and made to close the door again.

He put his foot forward to stop me. "Why won't you just let me in? I'll help you sleep. You know I will."

"Because you're my fucking enemy, Ax. Not to mention fucking crazy."

"That didn't stop you yesterday," he said, but his smile dropped a bit.

"Yeah, well, that was a moment of weakness," I lied.

"No, it wasn't. You loved every second."

Shit, that was true. Didn't mean I was *ever* going to admit it to him, though. I crossed my arms in front of my chest.

"I can't fucking stand to look at your face, you know that?" Because I got turned on by the madness in his eyes which was wrong on too many levels to count.

"Oh?" he said, raising his brows. "Then whose face would I have to wear for you to let me in tonight?"

"I don't know. Chris Evans. Chris Hemsworth. Chris Pine." I shrugged. "Any Chris would do, really."

The asshole grinned. "Hold that thought," he whispered and moved back to his room so fast, it caught me by surprise.

"What the…"

Five seconds later, he was out the door and in front of me again. "Turn around, Damsel."

I waited a second for him to say he was kidding, and when he didn't… "No fucking way."

"Turn around," he repeated in that hushed voice of his that had my arms covered in goose bumps.

What the hell was he up to?

And why was I even turning around?

Too late now. A piece of black fabric was right in front of my eyes the second I turned my back on him.

"What are you doing?" I asked breathlessly, but I already knew.

"I'm blindfolding you, Damsel. That way you don't have to look at my face at all, and you can imagine whichever Chris you want." He tied the blindfold behind my head…and I still wasn't moving.

"No," I said, shaking my head.

He put his arms on my shoulders and pushed me forward, into the room. Then he closed the door behind him.

"Let me make you feel good, Damsel," he whispered from behind me, right next to my ear, before he grabbed my earlobe between his teeth and bit.

Electricity buzzed on my skin instantly. Shit. What the hell was I going to do now? I knew what I *should* do—take that blindfold off and kick him out.

And I tried to do that. I tried to focus on anything other than him—even the whispers in my head for once, but they were barely there. I already drank too much, and I could barely hear them.

His hands moved down my arms, his touch rough, fingernails scratching my skin, just like I liked. And I really didn't want to be alone with my thoughts until sunrise. I couldn't see him at all—that blindfold was pretty tight.

It's not like we could do something right now without word from the covens, anyway. Why not just let him make me feel good when I didn't even have to see his face? I could pretend it was someone else. It would be easy.

His hands moved to my waist, and he squeezed tightly, almost breaking my ribs. My lungs emptied and my thighs clenched. Those fucking big hands of his.

"What do you say, Damsel? May I?" he whispered in my ear again. Such a nice guy, asking for fucking permission.

I must have lost my fucking mind on this trip because I felt myself nodding.

That's all the confirmation he needed.

He grabbed my crop top, pulled it off me in one movement, and unzipped my skirt and pushed it down in the next. Fuck, I even liked the way he took my clothes off. There one second, gone the next. No time wasted.

He still stayed there behind me and hooked two fingers in my underwear, before he started pulling them down slowly. The low growls he let out vibrated straight to my clit. I fisted my hands tightly, still hoping that some part of me was going to force me to get out of this trance, kick him out and be done with it, but it wasn't meant to be. My panties fell to the floor, and his hands ran up my thighs. My back arched as I moaned, my ass pressed to his pelvis. He was already hard, and I felt all of him. In my mind's eye, I saw his cock in perfect detail and my thighs clenched harder.

But then his arms were under me and my feet no longer touched the floor. He carried me forward, and even though I was blindfolded, I was perfectly aware of everything around me. I knew he was taking me to the bed. He lay me down on the pillow without word, just breathing as heavily as I was.

I heard him unbuckle his belt before he got in the bed with me, knees on either side of my waist. I was so warm, I was afraid I'd catch fire any second. I waited for his hands to fall on me, like being touched by him was the fucking purpose of my life.

But instead, he grabbed my hands and pulled them up. The leather of his belt was around my wrists.

"What are you doing?"

"Tying your hands," he said, and I was too stunned to even stop him until he tied the belt around my wrists and to the bed's headboard tightly.

"Why? Are you afraid I'll hurt you?" I teased, but I was actually a bit excited. I'd never been tied up in bed like this.

"No, Damsel. I just want to take my time with you without interruptions," he said chuckling, then moved lower on the bed. I felt his every movement, and suddenly, I was perfectly aware that my wrists were tied and I was blindfolded, completely naked while he looked down at me. Taking his fucking time.

I wanted to be embarrassed. I really did. But his fingertips ran over my stomach, just a ghost of a touch, and my hips moved up instantly, and my legs spread to the sides.

"The way you react to my touch is fucking exquisite," he whispered under his breath.

"Stop talking. I'm trying to imagine someone else here," I said before I allowed myself to blush. Because he was absolutely right. The way I reacted to him was completely senseless.

"As you wish, Damsel," he whispered, then moved his hands up to my breasts. He grabbed my nipples between his fingers, rolled them for a second, then pinched them hard. A moan escaped me, and my back arched again, legs spreading wider all on their own. Fuck, I wanted to see his face so badly. Instead, I squeezed my eyes shut and held onto the belt keeping my arms up. I didn't need to see him. Feeling him was more than enough.

The heat of his body spilled over mine when he leaned closer and closer. I held my breath, perfectly aware of him, until I felt his tongue, wet and hot, flick over my nipple. My legs wrapped around him instantly, and I pulled him down, but he resisted. With his hands underneath my thighs, he forced my legs to the sides again.

"Not so fast, Damsel," he whispered, warm breath blowing on my wet nipple.

"For fuck's sake," I said, raising my chest so he could take it into his mouth again. And he did. His swollen lips closed around my nipple, and he sucked. I pulled on the belt so hard, the wood of the headboard creaked.

"Don't make me tie your legs, too," he said, slapping my nipple with the tips of his fingers. I don't know why every time he touched me made me feel like I was on fire, but I didn't even care right now. I was wet and I was ready. I just needed him to be inside me so I could get my release.

So, the moment he closed his mouth around my other breast and bit my nipple, I wrapped my legs around him again. Growling, he bit and sucked and dug his fingers in my thighs, making me cry out louder each time. But he still wouldn't let me pull him to me. I needed to feel his weight on my thighs, his cock against my pussy. I needed it *now*.

But Ax hadn't been kidding around.

"My greedy little slut," he said chuckling, and the next second, I felt him pulling the sheet from under me.

"Ax," I breathed, so ready to break the headboard and just jump on him like a madwoman—but then I heard the sheet tearing.

"I'm gonna take my time with you, Damsel," he said, his hands around my ankle. He pulled my leg to the side, then wrapped the cotton sheet around it tightly.

I groaned. "Are you fucking kidding me?" He was really going to tie my legs, too?

"You're being naughty. You deserve a little punishment," he said, then moved on to my other leg, yanking it to the side.

"You know I can break this bed without effort, right?" And I made a point of pulling the belt until the headboard creaked again.

"But if you do, I'll stop," he said. Blood rushed to my cheeks, the words at the tip of my tongue, my instincts demanding I pull my limbs so hard that the entire fucking frame of the bed would be in pieces. "If I stop, you'll never know what my tongue in your pussy feels like."

Oh, hell.

Screw my instincts—I didn't move an inch.

My eyes squeezed shut under the blindfold, and I felt the heat of him again when he climbed on the bed, right between my spread legs.

"You really are a sight to see," he said in wonder, and the tip of his finger ran up my wet folds. I was so fucking doomed with this guy. "Hold still for me, Damsel."

My body must have been at his command because I stopped moving again completely.

I felt his warm breath right on my wet folds as he came closer and closer. He growled like an animal before he flicked his tongue over my clit.

Yep. Definitely doomed.

My soul was about to leave my body when he dove in violently, making out with my pussy the way he did with my mouth. He was relentless, merciless, biting and sucking and flapping his tongue everywhere at once. I cried so hard my throat was a bit sore, and though I wanted nothing more than to get rid of that belt and grab his head, press it onto me harder, I resisted. No way could he stop now. I'd die for real.

So, I took it, let the pathetic belt and the torn sheets hold me wide open for him while he feasted on my pussy, then employed his fingers, too. Ax wasn't gentle. He didn't play around. One second he let go of my folds, and I heard the sound of him licking his finger, and the next, that same finger was inside me all the way.

The orgasm built up so fast, it made me wonder why in the world I'd ever thought it was *hard* to make me come. It really wasn't. He pushed another finger inside me, and I couldn't stop the outburst if I tried. I cried out so hard, the whole hotel probably heard me, but I didn't care. The feelings took me high, away from the bed and the hotel and the whole fucking world before I came back down again, and his tongue was devouring every drop between my folds. The way he growled you'd think he was drinking human blood straight from a vein.

"That was less than thirty seconds," he murmured against my thigh before he bit it.

"Fuck you," I said, the blood in my veins boiling again, half from anger, half from embarrassment. That had been *more* than thirty seconds. At least forty.

The asshole chuckled, trailing kisses up to my pelvis. "Don't be rude, Damsel. I'm doing the fucking for now."

He rose and I felt his eyes burning every inch of my skin as he watched me, breathing heavily, heart racing in my chest, which he heard. He heard and saw exactly what he did to me, and as much as it pissed me off, I could do nothing but wait.

Because I needed more. Just a little more, and I'd be fine.

"I fucking hate your guts," I told him, and my back arched when his hands cupped my breasts and squeezed tightly.

"Really," he whispered, climbing higher, planting his knees on the sides of my waist. Gods, I felt so small lying there like that, desperate for him. And I loved every second. "You hate this?" he said and pressed his cock right between my breasts before he grabbed them and pushed them up around it.

Fuck.

"You hate this, Damsel?" he said and fucked my tits as he pinched my nipples hard enough to make me cry out.

"No, I love your cock. I just hate you," I said, trying to sound as hateful as my words, but I just sounded breathless instead. He kept going, faster by the second. His smooth skin sliding against mine, the tip of his cock piercing its way between my breasts as he held them tightly together, the feel of his thighs squeezing my ribcage… I was dying to take that stupid blindfold off and see it.

But Ax moved farther up, letting go of my breasts, grabbing my chin in his large hand.

"Open wide for me, Damsel," he said, but he never gave me the chance. The tip of his cock pressed against my lips and forced them open. He thrust hard, mercilessly, and his cock was all the way inside my mouth in a second, the tip of it grazing the back of my throat.

I gagged, but he didn't move away, kept himself right there, pressing into me for a good two seconds.

"That's right," he breathed, closing his fingers around my neck when he thrust back, then in again, even harder. "Take all of it, Damsel." Every time the tip of him pressed into my throat, it felt like I was choking in the best possible way. He didn't give me the chance to run my tongue over him slowly, to feel every inch of him the way I wanted to. He didn't care whether I could breathe properly or not. He just kept going, taking and taking and never once slowing down.

Eventually, he let go of my neck and held himself on the headboard, then fucked my mouth just as violently as he did my pussy. There was no gentle with him and I loved that. I loved that there were no feelings involved, just raw sex. We took pleasure and that was that. No meaning. No nothing.

Tears streamed from my eyes as he continued to thrust himself inside my mouth, each time as deep as it would go. The sounds he let out filled my head, those sexy moans and animalistic growls. His balls slammed under my chin and his pelvis pressed against my nose as he kept going, trying to fucking break my skull in half. The bed creaked the more he moved, and if he didn't stop soon, it was going to let go of us.

I could barely breathe, and my throat was fucking raw, but I never wanted to stop. The way he filled me was incredible, and my own pleasure was already taking over me.

But then he raised up a bit, grabbed the hair on top of my head and stopped thrusting. Knowing that I wasn't going to get a better chance than this, I took advantage of the fact that he wasn't moving for a second, and licked his cock slowly, grazed it with my teeth, then sucked his tip until I felt the salty pre cum spilling out of it.

He hissed, tightening his hold on my hair.

"Fuck, Damsel," he said, then brought his cock back in my mouth slowly. He liked it when I tasted him, so I kept going, sucking and grazing and flicking my tongue, but it didn't last long. He pushed himself back, and his cock was gone, no longer within my mouth's reach.

"More," I demanded, sticking out my tongue, but he moved lower instead.

"Your mouth's greedy, too," he whispered, running his hands down my stomach. "How am I gonna satisfy you when you need so much?"

I was going to tell him, but then he reached behind and pressed his thumb on my clit, before he stuck two fingers inside me all the way. I cried out, pushing my hips up.

"I wonder if your ass is greedy, too," he whispered.

Shivers danced on my skin. I was so ready to come, it was ridiculous. But if he was going to fuck my ass, I was going to see it. Fuck the blindfold—I needed to see it.

So, I pulled my hands down hard, and the wood of the headboard gave instantly.

Ax grabbed my wrists lightning fast.

"Damsel, no," he warned.

"I want it off me," I said through gritted teeth.

"But I'm not Chris Evans." I heard the grin in his voice, but when I pushed his hands away this time, he let me.

"I know, asshole." Once the belt was finally off me, I took the blindfold off, too, to find him sitting over me, knees to my sides, his cock on my chest.

Fuck. Just the sight of him made my clit throb painfully.

I reached for it immediately, but he was faster. He grabbed my wrists again and pulled them to the sides, pressing his weight onto me.

"Who were you thinking about when you were screaming just now?" he said, grabbing my bottom lip between his teeth.

"Chris," I said, and my hips moved up to meet him, but he pushed them down.

"Liar," he said, running his tongue over my lips. "Tell me, Damsel. Tell me…"

"*You*," I spit, so pissed and so turned on, it was a miracle I hadn't collapsed yet. "I was thinking about you, asshole."

He grinned and his bloodshot eyes sparkled again. He let go of my hands and raised up, settling between my legs.

"Good girl. Now let me earn it one more time." Grabbing his cock in his hand, he positioned it and thrust his hips forward within a second, burying deep inside me. It was like he lit all my insides on fire at once.

He raised up, grabbing my hips in his huge hands to keep me in place, and pounded into me fast, his eyes closed and head thrown back. I shouldn't have liked the sight of him, so lost in the bliss, as much as I did, but the pleasure had already consumed me so I didn't care about thinking straight. It took me another ten seconds to rip the sheets from around my ankles. When I did, I tried to sit up and wrap my arms around his neck. He didn't let me.

Instead, he brought my legs up and pushed them against my chest, then slapped my ass hard. "I need to feel all of you, Damsel," he whispered, and he brought his hand to his mouth, sticking his middle finger inside and sucking. He looked so damn sexy like that. "I need to own all of your holes. You got a problem with that?"

He must have been out of his fucking mind. "If I did, I wouldn't be here begging for it."

His face broke into a huge smile and he stuck his finger halfway up my asshole. My eyes squeezed shut and my head fell back. Pleasure and pain collided inside me, taking my breath away, but he didn't stop. He pulled his finger out just a bit, then thrust it in all the way.

"That's so fucking tight, Damsel," he whispered as he moved his finger in and out of me. He pushed my legs down harder until my knees touched my chest. "Your ass is just as greedy. I fucking love your hunger."

He pulled his finger out of me, took his cock in his hand, and brought the tip of it close.

I had my eyes squeezed shut as I waited, all my being hanging onto the moment I felt him inside me.

"Do you want me to take it slow?" he whispered, pressing onto me just a little bit to give me a taste. And it hurt. My gods, it hurt so beautifully.

"Don't you dare hold back on me now," I warned him. I didn't need slow. I needed to feel all of it—pain and pleasure together.

Ax didn't hesitate. He thrust his hips while he held his cock in place, and the tip of him was inside me. I cried out, wrapped my arms around my legs tightly, and held my breath. He growled and moved back a bit, before he thrust himself forward again, entering me halfway. Fuck, how it hurt. The pleasure was fucking mind-blowing. I wanted to move but my body was frozen, all my muscles clenched tightly. All I could do was wait for him to move—and he did. He pushed himself inside me a little harder each time until he stretched me all the way and was inside me to the base. I cried out so much, and the pain mixed with the pleasure had my entire body shaking.

He stopped moving for a second, letting me adjust to the size of him, then took my legs and brought them up, resting my heels on his shoulders. He ran his hands up and down my legs, and I opened my eyes to see his closed, his face completely relaxed, like he was in pure bliss.

"Ax," I breathed, moving my hips away just slightly to test the pain. It wasn't half as bad as I thought. "I need you," I whispered. "I need you to keep moving."

"I'm gonna come faster than you," he said, planting kisses on my foot, but he moved back a little bit, too.

"I don't care. Keep moving," I begged, and his fingers dug into my thighs before he pushed himself back, then slammed inside me again, all the way.

I screamed. My eyes were locked on his as he moved faster by the second, fucking destroying my body with his cock. His fingers reached between my legs and he pressed them to my clit, playing with it for a second. His eyes were on fire. His skin was on fire. And I was right there, burning with him.

He grabbed my ankles and pulled my legs to the sides slowly, as if he were afraid he would hurt me. He did—and that was the point. I liked the pain he gave me. I fucking loved it.

When his fingers came down again, they didn't just stop on my clit. They went all the way inside my pussy, too. Every muscle in my body clenched hard, and he threw his head back again, moaning.

"Fuck, Damsel. I want to be everywhere inside you," he whispered, slowing down his pace. He pulled his cock out of me and thrust his fingers in, and when he pulled them out, he moved his hips forward again. It was the perfect rhythm, and I was so full. I was completely full, and I never wanted to stop.

"I can't take it," he said through gritted teeth, pulling out of me. "I need you to come again. I need to feel you clenching around my cock." And without warning, he buried himself in my pussy again, all the way. The pain was no longer there, and the pleasure climbed impossibly fast now. I'd loved the feel of him in both my holes, but I needed the release, too.

So, I pushed myself up, and this time he didn't stop me. He held me by the waist as he straightened his legs under me, and then I was straddling him, holding onto his wide shoulders as I moved, my clit pressing to his pelvis every time I took him in all the way.

He gripped my ass with one hand and grabbed a fistful of my hair with the other to keep me in place. We were forehead to forehead, looking into each other's eyes as we moved, with harder, more desperate thrusts by the second.

When I came, I dug my fingernails into his back hard as the pleasure wreaked havoc on my insides, wiping my mind completely clean again. He held my hips down as he pushed his up as far as they'd go. Then he let go, too. We held onto each other, still moving slowly as we rode the high. It was hands down the best sex I'd ever had, and as senseless as it was, I wanted *more* the moment we stopped moving.

Our hearts were racing, beating in perfect sync, and we could barely get enough air in our lungs still. His hands were on my face, and he planted kisses on my cheeks, my lips, my eyes. Every time his lips touched my skin, I felt…*weaker*.

And that was my cue to get the fuck off him.

It was already done. The sex was over. It was finished.

Pushing myself back on the bed, I spun around and jumped to my shaking legs as fast as my body allowed.

"You're welcome, Savage," I said with a wink, just like he said to me the morning before.

It took him a second to smile—he looked *surprised* first—but it didn't quite reach his eyes, and he didn't say anything back.

"Be gone by the time I'm out," I said and slipped into the bathroom, slamming the door shut behind me as if I were suddenly *embarrassed*.

I wasn't. Not even a little bit. Sex was not something to be embarrassed about.

What I was, was turned on still, and a bit freaked out because as it turned out, Savage Ax just might be right. No matter how many times or in how many ways he fucked me, it felt like I was never going to be satisfied.

15

Find her at all costs.

A text. That's all Jones could do for me—a fucking text. Not a call back—*a text*. And a ridiculous one at that.

Find her at all costs. How the fuck was I supposed to do that when I didn't know the city, the people, or the person I was supposed to find?

"Anything?" I asked when I walked out of the hotel the next night and found Ax in the parking lot, waiting.

"Nothing. They just want her found."

I flinched. "Same."

"Back to the apartment. That's our best hope of finding a lead," he said and started walking.

"Yeah…" I had my bag full of those tiny liquor bottles from the minibar, but I didn't dare open one yet. I wanted to see that apartment with a fresh eye and sharp mind first. If we had any hopes of finding that vampire, we needed to find something in there.

The streets were much more crowded now that it wasn't the middle of the night. The neighborhood buzzed with people, not just groups of guys hiding in plain sight and smoking weed, but plenty of regular people going about their business. It made me nervous that someone had found that apartment already and had called the human police or something. Unnecessary complications.

But to my surprise, once we got to the eleventh floor, we found the apartment exactly as we left it the night before. How curious.

"Somebody else has been in here," Ax said the second he stepped through the door. "Another vampire."

"From the covens?" I wondered, closing the door behind me. I smelled the scent right away—rust and rot and some kind of nasty perfume mixed together.

"Probably," Ax said, stopping in the middle of the ruined living room.

"Isn't it strange that the police haven't been here yet? How long ago did this happen?"

But he shook his head. "There's no blood. Nothing but the scents, and if I had to guess, sorcerers were here about three to four days ago."

Yeah, I thought the same. "Right, then. Let's get to work."

I dropped my bag by the wall, took off my jacket, and started inspecting every little thing in that place.

Even though I was focused, I still felt Ax's eyes on me every few seconds. It was ridiculous that I knew every time he looked at me, like my body was so in tune with his, when I just met him three days ago. Gods, the sooner we got this over with and went back home, the better I'd feel.

Physically, though, I felt way better than I did two nights ago. Even the voices in my head weren't as loud tonight. *Way* better, and not that I'd ever tell him that, but it was *him*. It was the sex. I hadn't felt this energetic in a long time. And the fact that I hadn't had a drink since I woke up was further proof of how fucked up this whole thing was.

We found some unpaid bills in a drawer—Marie Louise Graham was the name of the person who rented this apartment. It wasn't a lead by any means, but my next bright idea was to speak to the landlord, see if he could maybe tell us something. Because no matter how many times I searched Google and social media, I couldn't find any account with the picture of that woman's face. It was just an assumption, though. I didn't know that it was *her* in the picture, but who else could it be?

"We need to find the closest group of sorcerers to this place," Ax said when he was done inspecting the bedroom and came back to the living room. I was just going over the last cupboard in the kitchen, but other than some delicious gummy bears, I didn't find anything else. Come to think of it, I was pretty hungry. It had been almost two hours of searching, and my stomach needed food. I hadn't eaten anything since that pizza last night.

And…blood.

I looked up at Ax, confused at my own self for a minute. I hadn't thought about blood at all since I'd woken up. That wasn't normal. Just yesterday, I was thinking I wouldn't even survive the day without drinking some, and now I'd *forgotten*?

What the hell had he done to me?

"And do what? They're not going to talk to us," I said, shaking my head to clear my mind. It was a coincidence. I was wrapped up in the case; that's why I hadn't thought about blood.

"Then we kill a few, and make the others talk," he said with a shrug.

I rolled my eyes. "You can't just do that."

"Sure, I can. Robert said whatever means necessary."

"Jones said the same, but I'm pretty sure they didn't mean we could start a fucking war between us and the sorcerers."

"We're not going to start a war," Ax said, coming to lean against the broken counter, arms crossed in front of his chest. Fuck, his face. His eyes were so full of color now that I'd seen him from close up and knew them in detail. The way he looked at me just now, so intently, it brought back memories that my body reacted to instantly. Like the way I'd kissed and licked and bit those perfect lips just last morning, and the taste of them—better than anything in the world.

If the way his heart skipped a tiny beat when he met my eyes was anything to go by, I'd say he was feeling the same.

Which was *very* problematic.

"Sure, we are. Go out there, kill sorcerers, have them try to kill us—that's how you start the war." I pretended to look over the drawers again, just so I didn't have to keep staring at his eyes. I was afraid they'd fucking hypnotize me.

"Not if we kill every sorcerer we find—after they tell us what we need to know, of course."

I turned to him again. "You're fucking mad." And plain disturbed.

"What? You don't think you can kill a bunch of sorcerers?"

"I know I can. That's not the point," I said. "You can't just go around killing people, Ax."

"Why the fuck not? We're looking for someone, remember? And if we can't find her…" His voice trailed off and he shrugged.

"We're not going to try to force sorcerers into telling us anything. They won't—it'll just be a bloodbath. We need leverage first."

"What are you afraid of, Damsel?"

I raised a brow. "Absolutely nothing in the world." Except myself, and the voices that were whispering in my mind even now. They were calmer for the moment, but that wasn't going to last. I knew how it worked—I'd been living with them my whole life.

The corner of his lips turned up a bit. "What are you hiding from me? You can tell me, you know. I won't say a word."

I laughed. "Are you insinuating that I should *trust* you?"

"Why not?" He was serious.

"Because you're not only a Sangria—you're Savage Ax. I am not stupid."

"You had no trouble with me being a Sangria or Savage Ax last night. Or the one before that." And he was back to grinning again.

I sighed. "It's just sex, okay? There's no meaning behind it. It's *just* sex. Stop trying to make it seem important—it isn't."

The way his face twisted suddenly you'd think I fisted him in the jaw. I waited a heartbeat for him to say something, and when he didn't, I gladly turned my back to him and went to inspect the living room one last time.

He was quiet for another few minutes, but eventually, he caved, just like I knew he would.

"Who was it?"

I stopped going over the old CD covers tucked in the drawer under the TV. "Who was what?"

"The guy that fucked you up like this."

Every hair on my body stood at attention. "Nobody fucked me up."

"Liar," he said without missing a beat. "Just tell me."

I stood up to face him. "There's nothing to tell, Ax."

"Then what have you lost?" I forced myself to roll my eyes, but he didn't care. "I'm just trying to figure you out here, Damsel."

Laughter burst out of me. He was a funny guy. "Good luck with that."

Suddenly, he was right in front of me. I hated it when he moved fast like that. He was too unpredictable.

"What have you lost?" he said, searching my face with those eyes that shone like gems. "I know you lost something. What was it?"

I smiled. He wanted to know so badly? Fine, I'd tell him.

Leaning closer until our lips were an inch apart, I whispered: "Everything."

Stepping to the side, I grabbed my bag by the wall and walked out of the apartment with no clear plan in mind still.

Three minutes later, he came out of the building and found me waiting on the sidewalk.

"You take east, I'll take west. Meet back here in an hour," I said, and I didn't wait around for him to say anything. I just took off running down the street. There was no telling what else he was going to ask me next, and I didn't want to hear it. If that made me a coward, so be it.

My first stop was at a butcher's shop. Even though it felt like I didn't need blood *right now*, I knew my limits. I was a vampire. Drinking blood was how I survived. So, I paid the guy fifty bucks just to fill my thermos with cold cow's blood, and when he started asking questions, I gave him another fifty. Five minutes later, my thermos was full, and I was ready to run.

Searching for sorcerers in a city this size was a bitch, especially when all I had was my sense of smell. Too many people around me. Too much blood, too many fast-food joints, and way too many cars, too. I was starting to think that it was going to take a lot more than an hour to find a sorcerer in this place.

Until I smelled Ax's scent, mixed in with strawberries. All the hair in my body stood at attention when I turned to find him on the other side of the street, smiling at me.

"Got them," he whispered, but I heard him even over the sound of cars. I recognized his voice now—I could hear it even from a bigger distance.

"Already?" How in the world had he found them in this place?

"This way," he said, nodding his head, before he turned to walk up the street again.

With a sigh, I followed. He was making me feel really incompetent here, but oh, well. What mattered was that we find that vampire and get the hell away from this world that just wouldn't shut up for a second.

I followed him for a good five minutes walking, and then he began to run. I had no trouble keeping up—I still had that energy coursing in my veins. There were humans all around us, but at that point I would rather they saw me than drag this on longer. If they saw me, they were just going to think it was their imagination, anyway.

Ax took us all the way to the edge of the city. Houses on either side of the wide street, surrounded by large trees as far as the eye could see. Cars parked in driveways, bikes and scooters left there on the grass. Plenty of people still walking about.

"Over there," Ax said when I caught up to him on the sidewalk. "Fifth house left."

The houses looked very similar, some two stories, some one. The fifth left was wider than most, white walls and big windows, all the lights turned on inside.

"You sure?" Not that I doubted his sense of smell, but there was nobody outside the house yet, and those sorcerers had probably already felt us. It was strange.

"Positive. They've got the house locked tight, like they're trying to keep something out," he said. "Or in. They wouldn't be able to feel us through all that magic. I can't even hear their hearts beating through it."

"Okay," I said, more to myself than him. "Okay. We're gonna go knock on their door and we're gonna ask them about Marie. That's it."

"That is *not* it," he said with a grin, making me turn to him.

"Ax, it's *very* important not to start a fight in there, okay?"

The smile dropped from his face instantly. "Are you serious?"

"Yes, I'm dead serious."

Suddenly, he leaned closer to me, squinting his eyes. "What the hell are you afraid of?" he whispered. "You scared off a fucking Vein spirit, Damsel. You got this. Besides, I won't let them hurt you."

It was my turn to laugh. "That's not what I'm worried about, you fool!" I said. "Just don't start a fight if you can help it. Okay? Just…*please*. Don't start a fight."

His lips parted like he had never been more surprised in his life. "Damn it, Damsel," he breathed, shaking his head. "Okay. I won't start a fight."

Did I believe him? Fuck no. I straightened my shoulders anyway. It's not like I had any other options. If it got to that, I'd figure out a way to handle it.

"But when we're done, you're going to tell me what you're hiding from me."

He started walking down the street and I followed, taking a few sips of the cold cow blood in my thermos. Fucking disgusting, but blood was still blood.

"Want some?" I asked Ax, but he shook his head.

"No, thanks. I drank."

"Really? When?"

"Half an hour ago."

I raised my brow. "From where?"

"A woman sleeping on her balcony in a rocking chair."

My jaw almost hit the floor. "Are you serious?"

"Deadly." He grinned.

"You took blood from a human?"

"Just a couple sips. She didn't even wake up. She won't be able to tell at all."

"But…but…"

"It's an art, I'll give it that. If you want, I could teach you. It's simple once you get the hang of it. And the strength, Damsel…" His voice trailed off as he breathed in deeply.

"Fuck," I whispered to myself—not because he'd done it, but because *I* wanted to do it, too. I'd never tasted human blood…well. That one time when I was a kid, and that's *after* they were already dead, but never since. If I could actually take blood from someone and not even wake them up from their sleep, not hurt them in any way…I definitely wanted to try it. And the whispers in my head all seemed to approve.

But the door of the fifth house on the left opened, and all my other thoughts cut off. We were still in the middle of the street, and there were a few people walking around us, clueless as to what we were. Not the man and woman who stepped out of the house, though. Both of them were sorcerers, and they had their eyes locked on us. Chills washed down my back at the reminder of what their magic felt like, but I shook it off. It was showtime. I prayed to any god who'd listen that we managed not to screw this up. Too badly.

"Remember what you promised," I whispered to Ax, and with my head high, I walked up to the sorcerers with a smile on my face.

16

The woman was about my height, blonde hair braided behind her back, blue eyes ice-cold. The man was taller, skinny, but there was something about his dull black eyes that made me very uneasy.

We stopped in front of the fence as they watched us from their porch. The smell was incredible—so much magic hung to this place, I might suffocate on it if I stayed here too long.

"Good evening," I said, clearing my throat. "My name is Nikki. This is my friend, Ax."

"You are not welcome here," the woman said without missing a beat, her voice just as cold as the look in her eyes.

"And we'd love to get out of your hair soon," I told her, then looked to the sides, at the humans who'd stopped walking and were watching us. Others on their porches, too. "But we really need to talk to you about something."

The woman raised a brow, but she looked to the sides, too. To the curious human eyes who watched us openly now.

"If we may come inside for a minute?" I asked, knowing that if a fight broke out here, there was a good chance that innocent people would die. But if I were confined inside a house…

The man and woman looked at one another for a moment before they both stepped aside.

"See that?" I whispered to Ax.

He grinned. "Good girl."

And why in the world would those words sound so *dirty* to me and make me think about sex?

Shaking my head, I opened the gate and walked up the driveway, extra slow. If they wanted to ambush me, I had to be prepared. Ax walked right behind me, and the sorcerers examined every inch of us as if they were trying to memorize every detail.

"Come on in," the man said when I stopped in front of the stairs to the porch. His voice was just as dull as his eyes. The way he kept his composure was pretty impressive.

Meanwhile my palms were a bit sweaty. I was plain nervous as I crossed the threshold of the house and the weight of all that magic settled on my shoulders. Shit. Maybe this hadn't been such a good idea. Being inside a house in the middle of a human neighborhood with two sorcerers?

No…not two.

The deeper into the well-lit corridor I walked, the clearer I heard the heartbeats now that I was on the other side of the magic shield. I heard all *eleven* of them.

Fuck.

The hallway ended into a large living room, with a kitchen on the left and eleven grown sorcerers scattered all over the place. I felt Ax stopping right behind me as he, too, inspected the many faces turned to us.

Eleven sorcerers. We were so screwed.

"Two vampires in the middle of Atlanta," an old man sitting on one of the peach-colored couches in the living room said. His grey beard reached all the way down to his chest. His brown eyes were light, like honey, and his wrinkled fingers shook as he waved for us to come closer.

Nobody even breathed properly, and every heart in the room was racing—including ours. But Ax and I still walked ahead, to the middle of the room, surrounded by sorcerers on all sides.

I swallowed hard. This was a bad idea.

"You're a long way from home," the old man continued. Despite his appearance, his voice was strong, crystal clear.

"We're here on behalf of our covens to search for a vampire," I said, as Ax sniffed the air around us, no longer curious about the people. "Her name is Marie Louise Graham. We just need to find her and bring her home," I told the old man.

He raised a white brow. "And why are you here, in *our* home?"

"Because she's been taken from her apartment. By sorcerers." I watched closely for a reaction. He didn't give me any.

"I see. And so you figured it was us because…?"

"You're the closest to her apartment that we found."

The bad feeling in my chest kept expanding. My mind kept calculating all the ways these people could attack me without my knowing about it until it was too late. Four grown men were behind me in the kitchen. By the time I stopped one, all three of them would have had the chance to hit me with their magic, and then…I'd have no choice but to fight back.

Sweat beads lined my forehead. I was really hoping it wouldn't come to that.

"In that case, I'm afraid we're going to have to disappoint you. We didn't take any vampire from their apartment. We watch out for these neighborhoods—we don't go looking for trouble," the old man said.

His words rang true. His heartbeat didn't race any faster than it already was. He wasn't sweating that I could tell, and he held my eyes like a man speaking the truth would. I had no reason to suspect him.

Letting go of a long breath, I nodded. "Thank you for your time," I said and turned for the hallway again. I caught a glimpse of Ax's wide eyes as I turned, but I didn't stop. The sorcerers didn't move an inch but all their eyes were on me.

But when I reached the middle of the hallway…something occurred to me. Ax was still there, probably hoping for someone to attack him, and he was even more surprised to see me walking back to him again.

"Here's the thing, though," I said, shaking my head. "You weren't surprised."

The old man looked confused. "Excuse me?"

"You were not surprised to find out that a vampire was living right in the middle of your city," I said. I'd met sorcerers before on our way here, and they'd all been quick to tell me that there were no vampires around here.

Not this guy. He hadn't been surprised. He hadn't even batted an eye. He'd simply pretended he didn't know, which was ridiculous. If he watched out for these neighborhoods, he would have known if a vampire lived in that apartment building, wouldn't he?

The worst part was that he didn't try to deny it. Instead, the old bastard raised his chin, and every person in the room raised their hands.

Through the corner of my eye, I could see Ax grinning widely. My heart skipped a long beat. My instincts were already taking over.

And then we all heard it.

It started as a tapping at first, and it was coming from right under my feet.

"What the…" I whispered, looking down at the linoleum floor.

The explosion came out of nowhere, and the sound of it was so powerful, it had my ears ringing. The strength of it shook the entire house instantly, a second before someone screamed.

All hell broke loose at once. Sparks and colorful smoke came at us from all sides. I barely had time to drop my bag and reach for the knives around my thighs before I jumped to the side, rolling on the floor to get to the kitchen counter. The house kept roaring, vibrating under me, and I heard the movement of the sorcerers as they jumped over the counter to get to me. With my eyes closed, I held onto the handles of my knives and waited for them to get closer. When they did, I raised up and swung my arm back with all my strength, focused on where their hearts were beating. I caught one on the top of his head, the other in the chest.

Fresh blood slipped down my hands, and I pulled the knives back before I turned around, just in time to see yellow smoke coming at me furiously. I jumped to the side again, but another sorcerer twice my size was already producing some red smoke in the palms of his hands while he looked at me with all the hatred in the world, then threw the magic my way with a hiss.

I tried to get away by jumping over the counter, but it still caught me on my left ankle, sending searing hot pain up my body lightning fast. I lost control of my leg completely, but I still had my hands. I still had my knives. And before the asshole could collect another ball of magic like that, I threw my knife at his face too fast for him to even see it. That's why my knife buried right in the middle of his forehead.

His magic was already withdrawing from my body, but I still couldn't move my leg. I pushed the two bodies of the sorcerers I'd killed to the floor, trying to get to the other side, to find Ax, to get the fuck out of here. We had to—the whispers in my head had already turned to screams.

But two women and two men were already on me. I rolled on the counter and to the edge. When I hit the floor, I jumped to my feet right away, still having trouble feeling the left one. But I saw Ax behind the sorcerers, slamming his fists onto the floor in the hallway like a mad man before a huff of blue smoke slammed right on his back and sent him flying against the wall.

Reaching for another knife, I forced myself to focus on the four sorcerers in front of me. Moving away from their magic was torture, and the more of it I felt, the more my insides heated.

Please, please, please, I chanted to myself, hoping that my fangs were the only thing that would come out of me tonight. I moved away and threw my knives, killed two of them and wounded a third before the last was able to hit me with his white smoke square on the chest. I flew in the air and hit the kitchen cupboards with the back of my head.

Stars in my vision. The screams in my head were relentless.

Something moved in my chest. It fought me for control. It fought to break right out of me, through my ribcage if need be.

No.

Gritting my teeth, I forced my eyes to blink until I saw in front of me again—saw the brand-new ball of white smoke coming together between the sorcerer's hands. I grabbed two more knives and threw them without really aiming. He had no chance of moving away. Both knives hit him in the chest. The magic disappeared from between his hands, and I shot forward, desperate to get out of there.

"Down there!" I heard Ax calling, and I only had a second to look at him fighting four sorcerers in the living room, moving too fast for their eyes to see as he got away from their magic.

And then I saw the hole in the middle of the hallway floor. The one the screaming was coming from. Had *he* broken the floor like that all by himself?

It didn't really matter. I jumped without looking.

Even before I landed, magic exploded once again, shaking the house, and pieces of the ceiling began to fall down on my head.

But I saw.

Down there, I saw a room with white walls, two beds, and plastic trays with empty dishes on them. I saw a metal toilet in the corner...and Marie Louise Graham holding a teenage boy in her arms next to it, crying and shaking in fear.

Then, something hard hit me right on the top of my head and sent me to the floor.

My consciousness must have slipped from me because I heard the voices, but they were so far away. I heard the growling of the demons that lived inside me much clearer. I felt the pressure of them trying to take over, to make me give up control.

I felt it all, and the panic grew by the second because I didn't know how to stop it. There wasn't enough alcohol in the world right now to erase them from my mind, and the more I focused on them, the more power they gained.

But just as I thought I was going to lose control, a warm hand wrapped around my wrist and pulled me into a sitting position.

I blinked, and the darkness of my mind disappeared to leave way for my surroundings. Ax's face was right in front of mine, his wide eyes pitch-black, his fangs coated in blood.

"*Get her and get out!*" he shouted before he let go of me.

My ears whistled, but his words made sense. Get her and get out. Out, where there was no magic coming for me. Out, where I wouldn't be forced to fight and lose focus, and then lose *control* of the nightmare I shared my mind with.

Out.

More people were jumping through the hole in the ceiling that had grown even bigger. Half the hallway floor had collapsed by the looks of it, and Ax was fighting all four of the sorcerers left, while the woman and the boy stayed in the corner.

I don't know how I made it to them without falling, but I reached out my hand.

"It's okay," I told them. "It's okay, we're here to help you. But I need you to come with me, okay? Just come with me."

It didn't occur to me to stop and check if this woman was who we were looking for. It didn't occur to me to check if she was actually a vampire. All I cared about was that we got out of there, right now.

And Marie must have seen something in my eyes. Her black ones were wide and bloodshot, full of tears, but she reached out and grabbed my hand in hers. I pulled her up and turned back to the middle of the basement. Ax was just a few feet away, fighting three sorcerers, the fourth already dead with half his neck torn out.

"Go!" Ax shouted without ever turning to me, as colorful smoke came at him without stop.

"We have to jump," I told the woman and made to grab her in my arms.

"No! Take him," she said, pushing the teenage boy into my arms. "I'll jump myself."

I didn't need to be told twice. "Hop on," I told the boy and turned my back on him. He climbed on me right away, arms locked tight around my neck.

I jumped. Marie jumped, too, and she landed right next to me. Definitely a vampire.

Then we saw the six sorcerers coming through the door of the house that shook so hard, it was going to collapse any second now. *Please, no,* I thought to myself, but it was already too late. The boy jumped off my back. I reached for my last two knives.

"Move!" I told Marie, and I started running forward, just as the sorcerers raised their hands.

But I never reached them.

The hallway floor right in front of the door collapsed beneath their feet, and it took all six of them with it. Black smoke came from behind me and whooshed right past my right ear. I turned to see Marie and the boy on the floor, inches away from where the next hole was.

I ran back just as Ax jumped out, covered in blood, eyes black and fangs sharp.

"Get out!" he told me, and red smoke slipped out from the hole in the ground. Ax ducked, and I tried to move away, but the wall to the side cracked. The floor shook harder, throwing me to the side—and right in the magic's way. It hit me in the face, slipping up my nostrils, getting into my mouth, into my ears.

My entire body was paralyzed. I didn't even feel it when I hit the floor. My chest vibrated. My ribcage threatened to burst open as I screamed. Even my heart stood still for the longest second, and my demons felt like black smoke tendrils spinning around my mind, claiming it for themselves.

Another minute, and…

A hand wrapped around my arm. My body moved and I was flipped upside down. The next second, the wind was on the side of my face. I forced myself to breathe deeply and realized the scent of magic was barely there. I tried to see where I was, what was holding me up, just to fill my mind with more distractions.

And I finally did.

I was over Ax's shoulder, and when he stopped abruptly in the middle of the street, I flew forward and hit the asphalt with the top of my head. The pain blinded me again momentarily, but I heard him breathing, heard his heart beating, and he wasn't the only one.

Pushing myself up with my shaking hands, I blinked and blinked until I saw the body of Marie right there on the sidewalk next to Ax. No sign of the teenage boy she'd been with, though.

The ground groaned again. Half the roof of the house collapsed. Fire burned somewhere behind it. About fifty humans were all around us, watching us, too scared to come closer.

Ax was breathing heavily, still on his knees in the middle of the street.

It was over. We were out. And I was still in control of my mind.

"We have to go," I said breathlessly, forcing myself to stand. Marie was here, and she was alive. Her heart beat, and she was breathing, though she was unconscious. That was more than enough for me.

"I'll carry her," Ax said, making it up to his feet. I pulled Marie by the hands until he could wrap his arms around her waist and pull her up to his shoulder.

One look around, and even more humans had gathered, the fear leaking from their pores sticking to my nostrils. In the distance, we could hear the police sirens approaching.

I looked at Ax and he nodded. We were okay.

Then, we turned around and ran.

17

Ax Creed

I fucking hated motels. It wasn't just the cockroaches I had to kill in the bathroom—it was the entire setting. The rust, the dust, the stained fucking mattress.

The unconscious woman in the room next door and the other who just got out of the bathroom.

Nikki Arella. The most curious woman I had ever met in my life.

I'd just gotten out of the shower myself, and all my attention was on her movements. She was in a hurry, too. She barely stopped moving for three seconds, possibly to check on the unconscious woman, before she walked up to the door.

We made it. We'd escaped from Atlanta, and we were now hiding in a shithole motel an hour away from it. It was as far as we could get without collapsing, even though we had another hour until the sun came up.

My jeans and jacket were a mess, but I could always buy new clothes. Damsel had lost her booze and her knives, though. That seemed to piss her off.

Putting a towel around my hips, I walked out of the bathroom just as she stopped in front of my door.

Despite everything, I was smiling when I went to open it.

There were a few cuts on her cheeks, nothing major. Some bruises on her arm and the side of her waist, too. Nothing she wouldn't heal from during the day. I'd fared far worse in that department, but she didn't flinch at the sight of my wounds. That shit didn't bother her. I was starting to think nothing really did.

Nothing—except whatever had stopped her in that house. Whatever stopped her every time we ran into trouble. And I'd been there, had seen it with my own eyes when she'd scared the shit out of a fucking Vein spirit. Not a single one of them had come after us since, which was a damn miracle.

So, why was she so afraid? I smelled it on her skin, even now.

She strode inside the room without a word and went to stand by the small desk across from the bed, arms crossed in front of her. Her legs underneath that black skirt looked good enough to eat. That crop top barely covered her tits and showed me her ripped stomach perfectly.

Ever since she took her clothes off at that waterfall, I'd been trying to keep my shit together when she teased me. I'd fucking failed miserably every time. She was divinely beautiful to look at—but it wasn't just that. It was the wild look in her eyes. The way she spoke. The way she swung those fucking hips when she walked. How confident she was in her own skin.

The way she checked me out without batting an eye, too.

Her eyes roamed down my naked chest and to the towel wrapped around my hips. I'd be a damn liar if I said I didn't enjoy knowing I did to her body exactly what she did to mine.

"Why didn't you move, Damsel?" I asked, sitting on the edge of the bed.

She raised a brow. "Are you angry?" she whispered. "Because you can punish me, you know. I've been very, very naughty."

My cock twitched under the towel as if by magic.

"You have?"

"I've been thinking about your cock since we got here." She batted those long lashes at me. I thought out of all looks, it wouldn't suit her to play innocent, but she fucking nailed it. Now I was imagining putting her over my knee and slapping her ass raw.

Leaning back on the bed, I shook my head. "You're trying to distract me." I smelled the truth on her—she *had* been thinking about my cock, but that's not the reason she was telling me that.

The corner of her lips turned up just a bit. The mischievous little brat.

"I tried touching myself in the shower, but it's just not the same," she said with a pout before she reached behind her to unzip her skirt.

My heart was already racing, my cock hard. Damn, she played my strings like a puppet master. And when she let the skirt drop to the floor, she wasn't wearing any panties.

A growl escaped me, even before she reached for her top and took it off. No bra either. She was completely naked in front of me, and I'd be damned if I'd ever seen a wilder beauty in my life.

Despite my better judgment, despite knowing exactly what she was doing, I stood up. Her grey eyes stopped on the bulge of the towel immediately and she licked those lips furiously.

"Turn around," I said. "Hands on the desk."

She did it without hesitation, showing me her backside. That perfect tight ass I could keep my hands on all day.

I stepped closer, analyzing every inch of her pale skin, my fingers itching to grab her already.

"I know what you're doing," I said. "I know you're trying to get your mind off things. I know you're trying to get *my* mind off things, too." And, fuck, it was working better than she even hoped. But I liked to think I still had some fight left in me. "So, tell me why you stopped, Damsel." I went a little closer so she could feel my heat, but I didn't touch her yet. It cost me, but I was trying hard here.

"Because I was scared." I heard the grin in her voice perfectly. Yeah, she was scared but not of the sorcerers. She was a much better fighter than I'd thought. She'd have had no trouble taking all of them out by herself, if she hadn't collapsed all on her own, if she hadn't looked like she was fucking drowning on air.

Stepping to the side, I took off my towel. "Bend over so I can see your pussy."

She turned her head to the side and met my eyes. "Give me a reason."

The blood in my veins was near a boiling point. It fascinated me how much power she seemed to have over my body. My mind, too.

I moved fast and slapped her across her butt cheek with all my strength. She cried out and her back arched all the way, giving me a magnificent view of her wet pussy. My, my. The imprint of my hand on her ass made my cock twitch painfully. She was a fucking sight to see bent over like that.

"Tell me what you were scared of," I whispered as I stepped behind her again and grabbed her hips, then pushed my cock against her ass.

Shivers ran up her back. I saw the small hairs on her skin stand at attention. I pressed onto her ass harder.

"Tell me, Damsel," I ordered, but she only moaned. Just the sound of her had me shaking with need. Better than a fucking porn star.

"You want to get fucked, don't you?" I asked, and she nodded her head as she moaned louder. "Then tell me why."

Her response was to push her ass back right onto my cock.

"Goddamn it, Damsel."

It was too much. The sight of her, the feel of her smooth skin under my fingers, her ass pressed against my cock, the way she was dripping…I couldn't control it.

I didn't want to.

Fuck it, she was going to have to tell me eventually, anyway. So, I grabbed my cock and pressed the tip to her clit. She cried out, completely enthralled by now, and bent over the old desk all the way.

There was absolutely no more fight left in me.

I thrust my hips and buried my cock inside her as deep as it would go.

Her entire body shook as she took me in. She was way too tight still, and it drove me fucking crazy. I held onto her hips, eyes closed so I didn't fucking come in a second. No, I had to make it last. There were only so many times I was going to have her. I had to make it count.

But the sight of her ass, my cock buried deep inside her, had my mind twisting. I slapped her other butt cheek and watched as her skin turned red. The imprints of my hands were on her skin now. She was *mine*, at least for tonight.

The second I moved, her pussy clenched around my cock as she moaned, holding onto the edge of the desk with all her strength.

"Don't do that, Damsel," I breathed, bending over her so I could bite her shoulder. No matter how hard I did it, it never seemed enough. And it didn't help that she fucking loved the pain just as much as I did. "Don't clench your pussy like that if you don't want me to come right away."

At that, she turned her head to the side. "Don't you fucking dare," she threatened.

I laughed. She was gonna be the death of me.

"My greedy little slut," I told her, and her pussy clenched around me again, making me growl. I let go of her hips and grabbed a fistful of her hair with one hand, and I pressed my fingers to her clit with the other. Having her bent over like that, I wasn't going to last. Not when her ass felt like that as I slammed into her. Her fingernails scratched the wood of the table, and she didn't hold back on the screaming. The woman next door must have been really out of it because she still hadn't woken up.

And I didn't really give a shit.

I pounded into her over and over again, pulling her hair, circling her swollen clit for a while. Then I pulled her up and I moved us away from the desk, my cock still inside her. I pushed her against the wall and she had no complaints. I grabbed her perfect tits, and I pinched her nipples hard until she screamed. The more she arched her back, the deeper inside her pussy I went. Fuck, I wanted to break something so badly. She felt so fucking incredible, I had no chance of ever resisting her. And the more I touched her, the better she responded. The more I pleased her, the better she felt. I wrapped my fingers around her neck and squeezed just a little bit, and she went wild, pressing her ass against me harder. I bit her shoulder and raised on my tiptoes so I could give her all of my cock, and she cried out louder. Simple words were good, but they weren't enough—it was all in the touch. I had yet to figure this wildling out, but I knew her language. I knew she loved to be touched.

I pounded onto her harder by the second, and when she came, the feel of her made my fucking mind explode. I didn't even try to hold back. I just held onto her tits and slammed into her for a couple more times before I came, too.

I held her against the wall as the feeling ripped me apart and pulled me back together again. We were both panting, and neither of us wanted to let go. I knew it when I pushed her hair away from her face so I could see her, and she leaned into me, eyes closed, completely surrendered to me. That's how I wanted her forever. Completely mine. In my home. In my bed. *Mine.*

But a few seconds later, she remembered herself, just like she always did. Pushing her arms against the wall, she moved, and I had no choice but to move away, too.

She turned to me, ran her fingers over my lips and smiled lazily. "Thanks, big guy."

Oh, the little slut.

The moment she made to grab her clothes off the floor, I pulled her in my arms and threw her on the bed.

"What the hell are you doing?" she said, bouncing up and down on the mattress a couple times.

"I'm not done punishing you yet, Damsel," I said, and climbed on the bed with her, grabbed her ankles and spread her legs. The sight of her pussy, skin red and raw, of her cum and mine holding onto her folds, already had my cock hardening again.

With a laugh, she lay down on the bed and I settled with my chest between her thighs, her tits right in front of my face. Fucking gorgeous. I could keep them in my mouth all day.

Flicking my tongue over her nipple, I played with it for a second, before I bit into it and sucked hard. Her hands were on the back of my head and she pressed me to her harder, as if she wanted me all the way inside her. Her back arched and her big tit filled my mouth until there was no more space left. So fucking soft. I kissed and licked and sucked until I completely forgot where I even was.

I ran my hands down her body, her long legs, dug my fingernails into her ass, and she writhed underneath me. She had her eyes wide open as she watched me, looking like she was in pain, even though her body was brimming with pleasure. She loved watching me devour her. She loved my hands on her.

So, I took my time with it. If I had a chance of breaking her defenses long enough to see the real her for a second, it would be like this. Damsel was very physical. And I'd be damned if I didn't want to be the same with her.

Her hands roamed down my arms, on my back, scratching the hell out of my skin. I loved the pain as much as she did. And when both her breasts were red and raw, smelled like they belonged to me completely, I moved down lower, to her smooth stomach, and traced the lines of her abs with my tongue. The sound of her moans was the best music I'd ever heard, and it motivated me to keep going. I moved slowly, determined to savor every second until I'd licked every single inch of her.

When I reached her thighs, she was already shaking. I bit her soft skin, ran my tongue across her folds, tasting both her and me. Just like it should be.

Damsel was completely lost. Her eyes were closed now; she no longer watched me. She grabbed my hair and pushed me to her as her hips moved up, mouth wide open as she moaned, breathing heavily, as if her whole life depended on me right now.

It was the best shot I was going to get.

Flicking my tongue over her swollen clit again, I watched her back arching, those tits bouncing as she went. Fuck, she made an animal out of me.

"Have you ever been mated?" I asked, trailing kisses up her pelvis. Surprised, she stopped moving for a second, but she recovered quickly. There was always a chance that she wasn't going to tell me shit. She liked her secrets. Held onto them tightly.

But as long as my hands were on her, as long as my mouth was on her, I knew she'd feel safe enough to share. Maybe just a little bit. And I was so fucking desperate for it, I could have stayed right here for as long as it took. Days, months, years.

"No," she finally whispered. I closed my lips on her clit and sucked gently. It was a struggle to keep my myself from burying my tongue deep inside her, tasting her the way she needed to be tasted, but I held back.

I let go of her clit and continued to kiss her thigh.

"Ax," she breathed, and it was a pleading.

"Why not?" I asked instead. If she wasn't going to tell me what held her back, I still wanted to know more about her. I wanted to know everything.

With a sigh, she shook her head, then tried to bring her pussy to my mouth, but I held her down by the hips, and continued to kiss her pelvis.

"Because it's not for me," she said, and I stopped to look up at her for a second. Her eyes were still closed, head on the pillow. "I was close once. It didn't work out."

I lowered my head and dragged my tongue from her center and up to her clit greedily. She cried out again, pushing her hips up, and I let her for a second. For both our sakes, I sucked on her folds and teased her entrance with the tip of my tongue before I moved to her thigh again.

An exasperated shout left her. "For fuck's sake, Ax," she said, but even though she was angry, she still pleaded.

I kissed her thigh then bit it to hold back a smile.

"How long were you with him?"

Just the idea of another man doing this to her—for real, in a way that made her feel as desperate as she was right now—had my blood rushing instantly.

"Seven years," she whispered.

That was a long time. I dove in and licked her clit furiously. She held onto the sheets for dear life, but I only gave her five seconds. The moment I let go, she groaned.

"Why didn't it work out?"

At that, she raised her head to look at me. "Because he betrayed me."

I dug my fingers into her thighs. My heart was hammering in my chest. She must have seen something in my eyes because she smiled.

"Don't worry. He paid the ultimate price for it."

"You?"

She shook her head. "No, I didn't kill him. But he died anyway," she said, bringing her hands to my face. "Now get to work," she whispered and pushed my head down on her pussy.

Relieved, but still angry that someone had the balls to betray her, I gave her what she wanted, but not for long. I needed to know more. So, I ate her pussy and thrust my tongue inside her for a little while, then let go again. Those groans of hers were so desperate, they fueled me.

"Why do you drink?"

"Because I love the taste of it." It was a fucking lie.

I raised my head higher. "The truth, Damsel. Otherwise, you can go back to touching yourself."

She flinched. "Sure thing."

Her hand was between her legs instantly, and she began rubbing her clit.

Her head fell back, and she moaned, her back arching as she picked up the speed. I was so fucking hard, it was painful, and it took everything I had not to stop her. I just watched her burying her fingers inside her pussy as her hips shot up and she cried out, the pleasure taking her higher by the second.

And I was fucking jealous.

I blew on her wet folds as she brought her fingers to her clit again, moving them in a circle. I had never seen a better thing in my fucking life.

"Ax," she breathed, sending shock waves up and down my body. The way she needed me was fucking delicious.

"Want me to do that for you, Damsel?" I whispered, keeping my mouth close to her folds so she could feel my breath.

"Yes!" she cried out, and I grabbed her hand to take it off her pussy.

"Why do you drink?" I said, touching her clit with the tip of my tongue only slightly.

"To keep my mind buzzing," she said breathlessly. Thank the fucking gods.

I dove in, sucking her warm clit hard, thrusting my tongue in and out of her the way her fingers could never do. This was *my* territory. I knew it better than she ever would.

Ten seconds later, just as she was about to come, I stopped.

"Why do you need to keep your mind buzzing?"

She cried out, frustrated. She brought the heels of her hands to her squeezed eyes.

"Because when I lose my shit, people die!" she shouted.

And her hands were shaking a bit, too. That's how I knew I was at her very limits. If I pushed her harder than this, she was going to break.

Finally.

I dove down again and grabbed her folds between my lips, while I stuck two fingers inside her all the way. It took her ten seconds to explode, and the smell of her alone had *my* mind buzzing. My cock was in pain, just as desperate for her as she was for it.

While she breathed heavily, wide open in front of me, I raised up to my knees and grabbed my cock in my hands. Her eyes zeroed in on it instantly.

"Where do you want this, Damsel?" I asked, and her lips stretched into a lazy smile right away, like I'd just given her everything she'd ever wanted.

"Stand up," she ordered. My heart raced when I jumped off the bed, and she followed, then kneeled in front of me. Fuck, the sight of her like that…

"Your mouth's greedy again?" I teased. Both her hands wrapped around my cock.

"Fuck yeah," she whispered, then licked my tip with her tongue. As much as I wanted to close my eyes, I kept them open and on her. Grabbing a fistful of her hair, I squeezed tightly, making her cry. Pushing her head back, I touched her smooth cheek and just gave myself a moment to memorize her every feature, because sometimes I wondered if she was fucking real. Those colorless eyes, those heart-shaped lips, that little pert nose combined together perfectly.

"Suck it like you mean it," I said, then I pushed my cock inside her mouth. She opened wide right away, and my tip touched the back of her throat. If this wasn't heaven, I don't know what was.

And Damsel didn't hold back. She used her teeth and her tongue and her lips masterfully, like my cock was made for her mouth. She gagged every few seconds, and tears streamed from her eyes, but she never slowed her pace. She was hungry, and she must have taken my words literally because she sucked all the fucking life out of me with that greedy mouth of hers. I was on the edge faster than I'd ever been in my life. No woman had ever sucked my cock the way she did.

"Damsel," I said, holding her head back by her hair before she could take me in again. She blinked the tears out of her eyes as she looked up at me. "I'm gonna come. Are you gonna chicken out or are you gonna swallow?" I teased, and she grinned right away, pulling my cock out of her mouth.

"Every last drop," she said, her voice hoarse. Her throat must have been on fire, but she didn't give a shit. She took me in her mouth again and true to her words, swallowed every drop of cum I let out.

***

The imprints of my hands on her ass were gone. I wanted them there again.

"You don't sleep, right?" she mumbled against my pillow. After taking a quick break to the bathroom, she'd claimed she was too tired to get dressed, so she'd crashed on my bed and hugged a pillow to her chest, giving me a magnificent view of her ass and back, her pussy peeking through just a tiny bit between her thighs. It was more than enough to get me hot again.

Fuck, this woman was really going to be the death of me.

I lay on the bed by her side, arm propped under my head because she'd stolen my pillow, too. For whatever fucked up reason, it made me smile.

"No, Damsel. I don't sleep."

"Good," she whispered and snuggled the pillow closer to her chest to get more comfortable.

"Who was he?" I wondered, and a whisper came out of me, even though I hadn't intended to say it out loud. It wasn't my business, but fuck, I wanted to know. Who would betray a woman like that?

Damsel didn't answer. I knew she wouldn't, and her breathing was even, deep. She was seconds away from falling unconscious, and the sun had already turned the sky grey.

I closed my eyes, too, welcoming the way my muscles ached a little bit. My wounds didn't hurt. Come to think of it, I could barely remember the fight now. It felt like it had happened days ago, instead of hours, which was *exactly* what she'd aimed for when she came to my door. And for the life of me, I couldn't find any pleasure in remembering the way I'd fought.

"His name was Ezra."

My eyes popped open, half of me certain that I'd only imagined I'd heard it.

But Damsel continued to speak.

"I knew him since forever. He worked in IT, was very good at his job, had a smile to die for. I'd always had a secret crush on him, but it wasn't until I was twenty—and drunk for the first time in my life—that I actually asked him out."

"You started drinking at twenty?" I teased. "That's awfully late."

She chuckled. "After that night, I didn't touch alcohol for at least a decade." My smile fell. "Anyway, I thought it was just gonna be a fling, but we lasted seven years. And then he sold army information to the Rubena coven, information that *I'd* given him, and he tried to blame me for it. His brilliant plan was to get the money and leave the Hidden Realm, and if I took the fall, nobody was going to even go after him when he disappeared. They'd just assume I'd killed him or something."

"What a fucking wuss," I whispered, shaking my head.

"Worst part was that it would have worked perfectly if one of his colleagues in IT hadn't noticed some missing codes in their program and hadn't tracked it back to his user ID. He told our commander, who then came looking for him. I thought we were out to take a walk in the western woods, but the Rubena coven was waiting there for him and the flash drive. Just as they made the exchange, and he told me he was *sorry*, Ivan came out with a handful of other soldiers."

She hugged the pillow tighter again, but it wasn't doing it for her.

Because she didn't need a fucking pillow. She needed a body to hold onto.

I moved fast, knowing she'd stop me if she could. I grabbed her by the shoulders and flipped her over until her head rested on my shoulder, and both my arms were wrapped around her waist.

"What the fuck are you doing?!" she hissed, trying to push herself off me, but my hands were locked together. No way could she break my hold.

And she was tired. Exhausted. Maybe she just didn't give a shit because after about fifteen seconds of struggling, she fell on my shoulder again with a sigh.

"You're a piece of work, you know that?" she mumbled against my skin.

I laughed but held onto her for a little while longer, just in case. Once I was sure she wasn't going to try to move away from me again, I ran my fingertips up her arm draped over my chest.

Her heartbeat immediately began to slow down and she melted onto me like her body was made for mine.

"Where do you come from, Damsel?" I whispered, running my fingers down her back next.

"From far, far away," she breathed, her eyes closed, half her mind already gone. She slept within seconds, holding onto me, perfectly comfortable the way she wished she was with that pillow.

I closed my eyes, too, and let my mind wander as I listened to her heartbeat.

18

Nikki Arella

My eyes opened to the dark room. A warm body was right next to mine. A big shoulder was under my head. The arm came down and the hand rested on my naked waist. The other hand was over my hip and my fingers were intertwined with his. His leg was between mine, his hard chest pressed to my back, my ass stuck to his pelvis.

Sleep refused to leave me, trying to pull me under, but it just didn't feel right. It had been four years since I'd woken up with somebody else in my bed. Four years.

So…

The morning before came back to me. Axel Creed. The way he'd played my body, the way he'd tortured me, pulled words out of me, then put me over his shoulder to sleep. I'd been too tired to try to push myself off. The warmth of his body and his shoulder had been way too comfortable.

In fact, I'd never felt more comfortable in my life, but it was probably just because I was tired from the fight and the sex.

I'd slept with Savage Ax. On the same bed, our naked bodies flush against one another.

I'd *slept* with Savage Ax.

Panic shot firecrackers inside my mind. I pushed his arms away and jumped off the bed within a second, completely disoriented still.

That's when his eyes opened. They were swollen and bloodshot, like he'd…

"Were you *asleep*?" My voice was high-pitched by the panic.

He said he didn't sleep. That's what he said—I remembered. I fucking *asked!*

He sat up on the bed, even more disoriented than me as he looked around the room.

"Looks like it," he whispered, rubbing his face.

"*Looks* like it? You fucking prick!" I shouted, rushing to the other side to grab my clothes. "You said you didn't sleep!" I had my clothes on in record time, and I prayed with all I had that the fact that I *couldn't* hear a heartbeat from the room next door didn't mean Marie wasn't there. It just didn't.

"I never do," Ax said, and he was on his feet, too, putting on his bloody jeans. "Fuck, Damsel—I never do."

I pulled the door open with my heart in my throat and opened the one of the next room.

Empty. It was empty.

"She's gone."

We'd had Marie right there, unconscious on that bed, and I'd let him distract me with sex and fucking *hugs*. What the hell was wrong with me?

"She couldn't have gotten far," Ax said from behind me, and the next second, he jumped off the railing on the other side of the corridor and landed straight into the parking lot.

I did the same. We looked at the people surrounding us for a moment, neither of us caring if they'd seen us jump off the second floor. I couldn't see Marie anywhere, but I could make out her scent. She still smelled like a fucking sorcerer, and it blew my mind.

But Ax must have seen something more.

"This way." He took off running toward the wide road where we'd come from the night before. Toward Atlanta.

We ran too fast for human eyes to even make us out, and it only took us two minutes to see her.

I stopped running, focused on breathing, on reminding myself and all my demons that she was right there. It was her—I recognized her long black hair, her scent, her height. She had her arms wrapped around herself as she rushed forward, walking by the edge of the road, back to Atlanta.

Ax jumped and landed right in front of her. She stopped moving instantly.

I sighed. *It's over. She's here.* Fuck, that had been close. So, so close.

"Hi, Marie," Ax said with a smile I'm sure he meant to be *polite*. Instead, he looked like he was about to devour her soul.

"Marie," I said, and once she turned and saw me, she started backing off toward the warehouse parking lot on this side of the street.

"Don't come near me," she said, her voice shaking, and she raised her hands toward us.

"It's okay. We saved you, remember? Last night. From the sorcerers," I said, keeping a good distance away. I didn't want her even more freaked out than she already was. We all needed a breather here.

But…the strangest thing happened, and if I hadn't seen it with my own eyes, I would have never believed it. *That's* how much I trusted Abraham Jones.

The tips of her fingers lit up with yellow smoke. *Exactly* like they would on a sorcerer when she used her magic.

My mind was a mess of thoughts, none of them making any sense. I looked at Ax, sure that I was seeing things, but when he met my eyes, he was even more shocked than me.

Marie Graham was a fucking sorcerer?

Oh, fuck. *Shit, fuck, crap.* We'd gotten the wrong person.

With a sigh, I took a step back, holding my head in my hands. "This is a mistake." A goddamn mistake I should have been smarter than to make.

"My brother," the woman said breathlessly. "My brother's still back there. I need to get to him, right now. You can't stop me."

"We're not going to stop you," Ax said, grabbing his hips as he lowered his head. "We thought you were a vampire—that's why we took you."

The woman shook her head, lowering her hands to her sides as she looked away, toward the road that would lead her back to Atlanta. Fuck, she was so confused. So scared she was shaking.

"Hey, it's okay. You don't need to be afraid," I told her.

She met my eyes. "I need to go back for him. Right now—I need to go back."

I nodded. "It's okay. You can go wherever you want. We're not going to hurt you, I promise," I said, feeling more miserable by the second. It was *her,* the woman in that picture. I thought for sure she was exactly who we were looking for—and now look what we'd done. We'd brought her all the way here. She was right to be scared out of her mind. "We can give you cab money, okay? It's a long way back to Atlanta," I tried again, though I knew that cab money wasn't going to make this right. And I remembered that I'd lost my bag, too—I didn't have any money on me anymore.

I looked at Ax. Did he?

But his eyes were on Marie, and he didn't look as desperate as a minute ago.

"Here's what I don't get. Why would those sorcerers keep one of their own in the basement like that?" His voice was calm, perfectly composed now. He took a step closer to her. "And why were you screaming? Why did you ruin the hallway?" Another step. "How did you know we were even there?"

The woman blinked, her eyes filling with tears. What the hell?

"I need to get to my brother," she whispered, and her whisper broke.

"How did you know?" Ax insisted, not smiling for once.

"Because I heard you."

I raised my brows. "In the basement?"

"Yes, in the basement," she said.

"But you're a sorcerer." Sorcerer ears weren't enhanced. Too many layers of concrete between the hallway and the basement, which was the reason why *I* hadn't heard *her* heartbeat.

Ax moved even closer to her, and she raised her hands again, yellow smoke coming out her fingertips.

"Stop!"

But he didn't. The next second, he was right in front of her, her glowing fingers on his chest. Ax didn't bat an eye. He was smiling instead.

Cursing under my breath, I moved.

"Let's just calm down, okay? There's no need to fight."

"How did you hear us?" Ax insisted. "We couldn't hear *you* at all. Just tell us how and we'll let you go." It sounded a lot like a lie.

The woman's chin quivered. "Because…because I'm like you."

Ax turned to look at me for a second, then back down at her hands again, that magic still hanging onto her, thickening the air.

"You're like me?" he asked her.

Her response was to squeeze her eyes shut and cry out a second before two thin fangs slipped down her upper lip and went all the way below her lower one.

I blinked and the view didn't change. I blinked and I was still looking at a sorcerer with fangs.

Ax burst out laughing. I shook my head, refusing to believe my eyes.

And the woman started running.

***

She sat on the edge of the bed in our motel room, right where she'd been unconscious when we first brought her here. Tears wet her cheeks. Her hands were no longer glowing, and her fangs were no longer in sight. It had taken Ax all of twenty seconds to throw her over his shoulder and run back to the motel room where we could talk. Make sense out of this. Just...*calm down*.

But it wasn't working.

"Explain this to me because I don't get it," I said, pacing around the bed. So far, she kept her magic inside her, but if she tried to attack, we'd have no choice but to stop her.

"She's a sorcerer. And a vampire" Ax told me, leaning against the wall, arms crossed in front of him, grinning ear to ear. "At least Robert was right. This was totally worth it."

I rolled my eyes. "Speak, Marie."

She shook her head. "I don't know anything, okay? I was coming back from work two weeks ago, and someone hit me on the back of my head. I passed out. When I woke up, I was...I-I-I..." And she waved her hands toward her body. "My clothes were torn. I had scratches everywhere. And I had fangs." Her shoulders shook as she cried in silence.

Fuck. I stepped closer, not sure what I was doing. "Hey, it's okay," I whispered. "Please, calm down. We'll figure it out."

"Somebody bit you—that's the most probable explanation," Ax said.

"Except vampires can't turn sorcerers," I reminded him. The magic in us and the magic in them were opposites. They couldn't coexist, hence why I knew Jones' theory about me was absurd. Sorcerers had the same kind of magic in them as Vein spirits, only in much smaller amounts.

"I'm not…I don't think I'm exactly like you," Marie whispered. "I don't crave blood."

I raised a brow. "What do you crave?"

She shook her head. "Food."

"So why were those people keeping you in the basement?" I asked the same question Ax asked her earlier.

"Because sorcerers hunt vampires," Marie whispered, and the way her hands shook made my stomach twist. "That's what we do."

"But you're one of theirs, too." Even if she really was bit by a vampire and it somehow worked in turning her, she was still one of their own.

Unless they hated vampires so much that her sorcerer half no longer mattered.

"I don't know," Marie whispered, shaking her head.

"What did they do to you there?" I asked, though I knew I shouldn't have. It wasn't my damn business, but the curiosity had already gotten the best of me.

The woman shrugged her hunched shoulders, kept her eyes on her lap. "They…they did rituals. Several different ones—I don't know what kind."

"But what did they *say* they were doing?" Ax asked.

"Nothing. They didn't speak to me, but I heard them talking one night. They said they were trying to *expel* the vampire in me, and they were going to try until it either worked or I died." Her voice broke again. "My brother saw it all. They kept him there every time they came. He saw all of it."

Fuck. My heart broke even though I didn't even know this woman. And it wasn't just because of what she'd gone through—who even tortures someone in front of their fucking brother?

But it was…something else, too.

How would sorcerers try to *expel* the vampire in her? There was no such thing.

Unless she really wasn't a vampire at all. Unless she was *touched*, like Jones thought I was.

I shook my head to clear the thought because it wasn't possible. I'd seen her fangs with my own eyes. She had enhanced senses, too—she could hear us from the basement. I couldn't argue with that, no matter what it sounded like.

"And what about your brother? Is he the same?" Ax asked.

"No—he's a sorcerer. Just a sorcerer," she whispered, squeezing her eyes shut. "I need to find him. I need to get to him—he's just a kid."

I squatted down in front of her. "Hey, calm down," I said, though *I* wasn't calm at all. "We'll go back for your brother. We'll—"

"No," Ax said from behind me. "There's a good chance that your brother's dead, but even if he isn't, our job was to find you. Bring you to the Realm."

"No!" she shouted. "I am not going anywhere without Marcus!"

"Lady, you—"

I moved and was in front of him in the blink of an eye.

"Don't."

He smiled. "Damsel."

"We're going back for her brother."

"Are you out of your fucking mind?"

"If you don't like it, you can stay."

"Our job was to find *her*!" he hissed, getting in my face.

"For fuck's sake, look at her!" I looked back at Marie, shaking, barely any strength left in her. She was completely torn apart. I couldn't stand to even see it. Hadn't she already gone through enough? None of this was her damned fault.

"Don't tell me you have a soft spot, Damsel," the asshole said, bringing his fingers to my face to push my hair back. I slapped it away.

"She's not going to come with us if we don't find him."

"So what? We knock her out and put her in the trunk," he said. He wasn't remorseful in the least—he didn't give a shit.

"No, Ax," I whispered. "She won't survive it."

He leaned closer and closer to my face until our noses touched. "Why do you care?"

It was a good question. Why would I care about this stranger?

The truth was, I shouldn't have. But I'd been in her shoes before. I'd lost my whole family. My whole town. I knew what it was like not to want to do anything other than get them back.

For mine, it was impossible. For her…maybe it could be done.

And *this* is why I hated doing anything other than drinking and forgetting. I could talk a big game, but give me a sobbing woman who'd give her life for her brother's in a blink, and I was a goner.

But I was already here now. And Jones was going to pay for this. Just as soon as we found her brother and got the fuck out of here.

"We can't do it alone," I told Ax. "Just help us, okay?"

"Damsel," he whispered, leaning his head to the side. "If you really think I'm going to leave your side now, you're more fucked up than I thought."

Despite everything, I grinned. "Here I thought you were a savage."

But he shook his head. "Baby, I've got nothing on you," he whispered and kissed the tip of my nose before he moved away.

Damn him. *Baby?* I hated that word, always had. So why didn't I hate it now, too?

The voice. I would blame it on his voice—again, because why the fuck not?

I wiped my nose, but it was useless. My skin was still burning where his lips touched it. I hated that he knew how to touch me so well. I couldn't wait to get back to my life and not have to be close to him at all.

"All right, sorceress. We're gonna go get your brother. But first, you're gonna shower because you stink," he told Marie. And he was right—she probably hadn't showered in days. Not that it mattered, considering what she'd been going through in that basement for gods knew how long. Her hair was greasy, the smell of sweat hanging onto her skin and clothes like perfume. I didn't mind, though. I trained with sweaty men and women on the daily. I was used to it. "And you're going to get some food in you, then show us what you can do. Because we're gonna need your help with this."

Marie immediately wiped the tears from her cheeks. "Deal." She stood up on shaking legs and locked herself in the bathroom.

19

Half an hour later, we sat on the sidewalk of the warehouse parking lot next to the motel, eating bad sandwiches and drinking soda. The meat smelled funny, but it's not like we could get poisoned. Any virus or bacteria that touched our body would be consumed by the vampire gene long before it had the chance to do any damage to us.

So, we sat there and we ate in silence. Marie's hair was still wet, and her clothes were a mess, but her skin was clean. Her face had been more dirty than I'd even realized before she came out of the bathroom, and now that she'd eaten, some color had returned to her cheeks, too. Her uptilted eyes looked more vibrant. More alive.

"How in the fuck did that happen?" I wondered out loud as I watched her chewing. "You were a sorcerer all your life, right?"

"Yes," she said, swallowing hard.

"Your parents, too?"

She nodded. "So were our grandparents. They raised us. And when they died, it was just me and Marcus. We've stayed together for the past two years without trouble because we keep away from other sorcerers."

"Why?"

She shrugged. "Just how it always was." Definitely not a good answer—but she was telling the truth.

"It should have killed you," Ax said from my other side. "The vampire bite should have killed you—or whoever bit you."

"It didn't," she said bitterly, then looked up at us. "How were you two turned?"

Shivers washed down my back instantly. That was not a story I liked to think about.

"Same as everyone else," Ax said before he changed the subject again, for which I was thankful. "You have fangs. You have enhanced hearing, but no blood craving. What else?"

She shrugged. "I don't know. It's only been two weeks. All I know is I woke up, clothes torn and wounds all over me like some animal had clawed my skin. I went home and took a shower, and then the fangs came. I started hearing the neighbors as if I were in the room with them. I smelled things in a way I never smelled them before. My sight, too—I could literally see the tiny spiders out on the balcony at the corner of the ceiling."

"Did you try to drink blood?" I asked.

"No—just the thought disgusts me," she said, twisting her face. Yeah, that definitely said a lot.

"Who did you tell?"

At that, she raised her brows. "No one. I didn't tell a single soul." And she meant it.

"So, how did those sorcerers know?" I wondered. "You smell like them. You don't smell like a vampire."

"We can feel your kind," she said, as if she were giving me news. "But there are also seers among us. Some of them sense things nobody else can," she whispered.

"Why take your brother, though?" Ax asked.

"Because he tried to fight them off when they came. They knocked us both out and took us. We woke up in that basement."

"How long?" I'd been punished in Redwood before for misbehaving and breaking people's teeth during sparring. I'd been punished for killing other soldiers, too. They'd thrown me in one of the holding cells and left me there for days, without food or water or blood. I hadn't learned my lesson, mind you—I *couldn't* if I tried—but I knew the feeling. It wasn't nice.

"I'm not sure. Maybe a week, maybe less," Marie said.

"And did they say anything? Did they tell you why they took you?" Ax asked.

"No—just that I was an abomination and that I needed to be stopped. That's it." I felt her shiver rushing down her back.

"Why not kill you, though?" I wondered. "I don't understand."

"I don't know," Marie whispered. "But I can't stay here any longer. They won't be the only ones coming for me."

"Don't worry. We're taking you to the Hidden Realm," I said, though I still wasn't sure how the fuck that was going to work out. A sorcerer in the middle of the Realm?

"As long as Marcus comes with."

Ax and I looked at one another. A vampire-slash-sorcerer was one thing. But just a sorcerer?

I stood up, the sandwich finally gone. "I'm gonna make a phone call. Be right back."

I moved closer to the warehouse and called Jones's number, hoping this time he'd pick up.

He did after the fifth ring.

"For fuck's sake—a *sorceress*?" I exploded even before he said *hello*.

"Calm down, Nicole," Jones said, his voice as unwavering as ever.

"She's a fucking sorceress—and she's got fangs. What the hell is this, Jones?" I turned and looked at Ax and Marie, still sitting on the ground.

"So, it's true," Jones said.

"Yes, it's true. You didn't even know for sure?!" Was he kidding?

"We heard, but it's kind of hard to believe something like it, don't you think?" he said. "So, you have her?"

"Yes."

"Good. And Savage Ax?"

"Yeah, he's here."

"Any trouble?"

"Not with him."

"Oh?"

"We did have to kill about eleven sorcerers to get her, Jones. We almost died."

"But you didn't." He wasn't even fazed. "What about the other covens?"

"Some tried to sneak up on us and shoot us with arrows. Tried to deliver us to a bunch of sorcerers."

A second of silence. "And?"

"Nothing. They'd heard about Ax."

"Ax, huh," he breathed.

I squeezed my eyes shut. That asshole could smell the way I talked even through the phone.

"Yes—*Ax,* Jones. We're on this fucked up mission together because of you," I reminded him.

He sighed as if he were suddenly exhausted. "Get the girl back here, Nicole. We'll talk about the rest when you get home."

"She wants her brother," I said before he could hang up. "She's not coming without him."

"Is he the same?"

"No, just a sorcerer."

"Leave him."

"No," I said, even before he finished speaking. "He's coming with."

"A sorcerer in the fucking Realm, Nicole?" And he laughed.

"I'm sure you'll figure out a way to handle it," I said and ended the call.

He called back before I even got to the others. I didn't bother answering. I had the feeling things were going to just get worse for me from here on anyway.

"Right, so," I said to Ax and Marie. "What exactly can you do? And how strong are you?"

She stood up, dusting crumbs off her lap. "I'm a sorcerer. I know spells. I have magic."

"How fast are you?" She only shrugged.

"Have you ever been in a fight before?" Ax asked.

"No, I—"

"Have you ever killed anyone before?"

"*No!*" she said, like I'd insulted her.

I looked at Ax. We couldn't rely on her for shit.

He sighed. "Right. See that warehouse over there? Throw the most powerful magic you can at it." And he pointed at the garage doors of the warehouse behind us.

"What—right now?" Marie already looked terrified.

"Yes, right now. We need to know. C'mon," he said.

"But there are people—"

"Forget about the people. Just hit that thing,"

She looked at me as if she were about to ask for help, but one look at my face and she raised her hands. I needed to know what she could do, too. How much I could rely on her. I already knew about Ax.

And as much as it pained me to admit it to myself, I wasn't afraid to go back there right now. I wasn't afraid because I knew *he* would be there.

I was in deeper shit here than I realized.

For now, I watched in awe as the ball of red smoke between Marie's hands grew bigger. The air was charged with the electricity of her magic coming to life around her. I stepped back instinctively. That shit hurt a lot. But Ax didn't back away. He went even closer, watching the swirling smoke with a smile on his face, his eyes lit up.

Fucking lunatic—but I found myself smiling, anyway.

And I dropped that smile immediately, reminding myself of who he was once more.

Marie screamed as she pushed her magic forward. A blink, and it slammed against the garage door of the warehouse with a deafening noise.

"*Woohoo!*" Ax called as we watched the smoke blow away and saw what the magic had done to the doors.

It had ruined them completely.

Alarms went off somewhere in the building. The doors were in pieces, and we could see the shelves full of cardboard boxes on the inside. People were approaching fast.

"It's time we got the fuck out of here," Ax said and turned for the street.

"How fast can you run, Marie?" I asked her while we followed, and Ax disappeared from our sight completely.

"I don't know!" she said, but she was already moving down the street, too afraid to stop now.

And she was pretty fast. Not vampire fast, because I could still see her, but she was definitely faster than a human or sorcerer. Yeah, she was definitely a vampire.

For now, it would have to do.

***

The neighborhood was quiet, not a lot of people outside. What was left of the house was barely standing. No police cars. No police tape. How strange.

"Stay here," Ax said before he disappeared behind the row of houses lightning fast. We waited at the beginning of the street. It didn't take him longer than three minutes to be back.

"Not a living soul inside it," he said, his breathing perfectly even.

"I need to go check for myself," Marie whispered and started walking ahead.

"The poor schmuck is probably dead," Ax whispered. If Marie heard him, she didn't turn.

"We have to try."

"Yeah—I got that. You're all soft and sensitive on the inside." He grinned.

"Don't be an ass. He was her responsibility."

"And you care about that—I get it. You've got such a big mouth on you, I almost believed it myself."

I smacked him on the chest. "What did the coven say?"

"Bring her back. Leave the brother."

I nodded. "Same. What did you tell him?"

"That I was going to bring him anyway."

I smiled. "Robert is probably not happy."

"I assume neither is Jones."

We both nodded. "Let's go check out the house. Hopefully I'll find my bag and knives in there."

We started walking, focused on our surroundings to make sure nobody was coming for us. So far, nobody was, and Marie had disappeared somewhere in the house already.

"You never told me you could kill like that," Ax whispered. "I saw you with those knives."

"Oh, yeah?" I grinned.

"You got me hard, Damsel."

I raised a brow. "You got hard by watching me kill people?" Was he fucking nuts?

"Fuck yeah. Sexiest thing I've ever seen." And he wasn't the least bit ashamed to admit it.

I shook my head, chuckling. "You're not well in the head."

"I'm starting to think I'm better off than you," he whispered, winking at me. If he only knew how right he was…

We reached the house, and it was an even bigger mess from up close. We heard Marie's heartbeat just fine when we went through what was once a doorway. Most of the walls had collapsed. The smell of burned wood and furniture stuck to my nostrils. Everything was ruined—and the big hole in the hallway floor was like an abyss threatening to swallow me whole. Last night, the six sorcerers who'd joined the party late had crashed into it. Their bodies, if they'd even died, were now gone.

We jumped over the ruined floor and all the way to the bigger hole deeper into the house, through which we could see the basement. Pink light shone somewhere inside it, and we saw Marie sitting cross-legged on the ruined basement floor, her magic glowing pink as she whispered something with her eyes closed.

The blood was still there, but the bodies of those sorcerers were gone. When I saw the handle of one of my knives in the debris near the broken kitchen counter, I almost cried with joy. They hadn't taken it with.

I managed to find four of them in the living room before Ax and I jumped down to the basement, where the glow of Marie's magic had almost faded completely. We didn't really need light to see. I found another one of my knives there without trouble.

And then Marie sucked in a deep breath, as if she hadn't been breathing at all until now.

"What?" Ax asked her. "What happened?"

"I've tracked Marcus. He's close," she said and stood up. "He's in the city."

"With who?"

"I don't know—probably sorcerers."

"And he's alive?" Ax sounded skeptical.

"Yes—he's alive, but he's unconscious," Marie said.

"How exactly does that work? How can you know?"

"Because I used his blood for the spell. Blood is the most powerful guide," she said, as if that was supposed to explain exactly how magic worked. "C'mon, let's go." And she jumped out of the hole in the blink of an eye.

I shrugged. "Sure. Let's go." I jumped after her.

"We're wasting fucking time here, but okay," said Ax, but he followed. My other three knives would rest in peace here in this mess forever. And my bag…

Just as I was about to jump over the hole in the hallway to the front door, I saw it. It was hiding under a big piece of concrete, the black fabric covered in dust, but it was there.

I hadn't been that happy in a long time. It was there—and two of the small bottles of alcohol I'd taken from the hotel room minibar were broken, but one remained. Good enough. My money, my thermos—all still there. Even my clothes. I was itching to get out of these ruined ones full of tears and blood, but I couldn't change until we found Marcus. Just in case there would be another fight.

But the strangest thing…as we followed Marie down the street, sometimes walking and sometimes running as she led us deeper into the city, I was…*calm*. Much calmer than I usually was when facing a fight. My demons were inside me, the whispers in the back of my mind like always, and even though I didn't trust them in the least, I…trusted Ax.

And that had to be the most fucked up thought that had ever occurred to me in my life.

"Over there," Marie said when we turned the corner into a busy street about fifteen minutes later. One side was full of shops, and across from it were apartment buildings, each about ten stories high. I had no idea in which part of the city we were, but apparently Marie knew where she was going. "He's in there somewhere." She was pointing at the third apartment building.

We kept moving, perfectly aware of the people walking by us. At least Ax and I were. The air was heavier and the scent of magic barely there surrounding the building. There were definitely sorcerers here. It became much more intense when we walked through the glass doors. My instincts were on high alert. My body remembered exactly what that magic had felt like, and it would do anything to keep away from it.

But Ax grabbed my arm before we took the first stair up.

"Do you smell that?" he whispered, and I sniffed the air deeply.

I smelled it instantly, the scent barely there, as if it were hiding beneath that of magic. Vampire.

"Covens?"

He nodded. "Most probably."

And even before I'd said the words, we heard the footsteps from a floor above.

"Lookie here," a man said before two other sets of footsteps reached my ears. I grabbed Marie and pulled her back, away from the stairs, and we saw the three vampires stopping at the top, smiling at us.

I knew them. I was bad with names, but I knew their faces. I'd seen them in the Realm somewhere, though I wasn't sure who belonged to which coven.

"Gerald Chase," Ax said, grinning widely, putting one foot on the first step, completely at ease. "I should have known they'd send you. I'm afraid I don't know your buddies, though."

"It's actually a surprise to see you here, Axel. Don't you stay in your tower all day, torturing people?" the man said, feigning surprise. The two others behind him had their eyes on me.

Ax laughed. "I do, actually. But it's not much different out here, to be honest. I get to torture plenty of people here, too—like I'm about to do to you if you don't get out of my face, Gerald."

If he didn't hear the threat in Ax's voice, he was a damn fool.

"The thing is, I need her, Axel," Gerald said, nodding his head toward Marie.

I leaned closer to her ear. "Now's the time for your magic shit," I whispered, and she immediately raised her shaking hands.

Yellow smoke began to come out of her fingers before any of us could even blink.

Gerald and his friends were shocked out of words—exactly what I was aiming for.

"Nice, isn't it?" I said. "If you're here to fight, just enough with the talking already. I'm fucking bored." I grabbed two of my knives from the holsters on my thighs.

"Aren't you that drunk Redwood bitch that always hangs out at Nameless?" the man standing to the left of Gerald said as he grinned.

Ax immediately turned to me, a sick smile on his face, that gleaming making his eyes look even more blue than usual. "He's mine," he growled.

I shrugged. "Have at him."

And he moved.

Fuck, he was really fast. One second he was there, and the next he was at the top of the stairs, in front of the guy who'd called me a drunk Redwood bitch. Gerald and the other friend were moving for us, but my eyes were stuck on Ax for a moment—the way he slammed his hand in the guy's chest as he tried to fist him in the face.

But Ax's hand was already *inside* his chest, and when he pulled it out, the guy's fucking *heart* was between his fingers. Blood dripped down to the floor fast.

Ax burst out laughing like a maniac.

I was the same because I was smiling, too. He was fucking brutal.

But Gerald and his friend were already on us.

Yellow magic shot from Marie's fingers just as they moved in front of us, forcing them to step to the sides to avoid it. The ball of glowing smoke hit the stairs and distracted the two vampires for a second. A second was plenty of time to throw my knife and bury it in the eye of the other vampire, while Gerald, with his fangs in clear view, came for my neck. I pushed Marie to the other side, throwing her against the mailboxes before I spun around and kicked Gerald in the thigh. He hissed and came at me again, while his friend pulled the knife from his eye. Shit—it hadn't gone deep enough. But even before he was done, Ax wrapped his arm around his neck from behind.

It took me no longer than twenty seconds to have Gerald on the floor on his back. I put my boot on his neck and he tried to push it up with all his strength. I gave him the pleasure, raised my foot just a bit, before I slammed it on his face with all my strength.

With a loud cry, he tried to roll to the side, giving me access to his back. I buried my other knife in the base of his neck before he could stand up. Then, I took the knife out, put him on his back again, and stabbed his heart three times, twisting the knife on the third. He was as dead as he could get. And I was all bloody. It had definitely been a good call not to change my clothes yet.

"See? That's how a fight's supposed to go. No colorful sparkly bullshit coming out of people's hands. Just pure strength and speed," Ax said, admiring what he'd done to the guy I'd stabbed in the eye—he'd taken his head off completely. Yep, that would get a vampire pretty dead.

Meanwhile Marie was sitting on the floor, arms wrapped around herself as her whole body shook. Shit.

"Hey, it's okay," I said, going closer to her slowly. "It's fine. We can go now. They're dead."

But when she looked at me, I saw that it wasn't the three dead vampires she was afraid of—it was *me*. And Ax.

Double shit.

I tried for a smile. "It's okay, Marie. Let's go get Marcus, okay?"

"More will be coming," Ax said, as if he couldn't see the terrified look on Marie's face. "They teamed up, those fuckers. Two are left. They probably teamed up, too."

"All the more reason to keep going," I told Marie, offering her my hand. When I saw how bloody it was, I made an effort to wipe it against my skirt. No use.

But she finally took it, swallowing hard.

I didn't want to freak her out—I wasn't here to hurt her. I would protect her with my life. But it was hard to convince her of that when we had to pass the two dead bodies, jump over the hole in the stairs her magic had made, then go over the third dead body with the still heart right next to the hand.

I looked at Ax. "Did you seriously pull his heart out, just like that?"

He shrugged. "It's my favorite way to kill. I can teach you if you'd like."

Despite the absurdity of the situation, I smiled, shaking my head. "Thanks, but I'm good." Fucking maniac.

The second we stepped onto the second floor, we felt the magic. So much of it, I literally couldn't breathe properly. It hung in the air, pressed against my skin as if it wanted to push me back—or warn me that something really bad would happen if I kept going.

"It's a ward," Marie said, raising her hand as if she could *touch* the magic with her fingertips.

"You sure he's in there? Because I can't hear shit." The entire third floor was locked so tightly, I couldn't smell anything or hear a drop of blood or a beating heart.

"Yes, I'm sure. I feel it," she said, pressing her hand to her chest. "Give me a moment."

She sat down on the stairs, closed her eyes and raised her hands. This time, the smoke that came out of her fingers was a light green color. It was almost calming the way it glowed and swirled, growing bigger by the second. It made me wonder what more it could do. I'd read the books, seen the movies. Artists presented paranormal creatures very differently from what they were. Like vampires—we are undead, but our bodies still live. Our hearts still beat. We still need air in our lungs to survive.

But they didn't really teach us anything about sorcerers, not in the Hidden Realm. All we knew is that they had access to the Veins, could summon incredible forces with their hands—and sometimes words—that could be deadly to a vampire and different creatures that sometimes escaped the Veins. I'd never even witnessed this magic firsthand until this mission, but now, as I watched the green glow and the smoke moving almost seductively, I couldn't help but try to understand it. How much power was really in that thing? What more could it do? I was sure magic could be used for more than energy blasts to fight with. Why did nobody ever even talk about it in the Realm?

Marie raised her hands toward the top of the stairs and let go with a weak cry, pulling me out of my trance. The entire building shook, knocking me against the wall, and Ax against the railing. My stomach twisted and the demons inside me roared.

Calm down, I told myself. It was just Marie. It was just—

Doors opened a floor above. Footsteps rushed to the stairway. I grabbed two knives, cursing under my breath, and pushed Marie down the stairs just as the first three sorcerers appeared at the top of the stairway. Their hearts raced same as ours, and their eyes glistened with hatred as they took us in. But they stopped for a second, and I tried to take advantage of it.

"We just want the boy," I said before they started attacking, hoping for once that things would go smoothly.

They didn't.

The sorcerers raised their glowing hands at us instantly, and Ax and I had no choice but to move.

Jumping up a flight of stairs was easy. Swinging my knives to cut through flesh was easy, too. But getting hit by that magic most definitely wasn't. Right now, I couldn't care less about what else magic could really do—I just wanted to keep away from it forever.

And more sorcerers were coming. It was chaos within a minute, and the more magic was inside me, the slower my movements became. But I kept on going—jumping up the walls to try to get away from the colorful smoke, popping up behind their backs to give myself a better chance at killing them before they killed me.

But the more they hit me, the more pain my body suffered, the louder the voices in my head, demanding my submission. I was losing strength. Ax and I went deeper into the hall to the right where the sorcerers were coming from, and my strength was giving up on me. I needed fuel. I needed my mind clear.

I needed to move the way Ax did—lightning fast, breaking necks with his bare hands as he went.

When I jumped and landed behind a woman's back, that's how I convinced myself to grab her by her blonde hair and sink my fangs in her neck.

Vampires didn't get the urge to bite sorcerers. The magic in them reacted against our own. Taking too much from them could kill a vampire, but right now I had no choice. Blood was blood, and even if the taste of it disgusted me, my body needed the fuel. I only took three mouthfuls from the screaming sorceress before I let go and stabbed her with my knife right between her shoulder blades.

The effect of the blood and the magic coating it was mixed. I moved back slowly, as if I wasn't in control of my own body anymore, until my back hit a wall. Dark spots in my vision. The sounds of the fight around me suddenly seemed so far away. I'd never drank from a sorcerer before, and for a moment, I thought I'd made a fatal mistake. No wonder vampires stayed away from sorcerer blood. My heartbeat was slowed down, my blood no longer rushing, and…my mind was empty, too.

The screams in my head no longer reached me. My vision cleared with every blink as my heart picked up the beating again. My body was weak, my limbs heavy, but when I tried to move, I could. My speed wasn't half of what it normally was, but…*my mind was empty*.

It was silent. Like that blood had shut out all the demands of submission. Like it had taken them right out of me completely. My gods, I'd never felt more powerful in my life, even though my hands felt like they weighed a thousand pounds. That's why I was smiling when the magic hit me in the shoulder and threw me against the floor, on all the bodies covering it.

"Damsel, move!" Ax called from somewhere on the other side of the hall. His voice was clear, and the sounds of the fight reached me just fine again. I pushed myself up, holding onto my knives tightly.

I heard Marie calling out her brother's name, and I barely saw her slip past Ax, who'd blocked the door of an apartment and was fighting two sorcerers on his own. A second later, she disappeared inside the apartment.

No more demons. No more whispers or screams.

And barely any strength left.

I kept on going. Kept on swinging my knives at the four sorcerers who were between me and Ax. I could barely stand, barely see, but I managed to stab one of them on the side of his neck, before the other hit me with his magic square in the chest. My feet no longer touched the floor. I flew in the air then slammed onto a dead body on my back. My ribcage hurt. My arms hurt.

For a second, I thought we wouldn't make it.

Shit, it *had* been a mistake. I'd been a fucking fool to bite that sorceress. My demons gave me strength. They gave me power. Speed. Sight.

And now…

"Keep moving!" I heard Ax's voice and turned my head just in time to see Marie with her brother right behind her, running over the dead bodies to the stairway.

Not over yet. It gave me the boost that I needed to jump to my feet.

"Go with them," Ax said, as he fought the last two sorcerers standing.

I wanted to help. I wanted to finish them while they were too busy fighting Ax, but I knew my limitations. That blood was still inside me. My demons were gone.

And I needed to keep an eye on Marie and her brother.

So, putting my knives away, I rushed down the stairs, seeing double until I reached the three dead vampire bodies we'd left by the entrance door. I grabbed my bag and walked out of the building without giving myself the chance to think. Humans were all around us, watching, terrified, and sirens went off in the distance. I saw Marie running, dragging her brother in the direction we'd come from, and I took off after them. I couldn't run fast yet, though my full vision was returning to me now that light, magic-less air was filling my lungs.

But as soon as I turned the corner, I found Marie and her brother frozen on the sidewalk. Ahead, about ten feet away, two men were standing there and smiling sneakily at them. At *us*.

Goddamn it.

Gritting my teeth, I reached for my knives again and stepped in front of Marie and the boy.

"What'cha looking at, fellas?" I asked the sorcerers, and even though I sounded a bit breathless, my hands weren't shaking. My aim would be true if they gave me a reason to throw my knives at them. I'd eat dirt before I let them get to Marie after everything I'd already gone through.

The men shared a look for a moment. "She's more trouble than she's worth," the one on the left told me, his big hands fisted at his sides, wide shoulders rigid. "Let us have her. You won't have to worry about her anymore."

I smiled. "Then come and get her, boys." I raised my knives, focused on their heads. I would aim for their foreheads, but anywhere close would do just fine, too.

But the men didn't summon their magic like I thought they would. A second later, I smelled Ax behind me, slamming his feet to the asphalt as if he wanted everyone to hear him coming.

"What do we have here? More people to kill?" His heart was still racing, and he still breathed heavily when he stopped right beside me. "It must be my lucky fucking night."

The sorcerers moved back a bit, then shook their heads. Still no glow around their hands. They weren't calling out their magic.

"We tried the nice way," the one on the right said. He was much smaller than his friend, but physical strength meant nothing when it came to how strong a sorcerer's magic was.

"Now, *he'll* be coming for you," said the bulky one.

Before I could even come up with something to say, they both turned around and walked away in a rush.

What the fuck?

I looked around for a moment, at the humans around me walking the street, and some of them were looking right at me—at my knives, at my body covered in blood. I put them away in my holsters when the sorcerers disappeared around the corner, and it didn't look like there were any more of them out here, waiting for us.

"Who's *he*?" I asked nobody in particular.

"The police are on their way. Let's move," Ax said. He turned and crossed the street without waiting for a reply. Marie and her brother were already following. With my head down, I did the same.

20

We rented a black van with plenty of space in the back and a full tank. Ax took the wheel; Marie and her brother were in the back, both alive.

We were going home.

"You sure about this?" I asked Ax when he turned the ignition on. Jones had been against cars—he explicitly told me not to travel in them. Ax said it himself, too, back when we were in the woods outside the Realm.

Gods, that felt like ages ago now.

But Ax didn't speak, only gave me a pointed look from the driver's seat. I thought it strange, and I was going to push harder, but when I lay back on the leather seat and closed my eyes for a moment, it was so…*peaceful*.

No whispers. No other presence in my chest. It was just me.

Ezra used to do that to me sometimes. When we lay together, and I focused on his breathing, on his heartbeat, it felt like I was all alone in my body, too. Maybe that's why I'd clung to him the way I did. Maybe that's why I'd imagined my whole fucking life with him before he went and stabbed me in the back.

Ax did it, too, but it was different with him. He chased away the whispers, but it was never *peaceful* with him. My own thoughts were in a chaotic state when he had his hands on me. The need for him was like a demon all on its own. It fucking possessed me, which was why I should stay away from him for good now that we were on our way back home. It wasn't long until I would never have to see him again, anyway. Everything would go back to normal. I had alcohol. I didn't need anything else.

"You drank from them."

I opened my eyes to the windshield and the darkness behind it. The car was moving, though I'd barely felt it. We were on a highway somewhere, with only a few cars in sight. In the back, Marie and her brother were locked in each other's embrace as they slept. Their hearts beat steady. The kid stank of blood and dirt and sweat, but neither of them were hurt badly. They just needed the rest.

"Yeah," I said with a flinch.

"Are you fucking nuts? That shit can kill you," he suddenly snapped.

Oh, so *that's* why he was pissed.

I looked at his profile, his eyes stuck on the windshield. "What do you even care whether I die or not?"

That shut him up quick. And he was right—sorcerer blood could kill you. But it was either that or going feral, so I made a choice. Honestly, if I'd known the kind of effect that blood would have on my mind, I'd have tried it a long time ago. Anything to keep those voices at bay. To keep the fear away.

"I don't. But I can't take them to the Realm on my own," Ax said after a minute. I flinched again, but he didn't see it.

"I needed blood or I'd have lost it." It was as simple as that. I didn't expect him to understand, obviously, but I also didn't owe him any fucking explanations.

"That would have been beneficial in a fucking fight," he said through gritted teeth. "People die when you lose it, right? That's what you said. Well, we needed those people dead, and vampires fight better when they're hungry."

I rolled my eyes. "I *know* that. I'm a fucking soldier." Master Ferrera himself trained me and I knew how beneficial it was for a vampire to be a bit hungry before a fight. Not hungry enough to lose control of ourselves, though, the way *I* was about to do. But the right amount of hunger made us more dangerous, our vampire instincts sharper. It gave the monstrous side of us more control. For me, that was bad news because there was more than one monster living inside of me—hence the reason Jones had sent me here. But Ax didn't need to know that. Nobody did. "Besides, I killed plenty."

"You almost killed yourself, too."

"What the hell do you care?" I said, but I wasn't angry. Not even a little bit. "I'm here, aren't I?"

"Fuck, Damsel," he said, gripping the steering wheel so tightly his knuckles were completely white. "Don't do that again."

"Maybe I will." If he knew how calm it was in my head right now, he would have understood.

"*Don't* do it again," he said, and for a moment, I caught a glimpse of the guy he was when he was pulling hearts straight out of ribcages while laughing his own out.

He didn't scare me. Nothing scared me except what was inside my head. But it made me wonder if he was maybe full of shit. If he *did* care more than he let on.

Which was plain ridiculous.

"Okay," I said, despite my better judgment. I just didn't have it in me to argue right now.

He was just as surprised as I thought he would be. He turned to look at me and probably expected me to start laughing any second, and when I didn't, he nodded. "Good."

I'd made the right choice saying what he wanted to hear. It was way less tiring this way.

"Where did you learn how to fight, Ax?" I asked after a minute.

That question took him by surprise, too. "Here and there," was his answer.

"Where did you get all those scars on your body?" His torso, his arms were full of them. He had one on his temple, too.

"Back in the good ole days."

I turned to him, brows raised. "You're gonna make me suck your dick before you give me your secrets?" He'd done the same to me, had pulled those words out of me by fucking torturing me. And the reminder sent shivers up and down my body that I tried desperately to ignore.

Just like that, his face transformed with a wide grin. "Not a bad idea, actually."

"Well, you can forget all about it. Not that curious, anyway." Though giving him blow jobs was one of my favorite things to do now, we were on the road. We were going to be driving all night. We weren't gonna stop.

"Liar," he said. "You're a fucking liar, Damsel."

That, I was.

But for my own sake, it was time to change the subject. He knew my scent too well by now to miss even a little bit of it—just like I knew his. "How much trouble do you think we'll be in when we get back?"

"Nothing we can't handle," he said. "We'll take her to them just like they asked. If they have something to say about the kid, they can say it to themselves. I won't be there to hear it."

I grinned. "Not even if you don't have a choice?"

"I always have a choice, Damsel," he said, his eyes on my bloodstained thighs for a second. "On most things, anyway."

"Now *you're* being naughty," I teased.

"All day, every day," he said without hesitation. "You want to punish me?"

Damn. "Fuck yeah."

"How?"

"I want to tie you up like the toy that you are, then take advantage of you fully." And wouldn't that be nice…

"Oh, Damsel." He chuckled. "You can tie me up any time you want. But I'll bring down the whole building if I see your pussy and my cock isn't buried inside it."

Fuck him and his dirty mouth that I loved. The best I could do was laugh, even though my thighs clenched, and I was soaking wet within seconds.

When his hand gripped my thigh, I looked at him, surprised. "What are you doing?"

"Those damn panties," he said, slowly inching his way up under my skirt. "They're in my way."

"Ax." Marie and her brother were in the back. Sleeping—but still. And he was driving.

"Relax, Damsel," he said, and when his fingers reached the hem of my panties, my legs spread to the sides as if by a fucking button. "I just want a little taste, that's all." And he slipped a finger under my panties, teasing my clit. Bringing the back of my hand to my mouth, I bit my skin to keep from moaning, but my hips moved against his finger anyway. Just like that. All it took was a damn touch, and I was completely helpless, my emotions all over the place.

"Ax, stop," I said breathlessly, even though my whole body was already moving in rhythm with his fingers. Fuck, how he played me. It wasn't fair.

"Close your eyes and breathe, Damsel," he whispered, and I did just that. My whole being hung on the way his fingers moved, and I didn't even care that we were driving anymore or that the siblings were in the back. I needed it. He touched me, and I'd burn the whole fucking world to the ground, too, just to get release.

"That's right," he whispered, his voice rough, sexy as all hell. "Keep grinding, baby. Your pussy's so fucking hungry." And he slipped the tip of his finger inside me. I bit on my hand harder to keep from crying out.

"You like that?" he teased.

"Yes," I breathed. I loved it every time he touched me.

"Good girl," he said, and…took his hand back, just like that.

I froze. "What are you doing?" Was he serious?

"That's enough, Damsel. Now you owe me. And later, when I bend you over, I'll collect my debt." He stuck his fingers in his mouth and licked them while he growled.

Fuck.

I was seconds away from giving him a piece of my mind. How dare he do that to me? Who the fuck did he think he was?!

But the siblings were still in the back. And we were on the fucking road.

Squeezing my eyes shut, I sank my nails in my palms and breathed. It wasn't worth it. If I made a fuss about it right now, I'd just sound desperate (which I was) and pathetic (which I also was).

But now I was turned on. More than that—I actually considered just straddling him while he drove. I wanted his cock so bad, it was ridiculous. Worse than the voices in my head.

Biting my tongue hard enough to draw blood, I reminded myself that this wasn't a game anymore. But in the back of my mind, something insisted that it was.

Soon, we'd be home. Savage Ax would forget all about me. And I'd be all alone again.

Wasn't that *exactly* what I wanted just minutes ago?

***

We drove for four hours straight and made it to a small town near Nashville, Tennessee. Marie and her brother were up, eating some of the bars I'd carried in my bag. The sun was half an hour away, and we were exhausted, Ax more so than me.

The blood of the sorceress must have been fading from my system because my head was already back to its original self, and I was craving a drink like never before. I drank the entire small bottle of whiskey I had left in two swigs, and it did get my head buzzing a little bit.

We stopped by an inn and rented two rooms. One for me and the siblings, one for Ax.

I couldn't wait to crash and pass out already, but the moment we stepped onto the second floor of the old inn, he whispered in my ear, "You've got a debt to pay."

And he disappeared in his room.

I'd be damned if my entire body didn't come alive at his words. I don't know what it was about that voice of his, but it pushed my buttons like nothing else ever did.

Still, I resisted.

Marie and the kid—that's what mattered. We'd had our fun. Now, we had them to take care of.

Marcus went into the bathroom to shower first. Marie sat on the edge of the twin bed, eyes stuck on the bathroom door, as if she were expecting it to explode any second. Her hands were still shaking a bit, too. I was bad with words, but I was still encouraged to give it a try because she looked so helpless. Helplessness sucked balls.

So, I sat on my bed opposite her, and cleared my throat.

"He's okay, Marie," I said, feeling like I was sitting on needles, especially when her wide eyes locked on mine and I saw the fear reflected in them. Anya would know exactly what to say to her to get her to calm down.

Damn, I missed that little brat. Half my mind was made up to give her a call, just to hear her voice. But I'd just worry her more, and there was no need for that. I'd see her in person soon enough.

"I know," Marie said, nodding her head. "He's a good kid."

"Looks like it," I said. "It's just you and him?"

"Yeah. Parents died when we were young. Our grandparents raised us. Grandpa died five years ago. Grandma, two." She shrugged like it was no big deal, but I heard the pain in her voice. It still hurt her. I understood that better than she knew.

"That's okay. You still got Marcus." Meanwhile I didn't have anyone.

"Yeah," she said, smiling. "He's so smart. And so talented. He's going to make something of himself. I've been working two jobs to make money to send him to college next year. He wants to be an architect." The big smile on her face said she was proud.

It made me smile, too. How nice would it be to have someone who loved you in that way? Who'd work two jobs just so you'd get a chance at becoming who you wanted to be. Simple things that meant *everything*, even though the best I could do was imagine.

"You're a good sister, Marie," I said, and I meant it.

"I can't let anything happen to him because of me," she whispered, looking down at her lap.

"Nothing will. I promise you, no matter what, we'll get you to the Hidden Realm." I meant that, too.

"And then what?" she asked, a terrified smile on her face, her eyes full of unshed tears.

"Then you'll meet Abraham Jones. He's one of the rulers of my coven. He'll help you."

She blinked and two tears slipped down her cheeks. "Really?"

I shrugged. "He helped me."

Slowly, she brought her hands to her face and wiped her tears. "What happened to you?"

"I was six. And alone." And *a monster*, but I didn't say that out loud. "He took me in. I had a roof over my head, food on the table every day, blood. He took care of me."

She raised a skeptical brow. "But now you're here."

"Yeah," I said with a nod. "Now I'm helping him." Even if I hadn't wanted to be here, and he'd practically forced me to come, I was always happy to help him. It felt like I was paying him back.

A minute later, Marcus came out of the bathroom. He lay down on the twin bed, and it was my turn to go clean myself up. The mirror said I looked a mess. The black eyeshadow was smeared halfway down my cheeks, and it was torture cleaning it up. My hair was in tangles, and my body was full of bruises and cuts.

Even so, looking at myself naked in the mirror had my mind filled with images of Ax towering over me, doing things to me that I didn't even know I could enjoy. That fucking savage.

I avoided the mirror until I was clean and dry, and walked out of the bathroom, dressed in my other, semi-clean clothes. The others couldn't be saved so I just put them in the trash can under the sink.

Tomorrow, we'd come really close to home. Tomorrow would be our last night together. Marie and Marcus were already breathing evenly, heartbeats steady. They must have been even more exhausted than I thought because they'd slept most of the ride here, too. I had nothing to do but sit there on that bed and wait for sunrise to knock me out. It wouldn't be long now.

But...what if I took advantage of this last night, too? I was never going to be here again. I was probably never going to even see Ax again when we were home.

Was I so desperate still as to go back to his room tonight?

Marie and Marcus were already fast asleep, holding onto each other tightly. The TV was on, on mute, but no matter how hard I tried, I couldn't keep my focus on it for longer than two seconds.

Meanwhile I could hear Ax's heart beating from the room across from ours. Calm. Steady. Waiting.

My flesh raised in goose bumps as my mind practically forced me to remember his touch in the car. The way his fingers had felt under my panties. How I'd been ready to burst within seconds.

The realization was like a slap to my face: I *was* so desperate as to go back to his room tonight, and I was no fan of sugarcoating things, not even for myself. That was just the simple truth.

"Fuck it," I whispered to the silent room. It was the last time.

I took off my panties, put them under the cover of my bed, so angry with myself I could burst. One thing I was sure of, at least— no matter how good he felt, I would *not* sleep in his bed today.

So, I opened the door and walked out, locking it behind me. He opened his before I had the chance to knock.

More than that, he was completely naked, his cock on full display, hard and ready for me. My body froze for a second, my eyes scrolling down the length of him involuntarily. Damn. Every inch of him was carved to perfection. Even his scars were beautiful. He truly was a sight to see.

More pissed and more turned on by the second, I stepped inside the room and slammed the door shut. This asshole had gotten under my skin, and now he was playing my body whichever way he pleased.

But two could play the game. So, when he reached out a hand to touch me, I slapped it away.

"Get on your knees."

He raised a brow, but his smile spread. And he didn't make me ask twice. He dropped to his knees right in front of me, looking like he was about to have the feast of his life.

He licked his lips and gripped my thighs when I stepped closer. I pulled my skirt up to show him that I was naked underneath it again, then I took his head in my hands and brought his face to my pussy.

His tongue was ready, warm and wet, circling over my clit like it knew my body by memory already. I threw my head back and moaned. The feel of him had me intoxicated within seconds. I was already seeing stars.

He put a hand under my leg and brought it up over his shoulder, and with the other, he held me upright by the ass as he devoured my folds. I pressed onto the back of his head harder as I moved my hips in rhythm with his tongue. Fuck, I could never get tired of the way he licked me.

"Deeper," I cried when he thrust his tongue inside me, and he complied. Thoughts spun in my head as my pleasure built up. All of my being was focused on him, the way he moved his tongue, the way he dug his fingers into my skin just like I liked. I was slowly losing control of my body and that feeling alone was pure bliss, no matter how wrong it was. This whole thing was wrong, and damn if that didn't just make it more intense.

He thrust his tongue in and out of me the way he shouldn't have been doing, and I cried out louder every second. My legs were shaking, and he must have felt it because he brought my other leg over his shoulder, too, before he stood up with his face still buried in my pussy, holding me up. I raised up my arms and touched the ceiling with my fingertips before he reached the bed and threw me in it. That short second of having his mouth off me was painful, but he didn't let me suffer for long. He climbed between my legs and pushed my skirt up like a man possessed, eyes bloodshot as he gripped my thighs and dove in again. I held him to me with both hands on the back of his head and moved my hips against his face, fucking his mouth until the orgasm ripped through me, breaking me to pieces. I don't know how he did it, how he knew how to lick me like that, but I'd never experienced anything more intense in my life. I'd been with five men before him, but nothing came even close to how he felt.

And as much as that pissed me off, he gave me no time to dwell on the past before he reached for the zipper of my skirt, then pulled it off me, throwing it to the floor. My crop top went next, and then we were both naked, panting as we looked at each other.

"Lay down," I ordered, and he grinned widely before he fell on the bed next to me. I'd been imagining riding him through all the drive here. It was time I made those fantasies come true.

He made himself comfortable as I put one leg over him and positioned myself on top of his hard cock. His hands were everywhere on me, touching and teasing, not as violent as before. He grabbed my hips and pushed his own up, pressing his cock to my wet folds, making me cry out again. I ran my hands over his chest, all those cuts and lines that decorated his skin like colors on a canvas, making for the sexiest chest I'd ever seen. Everything about him was burning hot, and I couldn't get enough of his heat.

Pushing myself a bit lower, I sat on his thighs and I grabbed his cock in my hands. I played with it a little bit, pressing it onto my pelvis as I jerked him off and he watched.

"You like that?" I asked, even though I already knew the answer. I could see it in his eyes, hear it in the way he moaned and growled.

"Yes, Damsel," he breathed. "I fucking love the sight of my cock in your hands."

I squeezed him tighter and watched how his breath left his lungs in a rush. I really liked that.

"I've been thinking about riding you the whole way here," I admitted. "I'm fucking crazy for your cock, Ax."

"Then ride it. Quit playing, Damsel," he begged and made to grab my hands, but I moved them away.

"I'll take my time," I told him, then slipped my legs between his and went lower, until my breasts were flush against his cock. I put it between them and squeezed them together hard. The moan that left him sounded like it was ripped right from his soul. He thrust his hips up and every time he did, I let out my tongue to lick the tip of him, keeping my breasts squeezed together tightly. I fucking loved the sight of it. When he did it to me two nights ago, I'd been blindfolded, but now, I saw all of it and I wanted to do it again. And again. And again.

But my pussy was on fire, and I needed him inside me right away, too. So, I climbed over him again, placed the tip of him at my entrance, then sat on him with all my strength.

"Fuck, the way you stretch me." All the fucking way. He filled every empty corner inside me.

"Clench your pussy, Damsel," he ordered, and I did. His head fell back on the pillow as he moaned, gripping my hips tightly as he held his up.

I began to move, slowly at first, before I picked up the pace. My clit rubbed on his pelvis, sending me right to the edge within seconds. I dug my fingers into his stomach, taking him as deep as he could go. I could move like that for days on him and never get tired.

My surroundings blurred and my skin was on fire as I rode him. I grabbed my hair and pulled it off my neck hoping to cool down a bit, and his hands moved up to my breasts instantly. He grabbed my nipples between his fingers and pinched hard. The way our bodies moved in perfect sync must have been a sin because it felt too good to be *good*. The orgasm had me wide open as it came over me, wrapping me up and sending me all the way to the clouds.

Before I knew it, Ax had sat up, his arms tightly locked around me as he thrusts his hips up, making my orgasm last a deliciously long time.

It only took him another minute to let go, too.

We held onto each other like we were lovers for real, and for the life of me, I couldn't bring myself to loosen my grip around his neck. He dug his fingers into my back, holding me to him, kissing my shoulder.

We stayed like that even after the high let us down, locked up in each other, just breathing each other in.

It was painful. I knew who he was. I'd seen him kill with my own eyes. I knew which coven he belonged to. I knew what would happen once we got back home. And that's why it hurt so much to be feeling for him. To be connected to him in this way. Because this hadn't been just sex. I don't know how I knew the difference, but I did.

Maybe it was the way we were desperate to hold each other close. Or maybe that sorcerer blood had messed me up more than I realized.

But when I let go of him, he refused to let go of me.

"Just give me a minute," he whispered under my neck, and my traitorous arms must have had a mind of their own because they locked around him again and squeezed hard.

I don't know how long we stayed like that, but eventually, he lay down on the bed, taking me with him, his arms never loosening. And I took it. There was a part of me that screamed at me to get up, get the hell out of there, but I still stayed on his chest like that, eyes closed, mind almost completely empty. Just this once, I wanted to allow myself to want what I wanted, consequences be damned. I just wanted to get lost in the rhythm of his heartbeat, the heat of his skin, the touch of his hands.

But even that minute had to come to an end. We were enemies. In our world, our covens were enemies. It had been a mistake to give in to him. It had been a mistake to let him touch me. I never imagined that it could come to this, though. It *never* had in the past. I never connected to anyone. I'd only ever connected to Ezra and look where that got me. That I'd want to lay in this man's arms for an eternity had never even occurred to me. That he'd know exactly how to touch me, how to kiss me, how to *speak* to me with his hands, had never seemed possible when I first met him.

I used to love being touched. A kiss on the neck. A touch on my back. A tight hug. It had always been the form of communication I understood best.

But after Ezra, I never wanted to be touched again. I never wanted to *feel* anyone. And now this guy was here, as if *he knew*. He talked a lot, but he really spoke to me when he touched me like this—gently, fingers brushing against my skin, small kisses on my head while he held me to his chest.

And I understood a little too well.

"Stay," he whispered when I'd had enough of my own self and pushed myself up. I looked down at him, at his wide blue eyes sparkling, and I saw myself in them, too.

"I can't."

Squeezing my eyes shut, I rolled off him and jumped off the bed. I grabbed my clothes from the floor and walked out the door without getting dressed first. If someone was in the hallway, I couldn't care less.

Too much. It had gone too far. And I needed to back the fuck off immediately.

21

Some mornings, it was very hard to tell dreams apart from reality. I could hear myself mumbling and crying, and even though I knew I was dreaming, it felt so real. The sobs that shook my chest felt authentic, and I somehow convinced myself that I was there again.

I was six and I had parents, people who loved me, a home, and then...they came.

My eyes popped open when a cold hand touched my cheek. I only had a second to register Marie's face, her eyes wide as she backed away from me slowly, her hand that had touched my cheek still raised.

I sat up and looked around the small room, struggling to remember how I got there.

"You...you were talking in your sleep."

I turned to Marie again, where she sat on the twin bed with her brother. They both looked at me like they were expecting me to jump them any second. Their fear of me made my stomach twist.

I'm not going to hurt you! I screamed at them in my mind.

"Just bad dreams," I said out loud instead, trying to rub the sleep from my eyes. This was what happened when I didn't go to sleep at least a bit drunk. The fucking *dreams,* as if the memories during the night weren't enough.

I stood up to go to the bathroom, my head weighing a thousand pounds.

"Grandma used to say that dreams always come to us when the universe is trying to tell us something."

I stopped mid-stride and looked at the boy. It was the first time he was actually speaking to me. His eyes, a copy of his sister's, were wide as he looked at me. Right now, he wasn't afraid. He was just curious.

It calmed *me* down a bit, too.

"Well, whatever the universe is trying to tell me, it's doing a damn shitty job," I mumbled and locked myself in the bathroom, regret already rearing its ugly head.

Poor kid. I didn't mean to be a bitch, but he had no idea what he was talking about. What I saw in that dream had already happened. It wasn't going to happen again. I just needed enough alcohol to get it out of my head and I'd be fine.

I was still washing my face when I heard Ax knocking on the door. Marie went to answer it. I smelled him perfectly and the hair on my forearms stood at attention instantly. The night before had been a mistake. I should have never gone to him. I should have never let him touch me like that. Why was it so easy for me to convince myself to do what *I knew* I shouldn't do when it came to him? Too damn complicated.

Now, the reminder of his touch was all over my body, and my skin still burned with invisible flames.

Yeah, I was gonna need *a lot* of alcohol tonight.

He didn't look at me differently when I walked out of the bathroom, but he did look different himself. A different pair of jeans were on him, these looser than the ones he'd ruined in the fights. They didn't look new and they smelled faintly of someone else, but they were clean enough. And the jacket he had on now was a dark brown, the leather worn around the hems, definitely not new. But it fit him perfectly, and as much as I wanted to ask who he bought it from, I kept my mouth shut. It wasn't my business.

He didn't say anything to me when we got our things and left the inn. He didn't say anything when we got in the car, either, just insisted that he wanted to be the one driving again. He didn't mention the night before at all, as if he'd already forgotten about it, and I was relieved. He knew that it had been a mistake, too. And it was never going to happen again.

"Is he your boyfriend?"

My entire body froze when I turned to the backseat to look at Marcus. We were parked at a gas station for gas, and Ax was in the store getting us some snacks. I'd almost forgotten he and Marie were even there.

"No," I said to Marcus, a bit too harshly.

"Your mate?"

His sister nudged him with her elbow, but he didn't mind. He still held my eyes.

I forced a smile on my face. "I don't have a mate, kid."

At that, he looked confused. Which made me wonder about what he'd heard the night before.

Had he been awake while I was in Ax's room?

Fuck, the reminder had my heart racing instantly.

"What's it like in the Hidden Realm?" Marie asked after a minute, and I was thankful for it.

"Just like any other place around here. There's a wall surrounding it, but you don't ever get to see it. The city is huge," I said. "We have stores, diners, restaurants, clubs—the whole shindig."

"Will we be safe there?" she asked.

"From sorcerers—yes." No sorcerer would dare cross the gates with that many vampires holed up in that place.

"And vampires?" Marcus asked.

"Vampires, too." Through the rearview mirror, I saw him give a look to his sister. He didn't believe me. "Hey—the rulers of our covens sent us here for you. Their word is law. You're under their protection. Nobody can hurt you." At least of that I was sure.

"What if we want to leave after a while?" Marie's voice was small, as if she were terrified of the words that came out of her mouth.

I flinched, but my back was turned to them so they didn't see it. "You're gonna have to talk to the covens about that."

"We just want to get away from sorcerers for a while, until things calm down. Until they forget about me," she continued. "We're not going to stay in the Realm forever."

Ah, shit. "You don't know that. Maybe you'll like the Realm." There's no reason anyone who wasn't a vampire would like the

Realm, but she was. Half, but still. Her brother, on the other hand...

Thankfully, before she could say something else, Ax came out of the store with two paper bags in his hands. He put them both on my lap as soon as he opened the driver's door, and the first thing I saw was the big bottle of vodka.

"Is that for me?"

He grinned. "Unless the siblings are alcoholics, too, then yes."

"Jerk," I muttered, but I was smiling. He knew very well that vampires can't become alcoholics. Our bodies regenerated too fast. I didn't crave alcohol because my body needed it—it all had to do with my mind.

"Next stop, North Dakota," he said when he drove the van ahead. "Let's just hope we don't run into trouble." And he gave me a sneaky look. I knew he meant the opposite—he *lived* for trouble.

"Don't worry. We'll see it coming," I said, shaking my head, and took a sip of the vodka. It was strong. It burned my throat on the way down perfectly, but it did leave a bad taste in my mouth. Nobody had ever brought me alcohol without my asking before. Ever. I always got my own.

"That we will," Ax said, eyes on the windshield.

Forcing my mind to clear, I settled on my seat with a big bag of chips on my lap, and the bottle of vodka in my hand. It was going to be a long ride.

***

Our next stop was *not* North Dakota. We drove for three hours straight without trouble. Then we stopped by a gas station again because Marcus and Marie needed to use the restroom. I wanted to stretch my legs for a bit, so I hopped out of the car and walked around the deserted road in the middle of nowhere before I sat down on the asphalt for a bit. The siblings wouldn't be long now.

The night was quiet, the sky over us dotted with a billion stars. I could see all of them because there were no skyscrapers and barely any buildings in the distance, except the old gas station. It was peaceful. I breathed easy. This was as close as I could get to real freedom.

Eventually, Ax got out of the car, too. I hugged my knees to my chest, perfectly aware of his every movement. He sat on the asphalt, too, right in front of me, legs spread to the sides of mine, elbows on his knees. He looked at the sky with me for a while in completely silence.

But my eyes went back to him in no time. I looked at his face, at his wide eyes as he stared at the stars, at his parted lips and his naked torso underneath the jacket. At the scars all over his skin, the tissue a couple shades lighter than his skin tone. I don't know why I found them so damn fascinating, but when I reached out a hand to touch them, I expected him to slap it away. I'd already asked him about them, and he hadn't told me, which was fine. It was none of my business, anyway.

He didn't slap my hand away, though. My fingertips ran over the lines of his scars, and I felt the breath leaving his lungs as the muscles on his stomach tightened. I heard his heart picking up the beating, too, just a tiny bit. I liked it, despite how fucked up it was.

"My parents got killed when I was a kid," he whispered after a little while, slowly lowering his head to look at my hand, at my fingertips tracing his scars. "I was sold to a mafia boss in New York City. He trained me for years, then put me to fight in underground cages." My stomach twisted in a million knots as he smiled. "I made him a lot of money."

"Did you want to?" I asked, as the images of him as a little kid, training to fight, and then later locked in a fucking cage with some monster, crossed my mind. It made me feel too many things at once.

"Sometimes," he said, then shook his head. "It didn't really matter what I wanted. I was his slave. He owned me."

It was like someone had stabbed me straight through the heart with my own knives. His eyes were wide, and there was a sadness in them I'd never seen before. It made him so *real*—a man, not just a murderous vampire who pulled hearts out of chests while he laughed. A man who simply became what life made him.

Slowly, he raised his hand and touched my knuckles while I continued to trace the scars on his chest.

"How old were you when your parents were killed?" I asked. Not that it mattered. I was just curious.

"Nine," he said, and the way my heart skipped a beat…it *did* matter.

"Why?" I whispered.

"My dad owed some money to the wrong people. He was just trying to make ends meet, and he couldn't pay them back in time. So, they came."

My eyes closed for a second. *They came.*

"And the people who killed them?"

"Oh, they're all dead." The way he smiled was heartbreaking. It showed me a side of him I couldn't have even imagined if I tried. He was damaged. Maybe just as damaged as me. I saw it as clear as the night sky and the stars blinking in it. It messed with my head even more than before, and suddenly, I *wanted* to tell him, too. For the first time in my life, I wanted to speak those words out loud willingly.

So, I did.

"My parents were killed when I was six," I said. "My whole town, actually."

I felt his eyes on my face, burning me, but I kept mine on his torso still.

"Who?"

"Vampires," I said, and it wasn't as hard as I thought it would be. It wasn't as hard to talk about it as it always was. "Jones found me. Took me in. Saved me."

"Did Jones turn you?" I shook my head. "Who did?"

I thought about it for a second. "I don't really remember."

Ax sighed. "When was that?"

"The night my parents died." His heart skipped a beat right under my fingertips.

"What was that like?" he whispered.

"It was…difficult." The pain of the shift and the blood cravings, the whispers in my head and the constant need to stay in control for fear of what might come out. They always had me feeling completely out of place. I never belonged anywhere, no matter how hard I tried. I was just too different.

"And the vampires?" Ax asked.

"They're all dead, too."

I wanted to say more. I wanted to tell him everything—but how could I?

How could I tell him that I'd killed them myself at the age of *six*?

Or whatever lived inside me had. Fuck, I was probably the only person in existence who had turned herself into a vampire. By accident, but still.

"Does it still hurt?" Ax asked, and my stomach twisted again.

"Sometimes. Other times it's hard to remember." And I couldn't say which one I preferred.

"Yeah. I forgot their faces a long time ago." He shook his head as if the idea was absurd, even though he knew it was real. "Come here," he whispered, and I moved without having to think about it. I dragged myself closer to him, then put my legs over his thighs. He crossed his under me, pulling me up until I sat on his ankles. We were chest to chest, arms around each other, and we just breathed. I rested my head on his shoulder and kept my eyes closed, focused on his heartbeat, on the heat of his body. He started to move his hands over my back, slowly, bringing one under my shirt and bra, pressing his palm between my shoulders blades to feel my heart beating.

A sigh escaped me—his touch felt so good. *I got you,* it said.

Then, he nudged my jaw up with his nose, and I moved my head up just slightly, and felt his lips on the side of my neck. It was barely a kiss—more just his lips pressed to my skin, warm and alive. *I understand,* it said.

I reached out my hand to touch his face, his eyes, his nose, his lips, the scar on his temple. We'd never really kissed, Ax and I. We had sex, and we kissed a couple times during it, but never a true kiss. Never *just* a kiss. And I wanted to try it. I wanted to know what he tasted like. So that when all of this was over, and life went back to normal, I could remember it. I wanted to remember it. I didn't want to forget, even if it was painful. So, I leaned my head back just a bit, until I could reach his lips with mine.

His were warm, soft, and the way he kissed me back was gentle. He held me tight against his chest, and we played with each other for a while, tasting, savoring, exploring. It wasn't sexual. It didn't set my body on fire. It just touched my soul. His tongue came out to lick my lips, and the kiss deepened, but it was still gentle. It was still slow—everything a kiss is supposed to be. We were one. Our hearts beat the same, our minds were empty, and our bodies knew exactly how to hold onto one another. It was the most beautiful thing I'd ever experienced in my life.

When we heard the siblings' footsteps approaching us, we stopped. Forehead to forehead, we looked at each other for a moment, saying what can't be said with words. We were a mistake. We were not meant for one another. My walls were unbreakable. His even worse. We were far too broken to be able to give anything good out into the world. But life somehow brought us here and that was okay. We'd always have the memories.

I pushed myself out of his arms while the siblings watched us from the other side of the car.

"I'm gonna use the restroom, too," I said and smiled at Ax. He smiled back. A brand-new smile this time.

I didn't need to use the restroom, but I went anyway. Because despite everything, I still couldn't let him see my tears.

22

When we reached North Dakota, we decided to take the day off. Marie and Marcus had slept in the backseat, but Ax and I still needed to close our eyes. He said he didn't sleep, but he did that one time. And even without sleeping, his body still needed the rest.

We'd be safe close to the border, and tomorrow, we'd reach the Realm in just a few hours. Everything would be over for real.

We chose a motel with the least number of cars in the parking lot. We settled on the second floor, and I had to sleep on the floor because there was just one queen-sized bed in our room. Ax was next door.

"You can sleep with Marie. I'll be fine on the floor," Marcus said, smiling.

"I'm a vampire, kid. I'm not gonna feel anything as soon as the sun rises. Don't you worry about me," I said, running my hand through his hair. I liked the kid. I liked his taste in music. He read books, too. I'd loved listening to his stories on the ride here. They had distracted me perfectly, too.

"I'm a gentleman," he said. "It's no bother."

Marie gave him an adoring smile from the bed.

"I'm glad you're a gentleman, but I'm no lady. I refuse your offer—thank you very much, sir," I said with a bow, and went for the bathroom. His chuckle made me smile, too.

The showerhead was rusted, and the plastic of the shower floor had turned yellow a long time ago. Even the mirror over the sink was broken in three places. Out of all the shitty motel rooms I'd been in the last few days, this definitely took the cake. But the water was clean and the toilet worked, at least.

Marcus insisted again that he sleep on the floor, but I would never let him. There would be bugs around here, and I didn't want them crawling all over his body. They wouldn't dare come near mine. Hopefully. If they did, I'd just squash them.

Eventually, he and his sister settled on the bed, and I put a blanket on the dirty carpet. They gave me one of the pillows, too, so it was comfortable enough. I closed my eyes, hoping unconsciousness would take me soon. And I listened to them whispering to one another.

They talked about their grandparents and about home. About school. Marcus was worried about his friend who was apparently bullied at school when he wasn't around. He was worried about school, too—about his future as an architect. There were no schools in the Hidden Realm, but there were certain people who dealt with all kinds of things. Maybe he could become an apprentice or something.

Except...he was a sorcerer.

Unease gnawed at my insides. How was he going to make it in the Realm? And would Jones and the other coven leaders let them leave after a while?

I didn't know. But I would be there. I would find out soon enough. And if I didn't like it, I could do something about it.

"Damsel."

I heard the voice slipping in my ear as if from a dream. My eyes popped open.

"Damsel."

Ax was whispering my name from the room next door. I looked at the siblings on the bed, still whispering their stories. They couldn't hear him. Not even Marie.

But I did.

I closed my eyes again—it would be just another mistake to go to him right now. I knew what he wanted because it was exactly what *I* wanted, too. I wanted to be with him. And it was wrong.

But he kept whispering my name over and over again, and the more time passed, the more pissed off I got. He didn't get to do this. He knew very well that what we were doing was absurd. He was a Sangria. I was a Redwood. If anybody found out about us at home, they were going to have a fit. Jones was going to have my fucking head.

Yet he wouldn't stop.

I jumped to my feet, so mad I saw red.

"I'll be right back," I told the siblings and walked out the door. Ax opened his the same second.

"What?" I spit. He only wore his jeans, but at least he wasn't naked. And without a word, he stepped to the side to tell me to walk in. I wouldn't have, but I didn't want any of the humans in the rooms next to ours hearing us.

So, I went inside.

The second he closed the door, he had me pressed against the wall, hands gripping my hips tightly.

"Ax, no," I breathed, eyes closed because despite the anger, I still loved the way his body felt against mine.

"It's our last night," he whispered in my ear.

"And it's a mistake—just like the others." He knew this very well, too. I didn't have to explain it to him.

But his grip around my hips only tightened. "I *need* you, Damsel," he said, then bit the side of my neck with so much urgency, my knees trembled. "I need you."

He needed me.

Every ounce of anger I'd felt until now drifted away, just like that. My heart squeezed and my hands shook. Tears I would never shed pricked the back of my eyes, as if my body already knew that I wouldn't walk away. Not now, when he needed me. And I needed him.

Grabbing his face in my hands, I pushed him back until I could see his eyes. They were bloodshot, no sign of the man he had been at that gas station anywhere on him. He just looked starved.

I kissed his lips, and I didn't feel their softness—just his need when he bit my bottom one.

"Then fuck me like you hate me," I whispered against his mouth. I didn't want touching. I didn't want gentle. It was just sex.

And he did exactly that.

His hands were under my skirt and he pulled my panties to the side before he pulled me up. My ankles locked around his hips immediately while he struggled to undo his zipper. We kissed like savages—both of us, biting and sucking until we drew blood. He didn't take his time. As soon as his cock was free, he brought it to my entrance and pushed his hips up until he was inside me all the way.

I bit his shoulder to keep from screaming, and he pressed me harder against the wall. I held onto his neck while he put his hands on the wall and thrust into me with all his strength. My body was on fire, and my pussy clenched around him just like he liked. He moaned into my neck and kept on going, until it felt like I had fire for real burning somewhere in my chest.

He slammed me against the wall over and over again, nearly destroying me from the inside. His hands came around me again, and he squeezed me so hard, I thought my ribs would break. Nothing about this was gentle. No touching or slow kissing—just raw need.

But…something was wrong.

That fire that kept on burning me from the inside was spreading unlike before, and when it reached my head, it turned my mind completely numb.

"Ax," I breathed because I needed to know if he felt it, too. But he didn't stop thrusting his cock inside me as deep as it would go. I held onto his neck, dug my fingers in his skin, tried to focus on the pleasure, but instead my focus went to my jaw. To my upper teeth. To the fangs that were slowly making their way out.

No.

My eyes opened, but I couldn't even see the room. I couldn't see anything but my fangs in my mind's eye.

The mating instinct. I wanted to bite his neck so bad, it hurt. It hurt worse than any magic I'd ever felt in my body, any broken bone, any wound I'd ever endured. The sound of his blood rushing in his veins was *everything*. I wanted to bite him. I wanted to claim him. I wanted him to be mine for the rest of eternity.

So fucking wrong.

I'd been with Ezra seven years, and every time we'd been together, I'd waited for this. I'd welcomed it. I'd *dreamed* about the day I'd get the instinct to bite him, take his blood, become his while he became mine forever.

And it had never come.

Now, as Ax slammed into me, I felt all of him, every little inch. I heard his blood and his racing heart, and I wanted it all. I wanted everything. I wanted *him*.

It took every ounce of willpower in my body to close my eyes again and grit my teeth. We were *not* lovers. We didn't care about one another. It was just sex. We were not mates. I didn't want a mate—and he didn't want one, either.

Wrong, wrong, wrong.

When he came, he cried out, face buried in my hair as he nearly broke me again with his hands. I took it, holding onto his body with all my strength until he stopped thrusting inside me. He let out a long breath and his arms loosened from around me, but I couldn't let go. He couldn't see my fangs. He couldn't know.

So, I held onto his neck for a while longer, until my heartbeat slowed down a bit and my blood stopped rushing. Until my fangs began to retreat back inside my jaw.

Tears filled my eyes, and these ones were too powerful to hold back.

"Damsel," Ax whispered, and it was a pleading. If I gave him the chance, he'd ask me to stay again.

I couldn't. *I wouldn't.*

So, with my head down, I unlocked my limbs from around him and pushed him away with all my strength. I didn't look in his eyes. I didn't wait for him to say anything else. I just opened the door and walked out as fast as my legs could carry me.

***

I lost everything once when I was a kid.

Then I lost everything a second time.

But none of it compared to the feeling that had taken over me last morning before I passed out at sunrise. The same one that had perfect hold of me now, too.

We were on our way again, clean and fed, and I couldn't even look at Ax. I couldn't breathe in through my nose, afraid his scent alone would get my mating instinct all riled up.

I'd never really *had* him, yet the feeling of loss that pressed against my chest right now was worse than anything I'd ever gone through. Especially when he kept looking my way every few seconds, as if he were expecting something from me. When he knew—*he knew* that there was nothing I could give him.

So, I just watched the road and drank. Then drank some more.

"How about some music?" Marcus said from the back of the van.

"Sure, kid," Ax said before he turned on the radio. Just the sound of his voice made chills rush down my back.

But he turned the volume up, and the music helped. The alcohol helped, too. And for the next hour, neither of us said a single word.

23

"We need to talk."

The whisper was so low, I barely heard it over the music. I turned to look at Ax, only for a second. The sight of his face hurt now, too.

How in the fuck had I let things get so complicated so fast?

"What?" I meant to sound bitter, but I just sounded afraid instead.

"We need to talk, Damsel." And he didn't sound happy about it.

I looked back at the siblings to find each leaning against the opposite window, sleeping.

"Talk about what?" I said, only to try to postpone the inevitable. Yeah, I was afraid. I was scared shitless—and already pissed off.

"You know what," Ax said. "You can't even fucking look at me."

I swallowed hard. "There's nothing to talk about."

"Fuck that," he spit. "There's plenty to talk about."

"They can hear you."

"They're sleeping."

"And you're about to wake them."

"I don't give a shit," he said. "Let them hear. I don't care."

"Then what do you care about?"

I felt his eyes when they stopped on my face, but I didn't dare meet them.

"I just want to know," he finally said.

"Know what?"

"How you feel, Damsel."

If someone had put a knife in my heart and twisted it, it probably wouldn't feel like this.

"Damsel," he said, but my eyes were stuck outside on the road. We were passing by a small town, with identical houses on either side, and it was two in the morning, so there were no people out. No fucking distractions.

"What the fuck does it even matter?" I spit, so angry my hands were shaking. "You're Sangria. I'm Redwood. We're fucking enemies."

"I don't give a shit what you are or what I am," he said.

I shook my head. "The covens—" but he didn't even let me finish.

"I will kill each and every one of them. I'll burn the whole fucking Realm to the ground if I have to, so long as you're with me."

My eyes squeezed shut. I believed every word he said because he meant it. He absolutely would, and I didn't know what the hell to do with it. He'd caught me completely off guard. I wasn't prepared for this.

"Look at me, damn it!" he hissed.

I couldn't. I could barely fucking breathe.

I needed air. I needed distance. I needed—

Everything suddenly came to a halt.

The car was moving, and then it wasn't. It suspended on air for a split second before it moved *up*. I saw it all play in slow motion, when the road disappeared and instead the night sky was right outside the windshield. I felt my body moving up and down as the car turned and turned, then spun in the air as if it weighed nothing. The screams coming from the back pierced my ears, and then I saw the houses behind the windshield, and they turned and turned until the car hit the ground again, upside down.

It was a while before the vibrations stopped, and I was able to make out my surroundings. I was hanging on the car seat by the seatbelt. My fangs were out, my demons rioting in my head, and I could still hear the car wheels turning, as if that had any importance.

"Nikki, help me," Marie cried from the back, and I turned to see Ax pull the seatbelt apart with his hands, before he turned to mine.

"Help them," I said, and grabbed my own seatbelt to tear it off me. The second it let go, I fell on the roof of the car with the back of my neck. Ax was already outside, pulling the door of the car on Marcus's side off, and I kicked mine with all my strength, too. It flew off the hinges and slammed against the asphalt, still rolling by the time I came out. I opened Marie's door and pulled it off, too, before I grabbed her. Her leg was stuck under my seat, so she screamed bloody murder and her fingertips lit up with bright red smoke. I let her go and pushed back my seat to give her space to wiggle her leg from underneath it.

When she did, I pulled her by her warm hands and dragged her outside.

Ax was standing in front of the car. White smoke came out of the hood, rising to the sky. The smell in the air was unmistakably magic, and the closer I got to Ax, the more of it I felt.

Then, I saw the faint chalk lines on the asphalt he was looking at.

"Fucking sorcerers," he spit, looking ahead at the street.

Empty. There were heartbeats in the houses on our sides, but nobody seemed to be up. No lights turned on.

"They're not coming out." The people would have heard a crash like that even if they were sleeping. It wasn't just the crash when the car hit the invisible wall of magic someone had put up here for us, but when it slammed on the asphalt again, too. Everybody should have heard that. Everybody should have been out to see what was happening.

Unless…someone had either spelled them—or spelled the accident site to keep the sound from reaching them.

"What now?" Marie said, holding onto Marcus's hand tightly. "Are they here? I can't see anyone."

"They're here, all right. Let's keep moving," Ax said, and started walking ahead, more pissed by the second. He crossed through the chalk line without trouble. Even though it still smelled like magic, it had done its job. It had held us back, and now it had faded. I barely had time to grab my bag from the upside-down car and follow with Marcus and Marie right behind me.

My fangs were out, my body ready for whatever was coming our way. Because someone was coming. Someone had known we'd pass through here. And that's why we should have dropped the damn car at our last stop and continued on foot. That way, they wouldn't have caught us by surprise. We'd have seen them, smelled the magic. We'd have taken a different route. Fuck, Jones had been right.

"They're here," Ax said, giving me a pointed look before he started rushing down the street. I sniffed the air deeply, and he was right. I could smell the magic and the blood not too far away.

And we saw him just as we turned the street corner.

He sat on a folding chair right in the middle of the street, a burning cigar in one hand and a flask full of whiskey in the other—though it was hard to tell for sure because of all the magic surrounding him. He had a cowboy hat on, brown cowboy boots, and a bright smile on his face. He couldn't have been older than thirty, but there was a sharpness in his light brown eyes that made me wonder if his smooth skin was any indicator of his true age.

"Who the hell is that?"

"That's Jacob Thorne," Ax said, grinning ear to ear.

Jacob Thorne. I knew that name. I'd heard it—he was a sorcerer who hunted monsters that came out of the Veins. Sorcerers who turned rogue. Vampires who escaped the Realm, too.

"So that's who those guys meant," I said in wonder. The two sorcerers we'd seen on the street in Atlanta had warned us that *he* would be coming for us. It never occurred to me that they meant Jacob Thorne. I'd honestly forgotten he existed until now.

"Savage Ax," the sorcerer said, his voice loud, echoing in my ears. "I've been wondering when I'd have the pleasure of meeting you."

Ax smiled like he was looking at an old friend before he started walking closer. I dropped my bag on the ground and turned to Marie. "Don't move," I told her and followed Ax down the street. It was eerily quiet around us. Houses full of people, yet nobody came out. Unusual, to say the least.

Jacob Thorne smoked his cigar and smiled as we approached.

"The pleasure's all mine, Thorne," Ax said when we stopped about ten feet away from where he was sitting. "I've heard plenty about you." His voice was composed, like he wasn't afraid in the least.

"And I've heard plenty about you, too," Thorne said, shaking his cigar at us, perfectly at ease. "Tell me—is it true what they say about you?"

"I don't really know what they say about me," Ax said, and the sorcerer raised his light blond brows.

"Last night, he pulled a guy's heart out with his hand and thought it was just the funniest thing in the world," I said with a shrug. "I'd say the rumors are pretty true."

"I would have loved to witness that," the sorcerer said.

"You're about to witness it on yourself if you admit to being the one setting up that trap for us," Ax said, pointing his thumb back.

"I'm afraid that wasn't me," Thorne said, raising his hand. "Honest to God." And he was telling the truth.

Which meant he wasn't the only one here. My eyes searched the street, the quiet houses, but there was nobody there. Plenty of hearts beating nearby, but they could have been the humans sleeping in those houses.

"So, you just happened to be sitting here in the dark in the middle of the street right where we were about to pass by?" Ax asked, and he sounded genuinely curious.

"No, I was waiting for you to arrive, friend," Jacob said.

"Why's that?" I asked.

"See, my employer tells me that you took something that doesn't belong to you." He spoke and the smoke of his cigar left his lips in puffs. Then he leaned forward and rested his elbows on his knees.

"She's one of ours," Ax said.

"Of course, she isn't. She doesn't smell like your kind, does she?" Jacob said.

Sweat beads lined my forehead. I already knew that whatever this guy would say to us, I wouldn't like it.

"She doesn't smell like us because of the magic. She's a sorceress, too," I said, hoping that was all there was to it.

But Jacob shook his cigar at us again.

"You see, you can't make a vampire scent disappear for long, not even with magic. I got my nose. I got my magic, too. For example, I can smell both your scents on each other's bodies." He smiled. "Are you mated?"

What the actual fuck.

"None of your damn business," I hissed. How in the world could he smell our scents? He wasn't a damn vampire. Were there spells that could enhance his sense of smell like that for real, or was it just a guess?

"That is true," Jacob said, nodding. "But I'm afraid I'm going to need Ms. Graham now."

"She's coming with us," Ax told him. "One way or the other."

Jacob threw his cigar on the ground and took a swig of the whiskey in his silver flask. Then, he stood up.

"Okay, then. If you manage to kill me and my people, it's only fair," he said, and just then, we heard the footsteps. A lot of people who carried those hearts we'd heard until now were coming from between the houses on either side of us. Sorcerers—ten of them. They stopped right behind Jacob and his stupid fucking chair.

An ambush. Whether these sorcerers lived here or they'd been summoned especially for us wasn't relevant. They were here now, and they weren't going to just let us walk away.

A cold hand wrapped around mine and I turned to look at Ax.

"Damsel, I need you to run now. I'll keep them busy," he whispered to me.

"No," I said before he finished speaking. "They'll kill you." It wasn't the other sorcerers I was worried about—it was Jacob

Thorne. No man who *knew* Ax would be so at ease in his presence. There had to be a reason for it.

"It's okay," Ax said, eyes sparkling with mischief. "I've had a good run. I've met you. I'd say it was fine."

My heart squeezed tightly, and I gripped his fingers. "Fuck that. You're not dying." No fucking way in hell. Just the thought of it...*no*. I would rather let my demons out to roam freely. Screw the whole damn world—he wasn't going anywhere.

"Neither are you," Ax said, and he meant it.

I smiled. "Things might get heated up in a minute, you know."

"Nothing I love more than your heat, Damsel. It burns me better than fire," he said, touching my jaw with the tips of his fingers. If he only knew what kind of *heat* I was talking about, he wouldn't be so sure.

"It was nice knowing you, Savage Ax," I said, squeezing his fingers one more time before I let go.

"Surely not just *nice*," he said with a grin, then winked at me. I winked back.

We either died tonight or we survived. And both of us were good with either option.

He turned to Jacob, and I ran back to Marie and Marcus, both of them shaking with fear.

"What's going on? Are they going to let us through?" Marie whispered.

"Listen to me. I need you to grab Marcus and I need you to hide somewhere, okay? Set up a trap or something. Use your magic.

But don't come out until we come looking for you. Can you do that?"

Marie was already shaking her head. "But-but—"

"Marie, it's okay. We'll come find you. You just need to hide until we do."

"We'll hide," Marcus said, not an ounce of hesitation in his wide eyes. "Don't worry about us. We'll hide."

"Nothing's going to happen to you," I promised. "Just keep hidden."

Marie was still shaking her head, but Marcus had her by the hand. She would be okay—she had to be.

I turned to leave, feeling heavier by the second. I really wanted to stick to them, but if I left Ax alone now, we were all basically dead. That wasn't an option right now.

"Nikki," Marcus called, and when I turned my head, he waved. "Thank you."

With his sister's hand in his, he ran back where we came from.

Thank you. What if we died and these people found them, locked them in another basement somewhere? That *thank you* would have been for nothing.

"So, how do we do this?" Ax called, his voice loud and clear. I rushed to his side, two of my knives already in my hands. My mind was a mess of whispers, my chest shaking with how fast my heart was beating. Because I knew. My body knew. We weren't going to get through this on our own, Ax and I.

"Whichever way you want, friend," Jacob Thorne said, a big smile on his face. He took off his cowboy hat and threw it on the ground, showing us all of his face. He was a handsome bastard, but that wasn't going to matter in a second. "We got time."

"Any plan?" I asked Ax.

He turned to me. "Kill them as fast as you can."

It was a damn good plan. I was going to stick to it.

24

I was perfectly aware of my surroundings as I ran. I smelled the magic in the air, saw the glow on the sorcerers' fingers aimed at us, and the big daggers in the hands of Jacob Thorne.

Magic came at us at the same time—ten balls of colorful smoke. We were too far still, so it was easy to duck and move out of the way. Then I jumped as high as my body let me and landed right behind the sorcerers and Jacob, their backs still turned to us. They might have had magic, but they weren't nearly as fast as we were.

By the time I landed on the ground on one knee, I had my knives turned and ready, and I slammed my arms back with all my strength, catching two of the sorcerers in the back before they even had the chance to turn to me.

From then on, it was a chaos of magic and color, blood and body parts right there in the open.

Sorcerers came at me left and right, throwing their magic at me, some with knives, too. And others with guns. They shot their bullets, and I moved away every time. Bullets were too slow for me, hence why we didn't even use guns back home. Too easy to see them coming, and the sorcerers who'd brought them figured that out in no time. They all turned to their magic. I used my knives and my hands and feet to get them off me every time they came close. A big guy with long black hair tied up behind his head grabbed me by the throat while his hand was still glowing with yellow light, and his touch seared me. I hissed and tried to stab him on the side of his neck, but his other hand stopped me, so I pulled up my leg and hit him right where it hurt the most. A loud sigh left his lips but his hold on me didn't loosen. And I saw the other sorcerers coming for me on my sides, so I had to move quick. That's why I stabbed him right in the arm then leaned my head down and bit a good chunk right off his forearm, until his hand was no longer on me. I slammed the tip of my boot to his face so I could move back, a split second before the magic of the sorcerers coming from my sides collided with one another—and exploded.

The blast of magic hit me in the face and threw me back. I hit the ground with the back of my head and bright stars filled my vision, but it was nothing compared to the magic still hanging onto my skin. The pain had my mind ready to explode, too, but I gritted my teeth and resisted. Not yet. Not unless I was absolutely sure we couldn't handle these people on our own.

Just as I made it to my feet, another ball of blue smoke came whooshing right past me. I threw my knife forward without really looking, and it hit the sorcerer right in the cheek. His eyes rolled on his skull and he hit the ground on his knees. The woman who'd been by his side screamed and came at me with her glowing hands. I jumped up again when she was two feet away from me and slammed my boot onto her face with all my strength. She fell to the side, rolling, and green magic hit me in the chest just as my feet touched the ground again.

My turn to scream as the pain set every nerve end in my body on fire. My legs shook, but by some miracle I didn't fall. It was like moving underwater when I reached for another knife strapped to my thigh. But when my hand wrapped around the handle, a body slammed onto my side and threw me down to the ground—the sorceress I'd kicked in the face. And she was still screaming right in my ear.

My demons went mad. She dug her fingernails into my skin and scratched the hell out of my neck. She had lost it just like I was about to. It took effort to slam my forehead to her nose, then push her to the side because that magic was still inside me and it had only begun to fade. Once she rolled off my body, I sat up and slammed my knife in her chest four times as she screamed, before another blast of magic hit me on the back.

Goddamn sonovabitch. They just wouldn't stop coming, and I was so tired of trying to keep control.

Pushing myself on my side, I tried to stand, tried to see, and it took a lot of blinks to make out the movement in front of me. Ax and Jacob were still fighting in the middle of the street, both of them bloody. His fucking daggers glowed orange as he swung them at Ax, and when Ax's fist connected with the man's jaw, it didn't go through. It was like he had some protective shield about his body, and every time Ax hit or kicked him, he couldn't reach him. What the fuck kind of magic was that?

But that wasn't all.

Behind them, at the beginning of the street, I could see someone else. I could hear another scream.

Marcus's.

My instincts were on high alert again instantly. Through the corner of my eye, I saw the two sorcerers gathering their magic between their hands, about to aim at me.

"Ax!" I shouted as I jumped to my feet, just to give him a heads up. He would see me running.

I ran with all my speed past the sorcerers, past him and Jacob, to get to Marcus. To get to Marie, unconscious, hanging onto the shoulder of a vampire I knew. A vampire of the Agana coven. I'd seen him in bars before—he loved alcohol just as much as I did. And he was about to make a run for it with Marie on his shoulder, while Marcus screamed and called my name, chasing after them.

I reached them slower than I'd have liked—there was still magic inside me, weighing me down.

"Drop her, fuckface," I hissed, breathing heavily, no longer an ounce of patience in my body.

"Rot in hell," the asshole spit and threw something at me—a knife, smaller than the ones I used. It was easy to lean my head to the side while it went past me. Easy to move, then duck, and bury both my knives in his thighs. He hissed, then screamed when I pulled the knives up all the way to his hips while they were still inside him. He grabbed my hair and tried to yank me to the side, but I was done with this bullshit. So, I just slammed right onto him, and the three of us went to the ground. Marcus grabbed Marie's hands and pulled her to the side while the vampire and I rolled a couple times, until I dug my knife in his stomach. Once he stopped rolling, I sat on him and didn't stop stabbing him until my arms threatened to give.

He was no longer moving. His heart was torn to pieces.

But Marie was in Marcus's arms a few feet away.

"Is she alive?" I asked when I stood up, pushing my hair out of my face.

"Yes, just unconscious," Marcus said, slapping his sister's cheek, trying to get her to wake up.

I turned to the fight again, only to see Ax fighting Jacob, and another four sorcerers throwing magic at him every few seconds. He couldn't move away fast enough, not when those glowing blades kept coming at him, too.

Wiping some blood from my mouth, I took in a deep breath and sprinted all the way to them. I slammed both knives on the back of the sorcerer about to summon his green magic between his hands. And once he was on his knees, I stabbed him on the back of his neck, too, just to make sure he wouldn't get up again. I moved closer to Ax and turned my back to him while the other three sorcerers came for me.

"More," he said, and I heard his voice, but I didn't know what he meant. I kept on fighting the sorcerers, using my body as a shield to keep the magic away from him while he fought Jacob. But I had to jump away from a sorcerer's knife and land behind him so I could take his feet from under him. Once he was down, I could see ahead and understood what Ax meant.

Seven other sorcerers were waiting in a perfect line barely ten feet away from us.

The one in front of my feet tried to get up, and I slammed my foot on his back, putting him down again. Another wrapped his arm around my neck from behind and pulled me, stabbing at the side of my waist three times before I bit his forearm and slammed my head back on his nose.

When he loosened his grip around me, I pulled him by the arm and picked him up. He was a heavy bastard, but I didn't have a choice.

"Get down!" I shouted, and Ax immediately ducked. I threw the body of the sorcerer forward, and he slammed right onto Jacob Thorne.

My legs were shaking. My arms were shaking. I could barely see straight.

"Ax," I whispered, and he was by my side as we moved back a couple of steps just to give ourselves a second.

"We're okay, Damsel," he said, but we weren't. He was bleeding in too many places, and he was breathing heavily, too. He must have been tired.

"I need you to make sure they make it to the Realm safe," I told him, holding onto his arm, eyes on Jacob and the other sorcerers as they prepared to attack us again.

"We'll take them together," Ax said.

"No." I stepped in front of him, grabbed his face in my hands. "I need you to promise me that you will keep them safe no matter what, okay?"

As if he saw something in my eyes, he was suddenly perfectly alert. "Damsel," he warned.

"Just promise me."

"I promise," he said without hesitation.

I kissed his bloody lips. "I fucking hate your guts."

And he smiled. "I hate you more."

I pushed him back. "Go."

"I'm not going anywhere." He tried to come closer again, but I pushed him harder, throwing him back a couple steps.

"*Go!*"

"What is happening over there?" Jacob Thorne said from behind me, and I turned to him, so furious I could burn holes right through that magic that shielded him. The asshole was smiling.

I smiled, too. "You should have left us alone."

"And we will—if you give us Marie Graham," the asshole said. "She belongs with us."

"She's one of ours. I saw it myself," I said as my head buzzed and buzzed, the pain so sharp it threatened to cut me wide open.

But if Jacob saw it, he didn't give a shit.

"She's not a vampire," he spit. "She was merely touched."

Everything inside me came to a halt in a split second. I couldn't even hear the sound of my own heart beating. "What?"

"She's been touched by a Vein spirit," he said. "She's not a vampire. We can help her."

A Vein spirit. *Touched*.

That night almost thirty years ago, when they came for us, when I saw my parents get slaughtered, something happened. Something…*came* to me. Something made a nest inside my mind, right before a vampire latched onto my neck, intending to drink me dry.

Something turned me, made me into something else. Something that could kill seven grown vampires and cut their bodies to pieces.

Touched.

Except vampires *can't* get touched, which was why Jones's theory was ridiculous. If I were really touched, I wouldn't have survived the shift. I would have died. And as for Marie…it had occurred to me, hadn't it? I'd thought about her being touched, too, in the beginning, but it hadn't made any sense. She'd literally grown fangs in front of my eyes. She didn't look *possessed* at all like someone with a foreign spirit inside them would. No—there had to be some other explanation, and I'd find it myself if I actually got out of here with my life.

"You understand," Jacob Thorne said, lips stretching to a smile. "You understand, don't you?"

Did it even matter?

"I promised Marie that I'd keep her safe," I said, more to myself than to him. If their version of *helping* her was to lock her in a fucking basement, no thank you. Abraham Jones could help her better. He'd never locked me in a basement before. He wouldn't do it to Marie, either, even if what this asshole said was true.

"You can't keep her safe. Not in the Realm," Jacob said, as if he knew exactly what he was talking about.

"Damsel, move," Ax whispered from behind me.

But I couldn't. I *wouldn't* move, not now. It was very clear to me that this man was not just going to let us get away. If we ran, he'd chase us. He wouldn't give up. The sorcerers that we could actually hurt were a different story, but not him. Neither I nor Ax could stop him alone.

So, I just turned my head back. "Go," I said for one last time.

And then *I* let go, too.

25

I spent every waking moment of my life trying to keep what was inside me under control. I'd slipped three times—once when I couldn't keep the whispers at bay. The other two times when they had tried to *teach me how to control it. It*—like it was a weapon they could wield instead of a monster, perfectly capable of rational thought. Despite my protests, they'd still made me try.

And all those times, I'd killed.

I'd killed mercilessly. I'd been brutal. A proper monster, something a true vampire could never be.

Yet the Redwood coven had never killed *me* for it. They were damn fools for that, but at least right now, I was glad they hadn't. Let Jacob Thorne kill me instead. I'd have gone leaving something good behind me this time, at least. I'd have helped someone in need of help. Which was all any of this was ever about.

I'd just…forgotten through the years.

Or maybe I'd willingly chosen to ignore it every time I filled my body with all the alcohol it could take. Either way, my eyes were wide open now.

And it felt *good*.

Gods, it felt so good to let go, to stop trying to shut the voices up, keep the demons locked inside me. Without my sheer will standing in their way, they came out. They took over my mind and my body, transforming me from the inside out.

Everybody held their breath as they watched me become a monster right in front of their eyes.

I'd only ever seen my reflection once in the training rooms in the coven castle. It had just been me, Ivan, and Master Ferrera when I'd chosen to give up control because they thought they could handle me. They thought they could *explore* me. I'd seen my face in the reflection in the windows. I looked like me still, except my skin was covered in black veins. My eyes turned completely black. My hair, too. My fingers became longer and grew claws at the tips. My body shrunk in size and my back arched all the way so that I didn't naturally stand straight—I was hunched over instead, on all fours. My toes developed claws, too, tearing up my boots. My skin became thicker, and my thirst deeper, my movements faster than that of a vampire.

"Holy Mother of God," one of the sorcerers behind Jacob whispered as she made a cross.

Jacob's eyes were wide open, lips parted. The sight of him didn't scare me now that I was *free*, standing on all fours right in front of him.

"Damsel?" Ax breathed from behind me, and I turned to look at him, just for a second. Just so he could see my face. He knew me better than everyone in the world now, and I wanted him to see this face of mine, too, before he left.

"Go!" My voice was transformed, too—that of a monster rather than vampire, almost robotic.

And as much as I'd have liked to push him back just to make sure he got moving, I wasn't in complete control of my body anymore. Whoever made me into this creature had its focus on Jacob and the sorcerers more than on Ax. When I jumped, I saw everything in slow motion. I felt the air, felt the movement of my limbs, and I landed right on Jacob's chest, taking him down.

For once in my life, my thoughts were in perfect sync with the creature, and we both wanted his fucking face cut off. But every time my claws connected with the magic protecting him, sparks flew, and I couldn't reach his skin at all, though I used all of my strength.

Jacob was terrified. So terrified that for long moments, he simply let me try to kill him as he watched.

Then I smelled the magic coming for me. It was so slow to my eyes now. So easy to move away from it, feel the heat of it as it passed me by. I jumped off Jacob and in front of the sorcerers, watching them for a second.

I wasn't sure what they saw when they looked at me, but they all turned their backs on me and started to run.

No time to waste. Grabbing the last knife I had in my holster strapped to my thigh, I held it up over my head with both hands and slammed it onto Jacob's chest. Sparks flew. It would have to give eventually. Whatever this was, he couldn't keep it going forever.

He knew it, too. That's why he finally pushed himself up and started to move his arms, those daggers with the orange blades buzzing with magic. I could feel so much more clearly when I was in this state. I *heard* the magic coming out of the engravings on those blades. The letters engraved on it were fueling the magic, and nothing short of making him drop them was going to turn it off.

It wouldn't have been a problem, except the sorcerers who had gone to hide behind one of the houses were throwing their magic at me from a distance. It was fucking annoying to whatever monster or spirit had hold of my body now, and it wanted them gone.

Jacob was still shocked at the sight of me, and he still swung his arms half-heartedly as his wide eyes took me in. So, when I jumped and slammed both feet on his shoulder to take him down, he didn't stop it. Couldn't stop it. He just hit the ground again and gave me enough time to look behind me and see that Ax, Marie and Marcus were already gone. The street was empty, save for the body of the vampire I'd killed, and those of the sorcerers we'd slaughtered. Good enough for me. I'd kept my promise.

Then I went after the sorcerers hiding behind the house. Once they were down, I could figure out a way to kill Jacob Thorne. His magic would run out eventually, and I'd be there to claw his heart out for hurting Ax. It would be the greatest pleasure of my miserable life.

The sorcerers were so slow, it was pathetic. One second I was standing on the shoulders of one of them, a guy with a long beard that I cut off with my claws while I dug them under his chin, and the next I was behind another, grabbing her by her long brown hair. I pulled her back and grabbed her head, twisted it to the side fast until I heard her bone breaking. Magic still came at me, but I was much faster than it. Much faster than they were at summoning enough of it to cause any real damage to me. I went through three more before I heard something moving behind me.

I turned, but it was too late.

Jacob Thorne was right in front of me, his glowing dagger inside my gut, the curved tip of it coming out my back.

I felt the pain. It consumed my mind completely. It burned so bad, there should have been fire bursting out from under my skin, but there wasn't. It was just Jacob, murmuring under his breath, waiting for me to collapse.

I wanted to let go, too. But whatever creature I'd become didn't care much for pain. My hands moved, and they slammed onto his chest hard. I heard the crack of the magic as he flew back and hit the ground a couple feet away, his dagger still buried inside me. But the blade was no longer glowing.

My lips stretched into a smile as I pulled it out. It hurt me. It felt like it should have paralyzed my whole body. All that magic…

But this other part of me that had come out didn't care much for it. It didn't find magic as painful as I did in my normal body.

I turned to the other side, to the waiting sorcerers, and threw the dagger forward without aim. It hit one of them in the chest, sending him right to the ground.

Jacob Thorne was already on his feet.

"What are you?" he whispered as he slowly approached me, armed with only one dagger now. I smiled again but didn't speak. I just waited for him to come closer. It was a done deal now. I'd heard the magic shielding him crack. A couple more of those hits and his blood was mine to taste. His heart was mine to pull out.

He was no longer shocked or surprised. He no longer gave me a second to hit him. He kept moving, one hand with his dagger, the other glowing with his magic, as he threw ball after ball of it at me. Half of them hit me, but they didn't slow me down.

Until the ground began to shake.

I saw the three sorcerers left standing on their knees, hands buried in the dirt, chanting in unison. I heard their words and I understood them. No—the monster understood them, even though they made no sense to me at all.

But the ground kept shaking, and in the blink of an eye, it collapsed from right under our feet.

Too late to jump. I fell, and so did Jacob.

Wet dirt all around me. I was completely disoriented for a moment, but when I raised my head, I saw the sky. I saw the large wall around the house, too. We were barely twenty feet below ground, in a hole that they'd made with their magic. The roots of the tree growing in the yard of the house opposite us were perfectly visible down there. Jacob held onto them to make it to his feet, then showed me his glowing dagger.

"I don't suppose we could talk, could we?" he asked.

I didn't waste breath. I just jumped at him with my claws ready and slammed right onto his chest. His dagger went in my waist this time, but the pain barely registered. We were going down, rolling in the dirt, my claws trying to dig through the magic shielding him, while he tried to push me off.

Then the ground groaned again like a living thing. It shook and it was impossible to keep my balance. I dug my claws into the dirt and slammed my feet onto Jacob's side with all my strength. His magic kept cracking, but the ground kept shaking, too.

"Stop," Jacob said, just as another sorcerer jumped into the hole with us. His hands were glowing red, his magic a huge ball of glowing smoke between them.

"No!" Jacob shouted, but he didn't stop. He released the large ball onto me, and it hit me right in the face.

Too much magic. It had been impossible to move away in time because of the slippery dirt and the vibrations of the ground. Too much blood lost.

Was I really dying? All it would take now was for Jacob to bury that dagger straight through my heart, and I'd be done for good. Whatever monster was inside me would have to find a new body to reside in—or die with me.

I'd finally be free.

Ax was safe. Marie and Marcus were safe, too. It was okay. I could let go—it wasn't that difficult to do, to be honest.

But my eyes still opened. The monster in me still struggled to be aware of our surroundings, to see what was happening, where Jacob and the sorcerers were… and I saw. Just a glimpse but I saw the concrete fence crumbling. The clouds of dust hanging over it. The huge pieces of concrete falling right onto us trapped in the hole on the ground. I saw them coming right at me.

And I could do nothing to stop them in time.

26

Ax Creed

My speed was not even half of what it usually was. I ran, but my legs were heavy. My whole body was heavy. Even when I saw the smoke rising into the sky, I couldn't move fast enough.

Damsel was still there. Whatever she'd become, she was still there. And now that that woman and her brother were safe, I could help her. We could kill Thorne. We could make it out together, same as we started it. I wouldn't have it any other way.

But the closer I got to the ruins of the entire fucking house, the more hope escaped me. Two sorcerers were kneeling on the sidewalk in front of the house they'd ruined, concrete fence wall and all. The pieces of it had filled up a hole in the ground half the size of a tennis court while the bright orange flames consumed them.

My heart skipped a beat. The sorcerers were barely breathing. I saw red, and when I grabbed one of them by the throat, he could barely open his eyes.

"Where is she?" I demanded. Why were the only hearts I could hear beating around me *theirs*?

The sorcerer didn't speak. He tried to push my hands away from him instead. I broke his neck and moved to the other. I grabbed him by the shirt and pulled him up. "Where the fuck is she?" I hissed at his face.

He looked at me from under his lashes, his warm breath blowing on my face. "Gone," he whispered. "They're gone." His hand rose just a little, his finger shaking as he pointed it right at the fire burning behind me.

I broke his neck, too, and threw him to the side before I went closer to the fire, the flames so high it looked like they were licking the night sky.

She survived it. She could survive anything. Whatever she was, she was strong. She could survive a house on her head, and the fire burning over it. She fucking *had* to.

The heat scorched my skin even before I touched a large piece of concrete half buried in the flames to pull it out. I gritted my teeth as I pulled and threw it to the side, then went for a piece of wood, what was once a door. Sirens reached my ears from a distance. I was bleeding, the skin of my hands and arms burned to a crisp. I barely had any strength, but I still had my ears. If I could just hear her heart beating, everything would be okay. I'd put the fire out somehow, then I'd pull her out of this mess and get the fuck out of here. She'd heal. In time, everything healed.

But the fire was too much. The heat of it melted the skin on my face, too, when I tried to reach deeper. The pain paralyzed me, and it was too much. I had no choice but to back away.

No heartbeat. I would still be able to hear hers even through the crackling of the fire. I knew it so well, would know the rhythm of it even if I were unconscious. I'd hear it through hell itself.

But not a single sound came from underneath the concrete and wood filling the hole. As if nobody existed under there—just the fire, a monster growing bigger by the second.

"*Damsel!*" I called at the top of my lungs. And I waited, ears strained. I waited to hear a single noise, a single movement, just *something*.

There was nothing.

My legs gave and I slammed my fists on the ground, screaming until I ran all out of voice. She wasn't there. They killed her. They killed my Damsel. They buried her under a fucking house, and they burned her body, too.

She was gone.

The only woman in the world I'd ever cared for, and now she wasn't here anymore.

Eventually, my strength gave. I couldn't even raise my arms anymore, and the sirens were so close. I knew I needed to get out of there before the humans arrived. Before more sorcerers got here.

I couldn't let them kill me now. They *all* had to die first to pay for her life. All of them.

So, I sat there, and I breathed in the smoke and the air filled with magic, eyes on the blazing fire, and I remembered. The first time I saw her, climbing up that waterfall, completely naked. The first time I touched her. The first time she smiled at me. The first time we were one.

The first time in my life that the mating instinct had taken over me. I'd had her right there in my arms, fangs ready to draw her blood, make her mine for good. I'd wanted to bite her so badly, my whole life had hung on the moment I'd taste her blood.

I'd always thought mating was not for me—and I believed it. Never once had I had the urge, not only to mate, but to be with another person for longer than a few minutes, maybe a couple hours at a time. Never, until her. She was everything I never even knew existed. I never even searched for her because I didn't think she could be real. She didn't try to be someone she wasn't. She didn't try to convince me or anyone of anything. She was who she was—who liked it, did, and who didn't...well, they could all rot in hell as far as she was concerned. It was just her—all anyone was going to get, for better or worse. She was my perfect. It didn't surprise me that she'd awakened my mating instinct as fast as she did. Out of all the women in the world, she was the only one who could tame me. The only one I would give everything for.

But I'd been a fucking coward. I knew she didn't want a mate. I couldn't do that to her without her consent. I'd wanted to ask for it, but she'd walked away. And I thought I'd have time. More time. Years, decades—however long it took to convince her that she belonged with me.

Look at us now. Worlds apart. Worlds we couldn't cross.

I should have bitten her then. She would have been stronger if we'd mated. I would have been stronger, too. We'd have killed Jacob Thorne and all his pathetic sorcerers in no time. If I'd only just bitten her...

The police cars turned the corner of the street I was in, behind them a firetruck. I raised to my feet and moved, running as fast as my body allowed, which wasn't much. But I managed to hide between the houses across the street, move to their back, and take it from there. I didn't care if someone could see me. If someone came close to me, I'd kill them. It wasn't my time to die yet. I'd made a promise, and I was going to keep it. Whatever it takes.

I found the siblings just as I left them, hidden in the basement of an empty house in the town. I'd broken the chains and the windows, and I'd put them down there where nobody could find them. And now that I was here, they climbed out.

"Where is Nikki?" Marcus asked, his fear alive, shaking his body.

"Nikki's gone," I said, but the pain wasn't there. It didn't stab me in the chest like I expected. It wouldn't—not yet. "We need to keep moving. Stay close."

I started walking back behind the houses to the woods surrounding them. It was going to take us another two hours to reach the border of the Hidden Realm. The sun was already turning the sky grey, but we'd make it.

And when we made it, I'd heal.

And when I healed, I'd be back.

They might have taken her from me, but they'd come to regret it. Because I was going to take them, too, one by one, until all of them were gone.

Then, there would be time for pain.

27

Nikki Arella

My eyes opened to a blinding green light. So hot, I could barely breathe. The memories of those pieces of concrete falling on my face came back, and I tried to move my hands in front of my face on instinct.

But nothing moved around me, except for a heart beating steadily somewhere close.

Where the hell was I? And where was all that light and heat coming from?

I blinked a thousand times before I was able to clearly make out the lime green glow of the magic surrounding me. So much of it. And there was…*fire* burning right outside it. That's why I was having trouble breathing. But no pieces of concrete were falling on my head. No flames reached under the magic. And my hands…they were clean. No black veins crawled on my skin. No claws—just my chipped fingernails.

I sat up, heart in my throat, trying to see what was around me. And I saw.

Jacob Thorne was sitting in the dirt, elbows resting on his knees as he watched me and smiled.

"Welcome back," he said, as if we were old friends. As if he hadn't tried to kill me just minutes ago.

Was it minutes ago?

I looked around, through the glowing magic that had wrapped us up in a circle, and I saw that we were still trapped. Flames all around it, burning hotter by the second.

"They brought the whole house down on us and set it on fire," Jacob said, shaking his head. "Fucking fools."

"You almost killed me," I said, looking down at my torso, my torn clothes. And the scars of the wounds he'd left on me with those daggers were still there, almost completely closed. No longer even bleeding. I healed as fast as the next vampire, but *this* fast? I'd never been wounded when the monster in me came out before, so I'd had no idea how fast *that* version of me healed.

"I saved your life, Nikki Arella," he said, and I looked up at him. "This is my doing. If it wasn't for this shield, those pieces of concrete would have smashed both our skulls. That fire would have turned our bodies to ash."

"Why?" I asked, no longer even angry. Just confused. And uncertain that this was even real.

"Because you've been touched, too," Jacob said.

Yeah, that wasn't news to me.

"I'm a vampire," I reminded him, just like I'd done with Jones. That night thirty years ago, even if the spirit had gotten to me *before* that vampire bit me, it wouldn't have worked. The moment the monster had taken over me, I'd bitten the vampire, too, on instinct. It's how I'd completed the shift from human to vampire before I killed him and all his friends—*after* they'd already slaughtered a hundred and three people in our town.

"I'll admit it sounds impossible, but you are. I saw it. I felt it," he said, and he meant every word.

Damn.

"And you want to *heal* me?" I asked Jacob, a small smile on my face. If his great plan was to keep me locked away in some basement, he was in for the surprise of his fucking life.

"No, I don't want to heal you," Jacob said. "But bad things are coming, Nikki. They have been for a while now. I've been trying, but I can't stop them on my own."

I held his eyes for a moment, expecting him to start laughing. He didn't.

"You've lost your fucking mind." Maybe some of those concrete pieces had gotten him before he put up that shield.

"Maybe. But I still need your help. Not just to get out of this mess, but to help me fight the evil out there in the world. The greater evil, one nobody even knows exists yet." He said the words as if they were undeniable truths. Whether they were or not was irrelevant—*he* believed them wholeheartedly.

"Fuck the greater evil. I'm getting out of here," I said, and tried to stand up, but it hurt everywhere. And the craving for blood had me seeing stars. Fuck, I needed blood. I needed it asap—and if I took his, I wasn't going to be able to rely on my body anymore. I'd tried that once. As tempting as it was to have my mind free of whispers, it wasn't worth it. Not now.

"You owe me, Nikki," Jacob said. "And if we can't come to an agreement, I'm afraid I'll have to pull this shield closer to me. All of *that* will fall on you." He pointed up. "You will be burned alive."

But his threats didn't scare me. "Then do it."

He paused for a moment, eyes wide with surprise. "You won't survive it."

"Try me."

With a sigh, he shook his head and smiled. Just like I thought—*empty* threats. "I won't. The world needs you, believe it or not."

"Fuck you." If he thought he could get into my head with his bullshit, he was dead wrong yet again.

"Then tell me what you want," he said, holding up a finger in front of his face. "What is the *one* thing you want most in your life?"

Ax, my mind whispered.

Fuck. Ax, Marie and Marcus.

Had they made it? Were they safe?

Yes, they were. Ax had taken them away. He'd promised me. He would take care of them no matter what happened to me here. If there was anybody out there in the world that I trusted, it was him, no matter how fucked up it sounded.

"Tell me what it is, Nikki. I can get it done," Jacob said.

My eyes squeezed shut as the memories hit me.

All I wanted was Ax. It was fucking ridiculous, too, because I couldn't have him. Not just because of our covens, but because of whatever monster lived in me—whether it was a spirit or not made no difference. I could never trust myself. I could never let myself *be myself.*

"Think about it. We've got time," Jacob said, leaning back on his fucking shield buzzing with energy, nearly suffocating me. And the heat of the fire burning outside it had every inch of my skin covered in sweat, too.

I did think about it, despite my better judgment.

All my life I'd been afraid of what lived inside me. Ever since I was a kid and I killed those vampires, I'd been afraid. When I grew up and killed three of the Redwood soldiers who'd had the misfortune to be in the training rooms with me, I'd been afraid. When I nearly killed Ivan and Master Ferrera, I'd been afraid.

Each morning I lay down on the bed with Ezra, I'd been fucking terrified that I'd wake up to find him in pieces.

Afraid, afraid, afraid. I'd always looked for people to make it easier for me—like Ezra. Being close to him had always calmed me down. Had given me purpose. Like, if I lived for him, I wouldn't have time to worry about myself.

And when Ezra was gone, I'd found a way to exist without having to be afraid every waking second. I'd found it at the bottom of a bottle of alcohol. It kept me intoxicated for long enough that I could be distracted by something other than the voices whispering in my head. And the longer I ignored them, the more power they lost over me.

But with Ax, it had been different. He never calmed me—he understood me. He never backed away, even when I was plain rude, even when I pushed him as hard as I knew how. He didn't think I was worthless because I drank alcohol and wore revealing clothing and talked like I didn't give a shit about anything in the world. The demons had been there with him…but so had I.

Was that why my mating instincts had come to life when I was in his arms? Was that why I'd had the urge to make him mine the way I never had before with anyone else? Was that why I felt less alone in his company, knowing he was just as fucked up as me? Because that made it almost *normal*. It wasn't just me—there was someone else out there who lived hanging on a thin piece of thread day in and day out, too.

"When did you change your mind about me?" I wondered. "You were dead set on killing me just minutes ago." Right until the ground had collapsed from under our feet.

Jacob smiled. "I had my dagger in you—twice. The magic should have killed you on the spot the first time." He even sounded like he was *in awe*. Whatever the hell that meant, I didn't even want to know at this point.

"I can't be touched," I whispered, more to myself than to him. All those reasons I always held close to my heart had to mean something. Especially when I saw that Vein spirit in that alley—I *couldn't* be like that, could I?

"I can't explain it to you because I don't know how it happened, but I know what I felt. The magic in you is that of a spirit. It's unmistakable," he said, and he was absolutely sure of every word.

Shaking my head to myself, I sighed.

What did it even matter if I was a touched or not right now? It didn't, not after everything.

"Say I believe you. Is there really a way to *heal* it?" I asked, mind only half made up.

Jones had always thought that a spirit had touched me, but he'd never once mentioned that whatever happened to me could be *undone*. If *healing* was possible, he'd know about it. I had no doubt that he would.

So why had he never even told me?

"No, that's not what I want to do. I told you—" Jacob started, but I cut him off.

"*Can* you heal it, though?"

I looked into his wide eyes as the wheels turned in his head, and he understood what I was asking.

"Yes," he finally said. "I think so."

"You *think* so, or you know so?" Because there was a difference.

"I know so," he said without missing a beat. "It's complicated. And long and painful. About fifty percent of sorcerers who are touched don't survive the process, but it can be done. Every spirit that latches onto a live being can be separated." He scratched his cheeks for a moment. "How long has it been?"

"Since I was six."

"And you're now…?"

"Thirty-five."

He flinched. "That's gonna be tough."

"But it can be done."

He nodded. "It can," he said. Just like that. "Is that your price?"

Was it? Did I really believe that—somehow—this man here could separate me from my worst nightmare living inside my chest? Did I really hope that I could ever be alone in my head, be free to have a fucking life? Did I really consider helping this stranger and expecting him to help me, too, so that I could go back to the Realm and to Ax?

Worse yet—did Jones really know about this and didn't tell me?

Because I believed it.

I witnessed it now as I stood there underneath a ruined house in flames, wrapped in a safe bubble of magic. The shields he'd had on his body—almost unbreakable—and those glowing daggers. He was stronger than anything I could have imagined. Not just glowing balls of smoke shooting from his hands. He had magic—*real* magic.

And real magic got shit done.

"Yes," I whispered. Yes, that was my price. I'd do whatever he needed done, if there was even the smallest chance that he could release me from this miserable existence. If there was the smallest chance that I would be free to go find Ax. Fuck the covens—if Jones or Sangria had a problem with it, we could leave. We could make our own place out here in the world. *As long as you're with me.*

"That certainly is good news," Jacob said and moved to his feet. He was over six foot three, so he couldn't stand completely straight. The bubble of magic wasn't high enough. "We will need to take a formal oath just so we know we'll keep our words," he said. "And we'll do that as soon as we get out of here."

I nodded. A formal oath wouldn't just be tied to me—it would be tied to him, too. It would be sealed with blood and magic so that neither of us could break out of our deal.

"If you cross me, Jacob Throne, I'll make sure you regret having been born," I said quietly. That was a promise he could be sure I'd keep.

"I'm not worried, Nikki." Not a hint of a lie in his voice. It made it really hard to doubt him when I could hear his heart and the blood coursing in his veins. "I'll make a small hole and try to put out the fire long enough for you to break through the debris, okay?" he said and raised his hands.

"Do it," I said and prepared myself.

Surreal. I was going to gods knew where with a sorcerer who could kill me in my sleep. I was going to be away from the Hidden Realm, away from Ax, away from anyone I'd ever known.

But not for long. There was a spark in me now—somewhere deep, but it was there. After so long, I finally felt a tiny bit of hope. Maybe I didn't need to live like this my whole life. Maybe I could really be *free*.

I realized that Jones was right about one thing, at least. Everything I'd gone through to get here, and everything that was waiting for me still, it wasn't going to be easy. It was going to be hard.

And it was going to be *worth* it.

THE END OF BOOK ONE

For more, please visit D.N. Hoxa's Amazon Page or

www.dnhoxa.com

Thank you!

ALSO BY D.N. HOXA

THE PIXIE PINK (COMPLETED)
Werewolves Like Pink Too
Pixies Might Like Claws
Silly Sealed Fates

THE DARK SHADE (COMPLETED)
Shadow Born
Broken Magic
Dark Shade

THE NEW ORLEANS SHADE (COMPLETED)
Pain Seeker
Death Spell
Twisted Fate
Battle of Light

THE NEW YORK SHADE (COMPLETED)
Magic Thief
Stolen Magic
Immortal Magic
Alpha Magic

THE MARKED SERIES (COMPLETED)
Blood and Fire
Deadly Secrets
Death Marked

WINTER WAYNE SERIES (COMPLETED)
Bone Witch
Bone Coven
Bone Magic
Bone Spell
Bone Prison
Bone Fairy

SCARLET JONES SERIES (COMPLETED)
Storm Witch
Storm Power
Storm Legacy
Storm Secrets
Storm Vengeance
Storm Dragon

VICTORIA BRIGHAM SERIES (COMPLETED)
Wolf Witch
Wolf Uncovered
Wolf Unleashed
Wolf's Rise

STARLIGHT SERIES (COMPLETED)
Assassin
Villain
Sinner
Savior

MORTA FOX SERIES (COMPLETED)
Heartbeat
Reclaimed
Unchanged

Printed in Great Britain
by Amazon